DESIRE
IN THE DEAD OF NIGHT

The fog swirled and spun in the center of his cell. Its spinning increased. A ghostly image began to condense and solidify out of the whirling mist.

She stood before him, naked, smiling sadly. Her eyes did not glow, they wept.

Slowly Dracula pulled himself out of his crouch. Cautiously he walked toward her. Why had he fought this for so long—for fifteen years? She was still as maddeningly desirable. He wanted to touch her, even if her flesh was cold. He wanted to kiss her. He wanted her to kiss him.

"Tzigane," he whispered, his voice strained and weak with the emotions which were boiling up inside him, violent emotions being released after all the years he had fought them.

And then his lips were on hers . . .

ASA DRAKE

Crimson Kisses

▲ AVON
PUBLISHERS OF BARD, CAMELOT AND DISCUS BOOKS

CRIMSON KISSES is an original publication of Avon Books.
This work has never before appeared in book form.

AVON BOOKS
A division of
The Hearst Corporation
959 Eighth Avenue
New York, New York 10019

First Avon Printing, February, 1981

AVON TRADEMARK REG. U.S. PAT. OFF. AND IN
OTHER COUNTRIES, MARCA REGISTRADA,
HECHO EN U.S.A.

Printed in the U.S.A.

dedicated to
Vlad Basarab III
(1430–   )
with undying thanks

He must, indeed, have been that Voivode Dracula who won his name against the Turk, over the great river on the very frontier of Turkey-land. If it be so, then he was no common man; for in that time, and for centuries after, he was spoken of as the cleverest and the most cunning, as well as the bravest of the sons of the "land beyond the forest." That mighty brain and that iron resolution went with him to his grave, and are even now arrayed against us.

BRAM STOKER, *Dracula*

Preface

❊❊❊❊❊

VLAD BASARAB III was once an innocent babe sucking warm life from his mother's breast, but he came to know Evil, came to be known by one single, lonely word.

DRACULA.

Even immortal, sacred monsters must have their beginnings.

Prologue

❖❖❖❖❖

22/23 APRIL
1440 A.D.

NAKED AND SHIVERING in the cold night air, the young girl stood at the center of the lonely crossroads and waited for midnight. Around her, the vast Transylvanian forest was silent and watchful. High above, ragged clouds scudded restlessly across the face of the moon.

It was Saint George's Eve, Satan's night, a night for black magic, a night for divining the future, a night when a young girl might conjure a vision of the man she would one day marry, if she had the courage to risk the darkness on this most evil night of the year. The girl at the crossroads had that courage for she was a gypsy, and like her mother and her mother's mother before her, she had been born a witch.

The girl was eleven years old. Her name was Tzigane, and her hair was straight and black and it hung down to her slim waist. Her pale green eyes glinted with excitement in the intermittent light of the moon.

"Soon," she whispered, feeling the tenseness growing within her. She hugged herself to ward off the cold. In her right hand, she clutched the small iron dagger her grandmother had bequeathed her. Around her neck, a small leather pouch containing rare herbs hung by a worn thong. Behind her, on the ground lay the clothing she had discarded.

Tzigane's excitement continued to build. She hugged herself tighter. Her body vibrated with every beat of her racing pulse. She felt it coming. She set her teeth and held her breath.

3

The night changed. A breeze sprang up, rustling the looming pines. Somewhere to her left, an unseen bird fluttered wildly among the treetops. A mile away, in the camp where her mother, father and tribe waited, dogs began to bark.

Tzigane exhaled explosively with relief. It was time. The witching hour had come.

The young witch knelt, facing east. Quickly she inserted the point of the dagger beneath the fingernail of the first finger of her left hand and jabbed. Hot pain shot up her arm, but she did not cry out.

She withdrew the dagger and examined her finger, nodding with satisfaction as blood oozed from beneath the nail. Using the bloodied point of the dagger, she drew a five-pointed star in the dirt, then let three drops of warm blood drip from her finger into the center of the star.

Tzigane sat back on her heels and stared intently at the dark stain within the pentagram she had drawn. "I give my blood to my loved one," she chanted, "whom I shall see shall be mine own!" She repeated the incantation twice more, then stretched out face down so that her forehead touched the blood in the star.

She closed her eyes and emptied her mind. She waited. In her mind's eye, a swirling mist began to form. Something moved within the mist. Tzigane's concentration deepened.

From out of the mist walked a young, dark-haired boy of aristocratic appearance, dressed in black. Something silver gleamed upon his shirt. He stopped, frowned, and stared at the gypsy girl.

"Who are you?" he demanded.

"Your future wife," she answered with a smile.

"I doubt that. You look like a gypsy, and a Prince of Wallachia does not marry gypsies," he replied with disdain. He frowned again. "How did you get past father's guards? You will pay with your life when they catch you."

"I am not really here," Tzigane laughed, "and neither are you. I am a witch, and this is a vision that I have conjured."

"Witches and visions do not exist," the boy said without the slightest hesitation. "They are superstitions, and I am above such things."

"Really?" Tzigane asked, amused by his typically male

disdain of the Unseen. "What is that on your shirt?" she asked, pointing at the silver design.

"A dragon," he answered proudly. "It is my father's emblem—the emblem of Dracul, the dragon."

"Sweet Satan," Tzigane whispered, suddenly chilled. Mixed emotions of fear and exultation pounded at her. The simple life she had always envisioned for herself had suddenly been destroyed, and in its place. . . .

Tzigane's vision faded as her excitement jerked her consciousness back to the lonely crossroads. She opened her eyes, rolled over onto her back, and stared up at the clouded moon. "Can it be, Sister Moon?" she asked in awed wonder. "Can it truly be?"

The gypsy witch named Tzigane scrambled to her feet, hastily threw on her clothes, then began to run back toward her camp, weeping hot tears of joy. She was eager to tell her parents and the others of her tribe about her vision and about her future mate, the Son of the Dragon, the Chosen One foretold of old in the sacred prophecies of their Lord, Satan.

Far south of Transylvania and the gypsy camp, beyond the southern mountains in the palace at Targoviste in the nation of Wallachia, a nine-year-old boy awoke from a dream and frowned in the dark. "Witches," he whispered with disgust. "Silly superstitions."

The boy turned over on his side and stared at the dying fire in the grate. Then his gaze shifted to the new black shirt which he had draped neatly over the chair beside his bed. The silver dragon embroidered on the shirt seemed to be alive in the flickering crimson light cast by the fire.

He smiled and closed his eyes, pleased with himself for not being frightened by the gypsy witch in his dream, thinking how proud his father, Dracul, would be of the way he had stood up to the witch, showed her his lack of fear, and made her go away.

Soon the young boy was sleeping again, but this time he dreamt of more worthy things, of battles and blood and the glories awaiting a future Warlord-Prince of Wallachia.

The witch was now forgotten.

NOVEMBER
1444 A.D.

1

✣-✣-✣-✣-✣

THE DUNGEONS of the Turkish fortress called Egrigoz stank
of death, disease, and decay. Spiders moved silently over
cobwebbed walls. Rats scuttled in shadows unpenetrated
for centuries by the cleansing light of the sun.

In the center of the dungeon's deepest torch-lit chamber
stood two Turkish soldiers, curved swords hanging at their
sides. At their feet on the filthy stone floor knelt a boy.
He was naked.

The boy's hands had been bound behind him, and his
body was forcibly hunched forward by a strap which held
his neck against a low, blood-stained block of scarred
wood.

He was a hostage, the thirteen-year-old son of the reign-
ing Warlord-Prince of a Christian nation north of the
Danube River, a nation called Wallachia. The boy's father
had broken a treaty with the Turks, and the boy had been
told he was about to die. His name was Dracula.

One of the soldiers leaned casually on the long shaft of
an executioner's axe and grinned down at the helpless boy.
The soldier had only one eye. "A Christian's sword took
my eye," he told the boy. "Now I will take your Christian
head." Chuckling cruelly, he lifted the axe.

Dracula did not entertain the guards by struggling. He
knew there was no escape, therefore he fought to keep
his swelling emotions under control and silently waited to
die. *I will not fear. I will not be weak. I will not fear,* he
repeated over and over in his mind, desperately trying to

9

crowd out the panic which threatened to engulf and shame
him.

The other soldier knelt and stroked the boy's sweat-
soaked hair. "Swear to serve the Sultan, and we will spare
your life," he said.

Dracula gathered the strands of his unraveling courage.
"You can kill me, but you will never break me," he hissed
through his clenched teeth.

Dracula closed his eyes and listened to the wall torches
sputtering in the dank, fetid air. He listened to the frantic
hammering of his heart, waiting for the blow to fall. He
continued to wait. Cautiously he opened his eyes.

The grinning, one-eyed soldier was still holding the axe
high overhead. Then suddenly, the man laughed and
brought the axe down with blinding speed and embedded
the blade in the block, less than an inch from Dracula's
nose. Both men laughed for a long time. Then the one-eyed
soldier bent down and ran his dirt-encrusted hand along
Dracula's sweating back. He leaned close to Dracula's face.

"If you remain stubborn, boy, I may not miss the next
time. Well? Will you swear to serve the Sultan? Or shall
I lift the axe again?"

Dracula forced himself to remain silent, forced himself
to ignore his raging panic, forced himself to repeat his
mental vow to be strong.

The one-eyed guard stood and lifted the axe. "What will
you wager that I can come closer than before without
touching him?" he asked the other guard with a wink of
his good eye.

"That's too easy," laughed the other soldier. "What will
you wager that you can trim his nose a bit without touching
the rest of his face?"

The one-eyed guard bent down again and examined
Dracula's nose. "It does seem rather long. Very well. I
will try to make it shorter."

The axe slowly went up, then came whirring downward
once again.

DECEMBER
1444 A.D.

2

THE WOMAN was called Djalma. She was sixteen and quite beautiful with long black hair falling below her shoulders and an olive-skinned body of budding perfection.

A few weeks earlier, Djalma had been a warm and pampered member of the harem of Sultan Mohammed II. But now she was sitting naked on a dirty straw mat in the dungeon of Egrigoz, shivering from the cold.

Despite her careful training in how to please a man, Djalma had made a serious mistake on her very first night with the Sultan. Partly from nervousness and partly from youthful exuberance, Djalma had laughed. She had meant no disrespect, but nevertheless the Sultan was insulted. Djalma was given a dozen lashes, then taken to Egrigoz and thrown into the dungeon to await her fate.

Djalma hugged her knees under her chin for warmth and cursed her luck. There had been no light in her cell since the single wall torch had gone out. But Djalma did not fear the darkness. She feared the guards who held her life in their hands. They had used her young body without mercy since her first night in the dungeon, but they had not seriously hurt her yet. Djalma feared that soon they would.

Djalma feared torture and mutilation. She feared death. Djalma feared the man the guards had promised to bring to her cell, for if she failed to please him, she would be made to scream and die slowly for the amusement of the men of Egrigoz.

Heavy footsteps echoed in the corridor. They came

closer. Djalma held her breath, praying they would pass by her cell. But they did not.

She heard the jangling of keys as her cell door was unlocked. "Allah be with me," she whispered, then began breathing slowly and deeply, tryng to relax.

When the door opened, she carefully kept her eyes lowered, fixed upon a crust of moldy bread on the floor. Men entered her cell. A guard placed a new torch in the wall bracket, then leaned over Djalma and hissed, "Do you remember what we promised you if you fail?"

Djalma clenched her teeth and kept silent. The guard ran his calloused fingers through her hair, then patted her on the head as he would a dog. "Have fun," he chuckled. The other guards also laughed as they left the cell and locked the door behind them.

Djalma kept her eyes on the floor and waited for the man to attack. She had grown used to their attacks. From the corner of her eye, she could see him standing motionless by the locked door. Panic threatened her. Why didn't he move or, at least, speak? If she failed to please him. . . .

She pushed away thoughts of failure for she was not prepared to suffer torture and death. She must succeed and survive. Perhaps a better look at her naked body would inspire him.

Djalma slowly uncurled her legs and stood facing the silent man, her eyes still lowered respectfully. She ran her fingers through her glossy black hair, then slowly moved her hands downward over her breasts, her belly, and her thighs. Now she stretched her arms high over her head and strained upward on her toes. Her fingers touched a thick spider web on the ceiling, and she suddenly jerked back, uttering a sharp cry.

The man by the door laughed contemptuously.

Djalma's anger flared, but immediately she reminded herself to control it. She clenched her fists for relief.

"Why do you stare at the floor?" the man asked. "Does everything frighten you like that cobweb on the ceiling did? Look at me."

Djalma's head jerked up, and she glared at the infuriating man. Her anger faded instantly as surprise took its place.

"I hate spineless women who fear their own shadows.

I hate any creature who shows fear," he said with aloof superiority.

"But . . . but you're only a boy!" Djalma exclaimed.

"I am a man. I am Dracula," he stated coldly. "But you are only a filthy Turkish whore."

He spoke her language with difficulty. Djalma recognized his accent. She had heard it once before.

"Allah be damned," she whispered fearfully. "He's a Christian virgin." Suddenly she knew that the guards would have their fun.

She was doomed.

3

THE TALL THIN BOY who called himself a man stood before Djalma. He was dressed all in black, his open cloak revealing a silver design on the front of his open-necked shirt. An aloof expression was on his face.

His forehead was high and domed, his nose a strong aquiline, his eyes deep-set and piercing beneath heavy, brooding brows. His lips were full and somewhat sensuous. Straight black hair, parted down the middle, fell to his shoulders, framing his pale face.

"A Christian virgin," Djalma repeated to herself. How could she, a Turkish woman, hope to please a boy whose Christian training had taught him to hate all Turks and to believe that sex was unclean and sinful? And yet, if the boy left her cell unfulfilled, she would be tortured to death. The insidiousness of the guards' plan washed over her.

The enormity of that revelation crushed her, and she sank down onto the straw mat and began to sob. But then hate and anger cut off her tears. She began to curse and scream, beating her fists on the dirty stone floor. Then she leaped to her feet and threw herself at the boy who was being used to destroy her.

She was nearly upon him, screaming insults like a demon, almost feeling her nails sinking into his face, digging at his eyes, ripping away his flesh. But suddenly he moved aside, and there was only empty space where he had stood. Unable to slow herself, she crashed into the heavy, iron-banded door and had time for just one final curse before she crumpled unconscious to the floor.

The darkness remained when Djalma opened her eyes. She moaned, believing herself blind, thinking that the guards had already begun her final torture by burning out her eyes. Her head ached horribly, throbbing with her pulse, threatening to explode with each beat of her young heart.

She moved slightly and felt the straw mat beneath her. Something warm was covering her. She touched it cautiously, not fully trusting her senses. It felt like a cloak. The boy had been wearing one. Could he have. . . .

"Boy?" she whispered. "Are you there?"

"If you call me a 'boy' again, I will take back my cloak," Dracula said angrily. "I am Dracula, son of Dracul, son of the Dragon, and heir to his Wallachian throne."

Djalma suddenly remembered the insignia she had seen on his shirt. "So, it is a dragon you wear," she mumbled groggily.

"Dracul can also mean *Devil*," he replied, "and many Turks have had reason to think of my father in that way for the Christian Dragon exists to kill Turks. You are a Turk, are you not?"

Djalma ignored the question. She had worse things to fear than death at the hands of a mere boy. He could have killed her while she was unconscious if that had been his intent. She tried to sit up, but her throbbing head forced her to fall back onto the mat.

"It irritates my jailers to see me wearing the emblem of my father," Dracula said arrogantly. "That is why I now wear the dragon at all times."

"I cannot see," Djalma said softly, more concerned with her blindness than with the boy's attempts to impress her.

"I extinguished the torch. The Turks probably have a spy hole through which they can watch me. Was that their plan? To find a weakness in me? To have me humiliate myself by succumbing to a Turkish whore?"

"I know nothing of what they planned for you," Djalma said wearily, "but you are probably right about the spy hole. Often, when I am doing private things, I seem to hear laughter coming from overhead."

"Of course," Dracula said knowingly. "But now they are as blind as we. They will find that I will not be broken by a woman any sooner than by their harsher methods. I have no weaknesses."

Djalma's heart fell. Her task seemed more hopeless than ever. "Why are you in Egrigoz?" she asked.

My younger brother, Radu, and I were sent here as hostages to guarantee that my father would not break a treaty with the Turks. But he broke it anyway. We will be executed when they tire of tormenting us, and my head will be returned to Wallachia without the companionship of my body," he said bitterly.

Djalma remembered that she, too, might be dead soon. "Aren't you afraid of dying?" she asked, her voice trembling slightly.

"Everyone dies," Dracula said tightly. "Do *you* know a way to escape the worm? I acknowledge my coming death in the absence of a means to escape it."

"Perhaps you will not die," Djalma said, thinking of herself. "Why should they wish to break your spirit if they intended to kill you soon? It would not make sense."

"Turks seldom make sense. Part of their fun is not letting my brother and me know whether or not we will be alive tomorrow. My brother cries a lot. He is weak. I never cry." Dracula paused a moment. "What was your crime?"

"I . . . I laughed at the Sultan."

Dracula exploded with laughter. "A crime worth the price of one's life!" he exclaimed.

"I do not think so," Djalma snapped angrily.

"You are a woman. Women never think anything is worth the sacrifice of their lives."

"Except having children," she said hotly. "If your mother had not risked her life to give you yours, you would not . . ."

Suddenly the cloak was ripped from Djalma's body, and Dracula stamped away toward the door.

"Allah protect me," Djalma whispered. What had she said wrong? Had his mother died giving him birth? "Wait!" she cried as Dracula began hammering on the door with his fists, calling for the guards. "No! You mustn't go! Please!"

Djalma hurriedly groped her way to the door and found him. She grabbed his wrists and stopped his pounding, but still he called out to be taken away. Desperately Djalma covered his mouth with her own. He struggled against her, pushed her away, and began shouting again.

Djalma threw herself on him and shoved him back against the door. She covered his mouth again and fought to lock her arms around his body.

Dracula grabbed her hair. Djalma screamed in pain, losing her grip. He jerked harder, and she fell to the floor.

He kicked at her in the dark. One of his boots found her stomach. She grabbed for his legs, found them, then jerked sideways. He fell on top of her.

Dracula tried to push away and suddenly felt his hands sliding over Djalma's firm, round breasts. Sensing a momentary hesitation in his struggling, she threw her thighs around his legs and encircled his back with her arms. She pulled him closer. He began to struggle again, but now she had a solid grip and was drawing him nearer and nearer, until at last she could kiss his lips. Her hot tongue darted into his mouth. His struggling became weaker. Then suddenly he began to return her kisses.

I am going to live! Djalma's mind screamed in triumph and relief. But then she heard the jangling of keys and the door to her cell being opened. She saw the guards rush in and begin to pull the boy away from her.

"No! Leave us! I will please him! I *was* pleasing him! More time! For pity's sake, more time!" she cried.

The guards merely laughed and leered down at her. "No more time," said the guard with one eye. "You have failed."

"No! Please! Please!" Djalma sobbed as the men jerked her to her feet. They dragged her into the corridor and began to tie her hands behind her back.

Dracula, held just outside the door by two burly soldiers, fought to still his racing pulse and clear his mind. He concentrated on his hatred for the Turks. He began to breathe deeply, calming himself, reassuring himself that the guards could not possibly know that he had been weakening and succumbing to the woman, and to powerful, unfamiliar passions.

He carefully kept his face impassive as he watched the binding of the woman's wrists and did not resist as the Turks propelled him down the hallway behind the squirming, screaming woman who had so nearly caused him to shame himself.

A potent memory teased him for an instant, a brief flaring of the passion he had felt growing within him while in the woman's embrace, but he quickly and ruthlessly crushed the reminder of his momentary weakness and concentrated on hating the woman and replacing all feelings of desire with feelings of hate and a need for revenge.

Dracula and Djalma were hurried down a flight of stone steps and into a large, vaulted room. Djalma screamed anew when she saw the ugly devices waiting to destroy her young, beautiful body. But while her beauty still remained intact, the guards intended to use it one last time.

Dracula watched as Djalma was bound spread-eagled and helpless, to a rough wooden table with thick ropes. He silently continued to watch as, one by one, the guards showed him what he had missed. But when they were finished and the torture was about to begin, Dracula quietly requested that he be allowed to help. The one-eyed guard grinned and handed him a red-hot poker.

Dracula calmly studied the glowing tip, then approached the sweating, struggling woman on the table. His eyes were locked upon her tear-streaked face.

He reached the table, carefully making certain that his hands did not tremble, then held the poker steady and pushed it down onto Djalma's naked flesh.

4

❋❋*❋*❋*❋*

RADU HEARD the heavy footsteps of the guards approaching his cell. He cringed in a corner, whimpering and biting his nails, praying for Christ to save him from the Turks. The door squeaked open. The Turkish soldiers pushed his older brother into the cell. Radu scrambled to his feet and ran up to Dracula.

"Vlad! I . . . I thought they had killed you for sure this time," Radu cried hysterically.

"Stop crying, Radu," Dracula hissed angrily. "Do not shame yourself in front of the Turks."

Radu continued to whimper.

Dracula hit him.

Radu fell to the floor and started beating his hands and feet on the stones, screaming that his brother was worse than the Turks.

Dracula shook his head in disgust, stepped over the squirming body, walked to his wooden cot, and lay down.

Laughing at Radu's tantrum, the guards left the cell, locking the door behind them.

When Radu had quieted, Dracula sat up and looked down at his eight-year-old brother. "Radu, I have warned you not to sob and weep like a woman before the Turks. You deserved worse than I gave you. Our father would have hit you more than once if he had seen your shameful display."

Radu got to his knees and wiped his streaming eyes. "Our father hates us! He broke the treaty! He wants us dead!"

"Do not speak ill of our father, Radu. He does what is necessary to preserve his throne, and a throne is worth more than the lives of two boys. Mircea is the eldest, and he is still by father's side. If father needs more sons, he can make them easily enough. I told you we were expendable when we were taken from our home. Why can't you be strong? You disgust me."

Radu looked closely at his brother for the first time since Dracula had been returned to the cell. Radu's eyes grew wide. "What do you have all over you?" he asked.

"It is merely blood, Radu."

"Yours?" Radu asked in alarm, thinking he might be next.

"No. It belonged to a Turkish woman—a whore. She no longer needs it. I helped to kill her."

"You . . . you did what?"

"I helped torture her to death. The Turks tried a new method to break me, Radu. I broke her instead. I remembered all our father taught us about the giving of pain. I prolonged her suffering longer than the Turks had thought possible. It took her a very long time to die, Radu, for she was young and strong and wanted very much to live."

"I . . . I thought you were dead . . . and that I would be next," Radu mumbled.

"How long was I gone?"

"Over a day and a half, at least."

"Yes," Dracula whispered tersely, "she was indeed very strong to have lasted so long." He did not add how beautiful she had been nor how he was still plagued by the teasing desire he had felt in her arms.

Dracula suddenly jumped to his feet and tore the wall torch from its bracket. Radu screamed and fell to his knees, thinking his brother meant to burn him. Dracula smothered the fire on the stone floor. The cell fell into complete darkness. Radu then heard the cot creak as Dracula lay back down.

"Why did you do that, Vlad? You know I am afraid of the dark."

"Stop whining, Radu, or I will bind and gag you," Dracula commanded, then turned his face to the wall and pressed his aching forehead against the cold stones.

"Are you going to sleep like that?" Radu asked fearfully. "You mustn't sleep covered with a dead woman's blood, or her ghost will come and haunt us!"

"I intend to wear her blood like a medal, Radu," Dracula answered wearily. "I do not intend to wash it off for a very long time. Each time the Turks see me, they will remember how I made Djalma scream. They begin to respect and fear me, Radu. One called me a 'Christian devil' during the torture. I believe that even they were sickened by some of the things I did to the woman. Soon they will forget that Dracula means son of the Dragon and will remember only the other meaning—the son of the Devil."

For a moment, silence filled the darkened cell.

"She was so beautiful," Dracula whispered, but so softly that his brother did not hear.

Radu suddenly heard an unexpected sound. "Vlad?" Radu cautiously whispered. "Brother? Are you weeping?" He did not hear the sound again and knew better than to ask such a dangerous question twice. Quietly, so as not to attract attention, Radu crept to his own cot and lay down. He decided he might as well try to sleep, for if the woman's ghost did come, he did not want to see it. He turned over on his stomach and buried his face in his hands, covering his ears with his thumbs to shut out the horrors of Egrigoz, trying desperately to imagine himself back home in his soft, warm bed in his father's palace in Targoviste.

On the other cot, Dracula was attempting to forget and trying to sleep, but each time he closed his eyes, the haunting image of naked, beautiful Djalma teased him. Then he felt his manhood stiffening, felt the desire he had experienced in her cell growing stronger, remembered her female scent, her warm breasts, her. . . . But then her image changed and became grotesque, mutilated, bloody, unrecognizable as something once beautiful and full of life.

As the sleepless hours crawled by, Dracula eventually found that he could no longer remember the beauty but only the horror. His manhood, however, remained painfully engorged with blood and desire.

Then he discovered that even with his eyes open, the image of Djalma's mutilated corpse remained floating before him in the darkness. The hallucination extended itself. He began to hear her screams. Suddenly his manhood exploded.

In the arms of a blood-drenched phantom, Dracula left his boyhood behind.

22/23 APRIL
1447 A.D.

5

❈❈❈❈❈

THE CAVE WAS LOCATED high in the mountains south of the Transylvanian village of Sibiu. Within the cave in a deep, smoke-filled cavern reserved for special ceremonies, a beautiful young gypsy woman, a witch named Tzigane, stood in the center of a ring formed by twelve, black-robed elder witches. They were waiting for the midnight of Saint George's Eve.

Seven years earlier on this very night, this young witch, then only eleven years old, had seen a vision of her future mate, the Chosen One of Satan. It was a vision which had irrevocably changed her life and set her on a path of service to her Lord Satan—a path which had led her away from her friends and family to the cave of the witches to be trained and tested.

Seven years of hard work and continual study lay behind her now. Only one series of tests remained. If she passed them as she had passed all the others, she would be deemed worthy to travel south into Wallachia to await the return of the Dragon's son. If she failed, she might not die, but she would certainly wish she had. It was very unwise to disappoint Satan and His followers. But Tzigane had no intention of failing.

Tzigane knew that she had seen the Dragon's son in her vision and that she was making no false claims; once she passed these final tests, the others would know it, too. Once and for all, she would have proven beyond a doubt that she was capable of fulfilling her part in Satan's prophecies

27

and that she really *had* been chosen by her Lord Satan to be the mate of His future King on Earth.

Of course, she could not blame the elder witches for their unspoken skepticism. Since the birth of the Chosen One nearly seventeen years earlier, many witches had come forth claiming visions similar to her own. Some had failed early in their training. Others—a very few—had reached the final series of tests which now faced her this night. They had all failed these tests.

But none who had failed remained on the Earth. Occasionally, on quiet nights when the realms of the Unseen pressed closest to the physical world, those who had failed could be heard screaming in their endless torment. Their pitiful cries seemed to come from a great distance away like faint echoes on the wind. Tzigane herself had once heard those screams, and the memory still chilled her soul.

Then an unsettling thought came unbidden to her mind. What if the others had not been lying? What if Satan truly had sent them a vision like her own? What if the vision was no guarantee of passing the final tests? What if her success depended solely upon her acquired knowledge and inner strength? What if. . . .

Tzigane angrily wrenched her mind away from the weakness of doubting. She must not fail. She would not fail. She was the chosen mate of the Dragon's son, and she knew she *would* share in Satan's glory!

"I will not fail," she whispered under her breath. "Satan, give me strength in this, my hour of trial," she prayed.

Tzigane suddenly felt a change. The witching hour had come. One of the elder witches, the leader of those who were still mortal humans amongst the coven, stepped forward.

"It is time, Sister Tzigane," the gray-haired elder woman said.

"Yes, Sister Lilitu," Tzigane replied softly, keeping her voice steady and her head high. "I am ready. Let it begin."

Lilitu nodded. "Your robe and sandals," she said.

Tzigane removed her clothing and stood naked. The witches stepped back, opening the way to a pit of hot coals. Tzigane did not have to be told what to do. She had done it once before without mishap. She was not afraid.

She walked to the edge of the long, narrow pit and

stopped. She breathed slowly and deeply, preparing herself, twisting her mind through the silent incantations she had studied hard to learn. Minutes passed.

Tzigane's skin glistened with sweat as waves of searing heat from the glowing coals at her feet bathed her nakedness. She sharpened her concentration and visualized her body beginning to glow and burn hotter than the fires in the pit.

Keeping her eyes tightly closed, Tzigane slowly moved her bare left foot forward and placed it upon the coals. It did not burn. Then steadily—confidently—she walked across the red-hot coals, turned, and walked back through the searing pit, unharmed. It was done. She opened her eyes.

Lilitu nodded. "Very well," she said. "And now the second test. Come." Lilitu lifted a flaming torch from a wall bracket and moved away.

Tzigane followed the elder witch out of the cavern and through a maze of passageways which she knew would eventually lead outside. The other witches followed behind. As she walked, Tzigane was careful to keep the fatigue caused by the exertions of the first test from showing on her face. She kept herself as calm as possible and worked on gathering her strength for the second test, wondering what it might entail.

Tzigane gasped as the freezing night air struck her naked, sweat-soaked body. She began to shiver. A light snow was falling outside the cave, and her bare feet began to throb as she waded through the blanket of numbing whiteness. She hugged herself for warmth and wished for her robe and sandals. What kind of test could this be?

She followed Lilitu to the edge of the nearby lake. The surface of the water was covered with a thin layer of ice.

Lilitu turned. "Enter the lake, Sister Tzigane," she said.

Tzigane's face betrayed her surprise.

"No," Lilitu continued, "you have never passed this test before. But you possess the knowledge to survive—if you have enough strength remaining to do so. Now enter the lake."

Tzigane stared at the icy lake and shivered again. She had no choice. She walked forward to the edge of the water. Did she possess the knowledge? She recalled no spell against the cold. Her mind raced. Had she forgotten a spell? No, surely not. But then, how. . . .

Perhaps there was no spell. Was this actually a test of obedience and pure physical endurance?

Tzigane dropped her hands to her sides and lifted her head. Hesitantly she placed her left foot on the ice, hoping it would support her weight, but the ice broke and her foot splashed into the freezing water up to her ankle. Tzigane's breath hissed between her teeth. She took another step. Her right foot broke through into the water, too.

"Walk forward," Lilitu ordered. "Submerge yourself."

Tzigane took another step and then another. Her teeth began to chatter and violent shudderings shook her body. Suddenly an idea occurred to her. Yes! That had to be the answer!

She closed her eyes and struggled to wind her concentration tight. Quickly she repeated the incantations she had used for the fire-walk, and once more she visualized her body growing hotter and hotter until in her mind she had become a living torch. Fatigue fought her, and she nearly lost her concentration. But then she gritted her teeth, clenched her fists, and the spell held.

Her discomfort faded.

Holding her concentration, her body trembling with the strain, Tzigane moved forward, the thin ice breaking up before her, until she was waist deep. She dipped beneath the water, totally submerged, then stood and walked back to shore.

She stopped before Lilitu, still maintaining her concentration and ignoring the waves of fatigue which were urging her to let go of the spell and relax. Ice began to form in her streaming hair.

Lilitu nodded. "And now for the third and final test. Once before you passed this test, Sister Tzigane, but you were allowed the use of your hands and voice then. That will not be the case tonight. Your mind and your will power alone must suffice if you are to survive this final test."

Lilitu motioned to two other witches. They came forward. "Place your hands behind your back," she ordered Tzigane.

Still concentrating on the heat, her eyes half-closed,

Tzigane slowly moved her hands behind her. She was vaguely aware that the witches were binding her hands at the wrists. Then a strip of cloth was passed around her head, over her mouth, and tied in place. Finally the two witches knelt and bound her feet together at the ankles.

Lilitu waited until the binding was completed, then spoke again. "For this final test, Sister Tzigane," she said, "you must summon a Strigoi and then banish it back to its realm."

Tzigane's eyes opened wide; her concentration was lost. The freezing air clutched her. Lilitu's words echoed inside her head. A Strigoi! Tied like this? Without the use of hands or voice? And already exhausted from the first two tests? It was unthinkable!

"If you survive this test, Sister Tzigane," Lilitu told her, "you will be released and honored as the most blessed of Satan's servants. Fail and . . ."

Lilitu propped up her torch in the snow so that Tzigane's efforts would be visible from a distance, then motioned to the other witches. "You may begin, Sister Tzigane," she said, then turned and walked away.

Tzigane watched the elder witches move back toward the cave. They stopped just outside the entrance and waited, looking back at her.

Tzigane had begun to shiver again. Her knees felt weak and shaky. She moaned softly beneath the gag at the thought of renewing her concentration. It would be an agony. For one horrible moment, she was sure she was going to fail, and her screams would join those of the others in the Strigoi's realm of endless torment. But then a spark of determination flared up deep within her. She *had* seen the Dragon's son. Satan *had* chosen her. She would show the elders the strength of their future Queen!

Clenching her fists behind her back so that the nails dug deeply into her palms, Tzigane began to grasp at the frayed threads of her weary mind and soul, seeking to order her thoughts and coil her concentration into a coherent force for the third time that night. Slowly she withdrew her consciousness from her aching body and sent her mind down a serpentine labyrinth of potentialities, projecting her thoughts toward the beast she had been ordered to summon.

The Strigoi were beasts not of the Earth. They dwelt in the Unseen, in the realms of the demons who were their cousins. Their touch was agony to a mortal human, even a mortal witch. Only the Undead amongst the witches— those who had died after a full life of service to Satan and had been resurrected to eternal physical life by His blessings—could suffer the touch of a Strigoi and remain unharmed.

Yet the Strigoi were subject to the control of mortal humans if the proper spells and protections were known. Tzigane knew the spells, but had now been denied the usual protections of hand gestures and voice commands. Should she be unable to control the Strigoi she summoned, it would grasp her in its burning talons and carry her back into its realm of eternal fire where she would scream forever without hope of release.

The bound witch trembled with her effort. She pushed her mind farther and farther from the world of mortals. Farther and farther and. . . .

White-hot pain washed over and through her. She swayed and nearly fell when she broke through into the Strigoi's realm of fiery torment. She began to chant the spell in her mind. Sweat broke out on her nude body despite the cold.

Now she could feel the beast approaching the realm of the Earth, nearing the gateway, beginning to emerge into a physical manifestation, coming closer . . . closer. . . .

High overhead vast wings beat the air, breaking the silence of the night. Tzigane's eyes snapped open. She looked up. A gigantic black form was hovering above her in the snow-clogged air. As it descended lower and lower, three glowing red eyes stared balefully and hungrily down at her. The air became foul with the stench of the nether realms.

For a dangerous moment, panic threatened to destroy Tzigane's control, but she stubbornly held onto the precious spell and concentrated even harder, her body quivering with the strain, her breath now coming in short, panting gasps.

The beast continued to descend toward her. Four leathery claws uncoiled from beneath the hovering monstrosity, reaching for her, coming closer and closer, the massive talons opening greedily, reaching, reaching. . . .

Tzigane closed her eyes on the horror and threw her last reserves of strength at the behemoth, ordering it to obey her, to return to its own world, to leave her unharmed.

Obey! her mind screamed out, *Obey!*

The stench was almost overpowering now, the beast was so close. Icy gusts of wind spawned by the creature's awesome wings buffeted the ground, sending Tzigane's ice-encrusted hair flying wildly around her. She again opened her eyes, but then wished she had not. The talons were only inches away, opening wider, preparing to close around her bound body and take her away.

The talons began to close. She screamed beneath the gag as bands of fire encircled her. *Obey!* she cried out with her mind. *Sweet Satan, give me aid!* she prayed in panicky desperation. The talons tightened further.

She struggled and writhed in the beast's fiery grip as it began to lift her off the ground. The unendurable weight of her failure pressed down upon her soul, threatening to crush her will to fight, to succeed, to live.

But one last spark of strength still remained deep within her, a hidden reserve of energy and stubborn determination she never imagined she possessed.

Her body stiffened in the talons. She locked eyes with the beast that was trying to take her to her doom. *Obey me in the name of your Master, Lord Satan!* she shouted in her thoughts, projecting the unspoken command like a bolt of lightning toward the beast's dull-witted brain.

The Strigoi seemed to hesitate. She felt the grip of the talons loosen slightly as she kept her eyes locked upon the Strigoi's while repeating the command a second time and then a third. But that was all she had left.

She felt the last of her deepest reserves slip away. Her body was no longer under her control. She slumped exhausted in the grip of the talons, and blackness claimed her consciousness. Her last thought was an insane hope that she might still somehow succeed where all others had failed.

Tzigane opened her eyes. Her naked body was wrapped in warm furs. A fire burned nearby. The fire . . . the Strigoi. . . .

She was afraid to move, afraid that it was a cruel illusion that would be broken if she moved, that she would then find herself in the Strigoi's realm of eternal fire, still in the grip of flesh-searing talons. But she did not feel burned. Cautiously, she moved her hand over her body. Her smooth skin was undamaged.

Slowly, Tzigane raised herself up on her elbows and looked around her. Her head spun as a wave of fatigue washed over her. But then it passed, and she recognized her surroundings. She was back in the special cavern where the final series of tests had begun.

Around the stone platform on which she lay knelt the black-robed forms of the Sisters of the coven. Nearest to Tzigane were the twelve elder witches who had witnessed her final tests. Beyond them were the other members of the community, both the living and the Undead. Their faces were to the floor, their hands clasped in front of them.

One of the elder witches rose and approached Tzigane. It was Lilitu. She was smiling, and her eyes were wet with tears of her joy. She gently embraced Tzigane and then knelt again, looking up at Satan's future Queen with an expression of awe and pride.

"Blessed be, Sister Tzigane," Lilitu said, "most blessed among the servants of Satan. We honor you this night. Truly, you are worthy. Even the Strigoi recognized your authority and gave you back to us."

Tzigane felt that she should say something dignified and solemn, but all she could manage was a weak smile. She had succeeded!

"Rest, Sister Tzigane. When you are ready, we will send you south into Wallachia to await the return of the Dragon's son, the Chosen One of Satan. But for now, most blessed of women, rest and regain your strength."

Tzigane lowered herself slowly back onto the furs and closed her eyes, her smile growing broader as the reality of her success began to solidify in her mind. She tried to sleep, but though her body was exhausted from her trials, her mind was too excited to sleep.

Lilitu sensed Tzigane's excitement. Smiling with understanding, Lilitu silently moved her lips, casting a spell of gentle sleep. Soon Tzigane's breathing became regular and deep as she slept.

Lilitu bowed her head and rejoined the others in their prayers of thanksgiving for the one called Tzigane, the one who was destined to fulfill the prophecies and lead the Dragon's son to his destiny of eternal glory in Satan's name, the one Satan had chosen to sit beside His chosen King upon the throne of the world.

NOVEMBER
1447 A.D.

6

❋❋❋❋❋❋

THREE YEARS OF IMPRISONMENT had not weakened Dracula. He had overcome the horrors and become the master, having survived unbroken and grown strong and hard in body, mind, and will. Furthermore, the rules of his imprisonment were now less strict and harsh, for although the Turks still hoped to use him one day as their pawn, they now knew it would have to be more on his terms than on theirs.

Dracula walked along the narrow corridor toward his room, carrying a manuscript he had found in the meager Egrigoz library. It was a treatise on the strategy and tactics of warfare, written by a general in the Turkish army. Dracula intended to study it thoroughly in order to add to his rapidly growing understanding of the Turkish mentality.

A warrior needed to know how his enemies thought, and Dracula's enemies were the Turks. He remained stubbornly determined to gain his freedom someday, return to Wallachia, and then invade Turkland itself at the head of a Christian army and become Christendom's greatest and most feared warrior. Indeed, Dracula's main source of amusement had become the thought of how fine the Sultan's head would look decorating the top of a pike.

Dracula turned to the right and down another hallway. Two guards saw him and made a sign to protect themselves against the evil eye. He ignored them as he passed by, though inwardly he felt greatly pleased for this was another indication of his successful efforts to become feared and respected by the superstitious Turks. Disobedient soldiers were often brought into line by the mere threat of placing them under Dracula's care in the Egrigoz torture chamber.

He opened the door to his room, then closed and locked it behind him. He was alone. His brother, Radu, had succumbed to the homosexual advances of the Sultan and was now living in the ornate luxury of the Turkish ruler's palace.

By Dracula's own request, his room had been austerely furnished with only a backless chair, a hard bed, and a rough, wooden table. A single candle set in an iron base, a bottle of red wine, and an iron goblet had been carefully placed on the table away from a neat stack of parchment sheets, a quill, and a container of thick, black ink.

The room was dimly illuminated by the flickering light of a dying fire in the grate. The small, barred window in the western wall of the chamber was dark for the sun had long since set.

Dracula laid the manuscript on the table, then lit the candle from the fire. He threw another log in the grate, sat down at the table, poured some wine into the goblet, and sipped the sweet, crimson liquid as he began to read.

When the candle had burned down low, Dracula rubbed his tired eyes and pushed the chair away from the table. He stood, pinched out the candle's flame, put a new log on the fire for the night, then sat on the bed and pulled off his boots.

He lay back in bed and closed his eyes. Soon he was asleep. He began to dream.

He was standing outside the house in the Transylvanian village of Sighisoara where he had been born. Mircea, his older brother by a year, came out of the house and walked toward him, smiling.

Dracula smiled in his sleep. It was good to see Mircea again. He ran toward his brother. They embraced.

Mircea led him to a pit that was full of muddy water. Mircea stripped naked and urged Dracula to do the same, but some uneasiness kept him from doing so. Dracula kept looking at the murky water in the pit, thinking he could see slim, serpentine shapes wiggling just below the surface. Mircea jumped in.

Mircea began to scream. Dracula pulled him from the pit. His brother's body was covered with writhing snakes. Dracula frantically pulled at the serpents. They came away with bloody chunks of Mircea's flesh impaled upon their fangs.

Mircea broke from Dracula's grip and continued to scream in agony as he ran toward another pit, this one empty and dug to the size and depth of a grave. He jumped in. The dirt which was piled beside the hole began to fall in upon him. In seconds, he was buried alive.

Dracula desperately dug with his bare hands. His fingers began to bleed, cut by the rocky soil. Then a cold fog descended upon him. He stood up.

A shape hovered just at the edge of his fog-cloaked vision. It seemed to be a man. He was beckoning to Dracula. He went toward the man, but for each step Dracula took, the shape receded a step.

Dracula began to run toward the man, but he receded even faster. Then the swirling mist parted, and he saw that the man was his father, Dracul.

His father's body was naked, bloody, and mangled. He smiled sadly at his son. His mouth moved, but emitted no sound. Then Dracul swiftly glided away into the fog, and Dracula was left alone.

Dracula jerked from his sleep. His body was bathed in sweat. He shakily got to his feet and walked to the table. Sitting down, he poured some wine into the goblet and swallowed it in quick gulps. He started to pour more, but then suddenly grabbed the goblet instead and threw it against the far wall of the room with a curse. It clattered noisily on the stones.

Dracula was angry with himself. It had been a long time since he had been wakened by a nightmare. He thought he had conquered that weakness, but never before had he dreamt of his father and brother, and never had he dreamt with such vividness, such a semblance of reality.

He drank more wine, this time directly from the bottle. The despair and sense of loss that the dream had spawned still plagued him. He whispered his father's name, then cursed his weakness. He decided that the only way to defeat the dream was to attack it, to examine it and study it.

Dracula had always laughed contemptuously at the idea of dreams containing knowledge of far away events or the future, therefore he decided that the dream must have originated within himself. He wondered if it could be telling him something about himself, something which he did not consciously know. In the dream, his father and brother had been either dead or dying. Was the dream telling him that he *wanted* them dead?

Dracula angrily pushed the thought aside and began to search for some other meaning. But he kept returning to the notion that he must truly want them dead.

Wearily Dracula got to his feet and walked to the barred window. A half-moon was hanging over the western horizon. Dark clouds scudded across its face.

The light from the fire was bright enough to show Dracula his reflection in the windowpane. He noticed how much he looked like his father. He had even grown a long, straight moustache like Dracul's.

He recalled a time long ago in the throne room of his father's palace in the Wallachian capital of Targoviste. His father had placed each of his sons upon the throne in turn and asked each one if he could feel his father's bones beneath him. None had said he could.

"I can feel them now, father," Dracula whispered in his cell, for he now realized that in order to gain his freedom from the Turks, the obstacles of his father and older brother might first have to be removed from his path.

Sadly he understood the nightmare. "I am no longer a child," he said quietly, "and once the child is gone, what need is there for the father?"

Dracula returned to the table and placed a sheet of parchment before him. He dipped his quill in the ink and began to compose a letter to the Sultan. It did not matter if the dream were true or not for he intended to convince the Sultan to free him and place him in command of a Turkish army with which he could invade Wallachia. If his father and brother were not already dead, he would kill them himself.

OCTOBER
1448 A.D.

7

✦✦✦✦✦

OUTSIDE THE SULTAN'S PALACE in Adrianople, Turkish soldiers waited impatiently for their new commander to appear. They grumbled and complained among themselves as they shivered in an unseasonably cold north wind. No doubt it was even colder north of the Danube in the Christian country of Wallachia, which was their destination. The soldiers were under orders to follow a young Christian there and help place him, if at all possible, upon his father's throne.

Their grumbling ceased as the youthful commander emerged from his final audience with the Sultan, Murad II. They snapped to rigid attention as their superiors barked the command. But the eyes of the men continued to look with suspicion upon the Christian who was called the son of the Devil.

They had all heard rumors about his expertise in the torture dungeons of Egrigoz, and any respect they felt for him was due only to fear for no one wished to learn first hand if the gruesome tales were true. One look at the pale, emotionless face with the piercing eyes, frowning brows, eagle-beaked nose, and cruelly set mouth was enough to convince the most battle-hardened veteran that the stories should not be taken lightly.

Dracula gazed out over the ranks of Turkish fighting men, his simple black clothes and cloak contrasting sharply with the ornate design of the Sultan's palace.

At a command from the Turkish officers, the soldiers

presented their weapons. Dracula nodded curtly and slowly drew his own sword. He returned their salute, then slid his curved blade back into its scabbard. He descended the palace stairs to his black stallion, a magnificent gift from the Sultan.

He swung into the saddle, galloped to the head of the assembled troops, halted, then nodded to his second in command. The march began.

Approximately one month after dreaming about his father and brother, Dracula had been informed that they had been killed by a Christian conspirator named Vladislav who had usurped the Wallachian throne.

Dracula's letter to the Sultan, which predated his knowledge of the deaths of his father and brother, had carried much weight, and after months of exchanging cautious letters, Dracula had been taken to the Sultan's palace in Adrianople to bargain with the Turkish ruler in person.

Eventually, he had been given his freedom and an officer's rank in the Turkish army in exchange for his promise to lead a force northward and take back his father's throne in the Sultan's name.

Wallachia was the geographic key to the rest of the Christian world, and with Dracula's support, it could become the Sultan's gateway to further conquests. However, the Sultan did not trust any Christian completely. Therefore, he refused to give Dracula the large army he had requested. Instead, he told Dracula to wait for Allah to send them an opportunity. Finally that opportunity had come when it was reported that Vladislav had led the bulk of his Wallachian army into Serbia in a new campaign. If that information was correct, Dracula could advance into Wallachia and take back the throne of his father with just a small contingent of cavalry and infantry.

Holding the throne would be another matter, for if the usurper, Vladislav, were not killed in Serbia, he would return to Wallachia and try to defeat Dracula's Turkish forces. But it was a chance worth taking, and Dracula did not hesitate to accept the challenge offered by the Sultan.

Now, as he led the Turks out of the city and along the road to the north, Dracula felt very pleased with himself. He was free. He would deal with his new problems as they arose. Surely he could gain the aid of his father's former staunch supporters. If not, and Vladislav returned with his army . . .

Dracula pushed away thoughts of defeat. A warrior had to take risks or nothing worth doing was ever accomplished.

Behind him, the soldiers grumbled and cursed as their eyes returned again and again to the tall, slim youth who held his head so high in aloof, Christian superiority. But then, at the end of their first day's march, the Turkish soldiers' dislike and mistrust of their Christian commander grew even stronger when word spread that Dracula was now wearing a threadbare black shirt—the shirt with the silver design.

The Turks all recognized the insignia. It was the emblem of the Dragon Society of the Christians, an organization dedicated to killing Turks. The youth's father had worn one, too. Many of the soldiers had been in battles against Dracula's father, and they bitterly remembered how their comrades were slaughtered beneath the Dragon Banner of Dracul.

The soldiers also knew that before giving Dracula his freedom, the Sultan had made him vow to never wear that hated insignia again. But now, a mere day's march from Adrianople, he was proudly flaunting his insubordination for all to see.

So much for the promises of a Christian, grumbled the men. Many prayed that Allah would see fit to cause some fatal accident to visit the Christian youth before they reached Wallachia.

But Allah was not listening.

8

✳✲✳✲✳

IN THE DEEP, DARK FOREST near the Wallachian capital of
Targoviste, from within a small, thatch-roofed hut, the
sound of a woman's laughter suddenly intruded upon the
silence of the night. The door of the hut opened, and a
beautiful young gypsy woman with long black hair and
flashing green eyes emerged into the clearing that surrounded the dwelling.

She began to dance naked beneath the silver rays of
the moon, swooping and leaping and weaving her lithe
body in time to rhythms only she could hear. It was a
witch's dance of joy.

Eventually she tired of the dance and stretched out flat
on her back, gazing at the moon, smiling up at the eternal
White Goddess who shined so serenely in the heavens.

"Sister Moon," the gypsy witch whispered softly, "can
you feel Tzigane's joy? Do you know? Did you dream of
him, too?"

Tzigane gazed at the moon a moment longer, and then
laughing happily, she rose and ran back inside her small
hut, the hut which had been built by her father and the
men of her former tribe before they had left her alone to
await the return of the Dragon's son.

For over a year she had waited, and finally she had
dreamed of him, tall and proud in his black and silver
dragon shirt, crossing the Danube upon a black stallion at
the head of a Turkish army, returning to claim his father's
throne, all exactly as predicted in Satan's prophecies.

48

Tzigane reached out with her mind and sought his, careful to keep her mental presence a secret from him.

Now that he was nearer, she found her future mate easily. She recognized his consciousness immediately as that of the small boy she had seen over eight years before in her vision. But Tzigane frowned when she probed deeper into his mind.

He had changed. There was a ruthless edge, a stony coldness within him now which made her vaguely uneasy. He was sleeping badly now, tossing and turning as he struggled with the problems of a warlord about to usurp a throne, a warlord straining to remain strong under the pressures of his first real command, a warlord who had yet to reach his eighteenth birthday.

"You must sleep. You must rest," Tzigane whispered, wishing it were possible to cast a spell of sleep strong enough to master the distance to his camp. But he was still too far away.

Tzigane withdrew her mental probe. Her joy was now mixed with sadness that she could not yet help him, that she still had some time to wait before she could meet him in the flesh.

But then the excitement of the first meeting began to consume her thoughts. She could see how it would be. She knew exactly when the moment would come for it had all been foretold in Satan's prophecies.

She could not get back to sleep. She rose and slipped into her simple black gown, threw her hooded cloak around her shoulders, then left the hut and began to run through the moonlit night.

Much later, just as the eastern sky was beginning to turn gray with the coming dawn, she reached the graveyard near the outskirts of Targoviste. Her muscles were aching, and her lungs were burning from her exertion, but she had reached her goal and was happy.

She found the sacred graves of the father and older brother of the Dragon's son. The two sunken mounds were unmarked. The murdered ruler of Wallachia and his eldest son had been buried shamefully in paupers' graves. But Tzigane knew the graves, could have sensed them even if she had not watched from a distance the day they were dug and filled.

The witch knelt between the graves and smiled. "Soon,"

she whispered to those who were buried therein. "He is coming, and only he may release you if the prophecies are to be fulfilled. You must be patient just a little while longer—just as I too must wait," she murmured, stroking the cold soil that covered the graves.

Tzigane remained by the graves, whispering gentle reassurances as she had many nights before, until the rising sun broke the hazy autumn horizon. Then she said her goodbyes to the two who would soon unknowingly fulfill their parts in Satan's prophecies and began to run back toward her distant hut, wishing that a spell existed by which she could speed up the passage of time, for although she had waited a long time already, she was certain that these last few days before she finally met the Dragon's son would be the longest ones of all.

9

THE SULTAN'S INFORMATION had been correct, and Dracula captured the throne of Wallachia without a single battle. Turkish sentries now walked the palace walls, and Turkish patrols kept watch along the routes by which the usurper, Vladislav, would return to Targoviste if he did not die in Serbia. Turkish guards stood at both sides of the throne upon which Dracula sat with his sword, the true scepter of a warlord's power, cradled in his lap.

The throne room was again as austere as his father had kept it. The ornate furnishings that Vladislav had installed had been taken to the courtyard and burned.

Dracula knew that he needed Wallachian allies. If Vladislav returned with his army, Dracula's force of Turkish cavalry and foot soldiers would not be strong enough to stop him. Furthermore, Dracula did not intend to keep the infidels in Targoviste forever. Having been seen in command of them had already damaged his credibility as a Christian in the eyes of his fellow Wallachians, and, if they stayed too long, he would never be able to garner enough local support to force them out and hold Wallachia against the Sultan, which was what he had intended all along.

But as yet, he had been unable to gain any local support. Those who might have been loyal to him for his father's sake were either dead or in hiding—all except one, a young woman, who was now being freed from the dungeon and brought before Dracula's throne. He hoped that she would prove useful in providing him the key to gaining Wallachian allies. At the very least, he hoped she could

give him the names of those traitors who had taken part
in the murders of his father and brother and lead him to
Dracul and Mircea's unmarked graves.

He heard the guards' boots clicking on the stone floor of
the corridor and glanced up. The guards entered the throne
room, supporting the woman and carrying her along, her
feet barely touching the floor. For a moment Dracula was
angered by their rough treatment, but then he realized
that they were only being kind. She could not walk on her
swollen, bleeding feet.

Dracula understood. His experiences in the torture
dungeons of Egrigoz had made him familiar with such
sights. The woman was young. Her hair was dark, though
he could not be sure if it were from matted filth or her
natural color. Her eyes were swollen shut. Her lips were
also swollen and cracked. The rags she wore did little to
conceal the tortured, half-starved body beneath—a body
which might have been beautiful once.

The guards reached the foot of the throne. Dracula
stood and stepped down from the raised dais to examine
the woman. He pried her mouth open and was relieved to
see that she still had her tongue, although several of her
teeth were either broken or missing.

"Has she spoken?" he asked.

"Yes," said one of the guards, "but only once. It seemed
to be a name. 'Mercria' or something."

Dracula's attention sharpened. "Could it have been
'Mircea'?" he demanded.

The guard shrugged, but the woman moaned and tried
to open her swollen eyes. Her head turned slowly from
side to side as if she were searching for something.

"M . . . Mircea?" she mumbled softly. "Mircea?"

Dracula smiled. "Yes," he nodded excitedly. "It *is*
Mircea!"

"Mircea?" she mumbled again.

"Follow me," Dracula ordered the guards. "We will
take her to my brother's old room. The women of the
palace will nurse her back to health."

Dracula walked quickly down the corridor and led the
way into the room he had shared with his older brother
so many years before. The guards placed the woman on the
soft bed.

"It is cold in here," Dracula said with a glance at the

fireplace. "See that a fire is started while I find women to care for her."

Dracula turned and strode back into the hallway, his pulse racing with excitement. He had hoped the unknown prisoner might help him, but if what he suspected were true, her aid was practically assured, and with it the possibility of acquiring the trust and loyalty of at least a few Wallachian nobles.

He suspected that the woman from the dungeon had once been his older brother's wife.

10

DRACULA FOUND OLD KATA in the kitchen, supervising the preparation of the evening meal. She hesitantly followed him b⌐ck into the corridor and curtsied with her gray head bowed low.

"It is good to see you again, Kata," Dracula smiled.

The old woman looked up and grinned, showing her toothless gums. "Thank you, my Prince," she said and curtsied again. "You are looking well. Such a handsome young man. Your father would have been proud, God rest him."

"Yes, God rest him," Dracula said. "You've nothing to scold me about today, Kata? You do not intend to pull down my britches and whip me for playing some trick on you?" he chuckled.

"Time changes much, my Prince."

Dracula let his smile fade. He could prolong the niceties no longer. "I need your help, Kata. I have freed a woman from the dungeon."

"Yes, I saw the guards carrying her through the hallway," the old woman said, looking down at the floor again.

"I want you to choose some women to nurse her back to health as quickly as possible. Will you do that?"

Kata hesitated a moment, then nodded, her eyes still downcast.

"Who is she, Kata?" he asked. "Was she Mircea's wife?" When the woman did not answer immediately, Dracula reached out and gently patted her on the shoulders, forcing himself to be patient. "Why do you hesitate?" he asked softly. "I can learn nothing from others here, but surely you will tell me these simple things?"

"I . . . Kata stammered, "I . . . If Vladislav returns and finds out that I helped you . . ."

"Surely he would not mind your telling me the name of this woman he tormented and the reason he chose to keep her alive."

"He is a cruel man, my Prince."

"I heard her speak my brother's name, Kata. Was she his wife?"

Kata's wrinkled face revealed her inner struggle. Finally she raised her head and made her decision. "Yes, my Prince. She was Mircea's wife. They were so happy together. We were all so happy for them. She was carrying his child when . . . when . . ."

"A child? Where is this child?"

"Dead, my Prince. It was born in the dungeon, and Vladislav killed it before her eyes." Kata began to sob.

Dracula clenched his fists at his sides and forced himself to remain in control of his emotions. He stepped forward and embraced Kata, patting her gently on the back. "I am here, Kata. It is all right now."

"Vladislav will return and . . ." she wept.

"He may be killed in Serbia."

Kata pulled away from him.

"What is troubling you, Kata?" he asked uneasily. "Why do you look at me as if I were a stranger?"

"Vladislav is cruel, but at least . . . at least he is a Christian," she whispered fearfully, crossing herself.

"Kata, Kata," Dracula said, shaking his head. "Do you trust me so little? Even you, Kata? I give you my word that I am still a loyal Christian. I will drive the Turks away as soon as I have enough local support. I tricked the Sultan, Kata."

Kata grinned uncertainly. "Tricked the Sultan, did you? You always could fool a person. Then you are still a good Christian?"

"Of course I am. Using the Turks was the only way I could gain my freedom and take back my father's throne. Do I not wear the Dragon of my father which dedicates me to killing Turks? Spread the word among the women, Kata. Tell them what I have told you so that in turn the men will know the truth and rally to my cause. With their help, I will first force the Turks to leave and then defend the throne against Vladislav. Will you do that, Kata? Will you tell the women?"

"I . . . I will tell them, my Prince. I promise."

Dracula hugged the old woman again. "Thank you, Kata. Can you tell me anything else that will help me? Do you know who helped murder my father and brother, or the location of their graves?"

Kata looked at the floor again and shook her head. "I am only an old woman, my Prince. I know nothing of the affairs of men."

Dracula decided it was useless to press her further. "One more thing, Kata. What is the name of my brother's wife?"

"Varina. They were so happy together. So happy." Tears filled the old woman's eyes again.

"Thank you, Kata. Now go and find women to help you nurse Varina back to health. And you won't forget to tell the women what I told you, will you?"

"I will tell them, little Vlad." Suddenly she realized what she had said and quickly added, "I mean my Prince."

Dracula laughed. "No doubt I'll always be 'little Vlad' to you, eh Kata?" he asked with a wink, then walked away.

Kata watched Dracula go, then hurried back into the kitchen. The other women turned expectantly toward her, anxious to learn what had happened in the hall.

"Our new prince says that he tricked the Sultan and that he will send the infidels away as soon as our local men give him their help."

"Do you believe him?" one of the women asked suspiciously.

"I have known him a long time," Kata replied proudly. "I believe him. I must go now and select women to help me nurse Mircea's wife back to health. Like a good Christian, our new prince has freed her, you know, and intends to care for her like a sister."

Kata cast a stern eye around the kitchen, then satisfied that all was proceeding properly, she turned her thoughts to Varina.

When she was gone, the other women began to talk.

"He's just trying to fool Kata like he always used to do," one woman said. "And he's trying to trick us into believing that he's still a good Christian after riding at the head of those horrible Turks!"

"I heard he intends to burn all the churches and put heathen altars in their place," said another.

And that was the story spread by the women. It made a better tale.

NOVEMBER
1448 A.D.

11

-][--][-*-][-*-][-*-][-*-

"I HAVE HEARD RUMORS that I intend to burn all the churches in Wallachia, Kata," Dracula said tightly. "That is not what I wanted the people to believe."

"I . . . I told them what you asked me to tell them," Kata said, fidgeting nervously. "They thought you were trying to trick me like you used to do. I could not convince them otherwise, my Prince. Women tell the tales that make the best gossip."

Dracula forced himself to remain calm. He reached out and touched the old woman's shoulder. "Thank you for trying, Kata. I do not blame you for the lies that have been spread. I am going in now to speak with my brother's wife."

"She is still weak, my Prince," Kata protested feebly.

"I would wait longer if I could, but time is my enemy. I must learn all I can from her right now. I have waited a week, but I can wait no longer."

Dracula entered the room, closed the door firmly behind him, then walked to the bed and studied the sleeping woman.

Varina's appearance had changed drastically. After just a week of care, her lips were no longer cracked and swollen. Her dark brown hair lay in soft waves around her head on the pillow. Her long-lashed eyelids were no longer dark and puffy, and her cheeks had gained a slightly rosy hue. Her hands and arms, wrapped tightly around a second pillow as she slept, now seemed less like a skeleton's.

"Varina?" Dracula called softly.

The sleeping woman stirred, then hugged the pillow closer, murmuring Mircea's name.

"Varina," he repeated. "I am Vlad, Mircea's brother."

Slowly, hesitantly, Varina's eyelids fluttered open. She turned her haunted brown eyes toward him and studied him for a moment in silence.

"I am Vlad, Mircea's brother," he repeated with a reassuring smile. "You are safe now, Varina."

Varina smiled weakly. "Kata told me what happened. Thank you for freeing me."

"I need your help, Varina," Dracula said. "I would let you rest longer if I could, but I do not have the time."

"Vladislav?" Varina asked with fear lining her face. "Vladislav is returning?"

"Not yet, and he may not. He may be killed in Serbia."

"And if he is not? Oh, God help me. I can't stand any more pain!"

"I will not let him harm you again. With your help, I may yet be able to hold the throne even if he does return. But if he returns and I have no hope of defeating him, I will take you with me when I leave."

Varina relaxed, reassured by his promise. "How can I help?"

"I realize this will be painful for you, but I must know the details of my father and brother's deaths, and the location of their graves."

Varina's eyes filled with tears.

"No one else will tell me, Varina. They all fear Vladislav too greatly to help me."

Varina brushed the tears from her eyes with the back of her hand, then nodded to Dracula. "I will tell you all I know. This pain is not as great as that which I suffered in the dungeon. My child . . ."

"Kata told me about your child. I am sorry, Varina."

She nodded again, then took a deep breath before continuing. "They . . . they tortured Mircea and made me watch, but they did not kill him. Then they made him watch as I was raped again and again and . . ."

Dracula waited for her sobbing to subside. "Can you tell me the names of those traitors who helped murder my father and brother?" he asked tensely.

"I will tell you the names I know," she said haltingly, "but please, I must finish telling you my story before I lose my strength. After I had been humiliated before Mircea, they threw him in a grave and buried him alive." She stopped for a moment and struggled to regain a semblance of composure. "After that, I watched them torture your father to death. Then I was taken back to the dungeon, and my own torture began."

"Where are their graves?" he hissed, fighting his own anger and pain. "I will bring my father and brother to the palace and give them a place of honor in the crypt."

"At last Mircea will return to me!" Varina whispered excitedly.

It was a moment before her words penetrated Dracula's consciousness.

"What did you say?" he asked suspiciously.

Varina's eyes had a faraway, dreamy look. "Mircea will return to me when you free him from those vines and that dreadful earth which covers him," she said quietly.

Dracula walked to the fireplace. He watched the leaping flames in silence. Had Varina gone mad in the dungeon? Could he really believe anything she told him?

"I am not mad," Varina said from the bed.

He turned and walked back to her. "You must rest. I will return when you have rested some more."

"I am not mad," she repeated. "There are many things which you do not understand. Do you not wonder why so many of your father's loyal supporters turned away from him and helped plan his overthrow?"

"Continue," Dracula said wearily, deciding to let her talk.

"Your father once offended a coven of witches. It happened a long time ago, and Mircea did not know the details, but the witches cursed him and his eldest son. They were condemned to return from the grave after death and live forever as slaves of Satan, as the Devil's Undead, as vampires."

"Varina," Dracula said angrily, "my father scorned all superstitions for the weaknesses they are. Vampires are superstition. Mircea is dead. He will not return to you."

"He *will* return to me. I hear him calling to me in my dreams, begging me to free him from the vines, to release him from his grave."

"Your torment in the dungeon has harmed your mind, Varina," Dracula said. "I have seen it happen before when the pain . . ."

"When you find their bodies, you will see that they are wrapped in wild rose vines which keep them from walking the night," she interrupted angrily.

"Finding vines would prove nothing," Dracula replied, "except that the story about the witches was known to other superstitious fools. Vladislav might have spread the tale himself to weaken the support for my father."

"You will see," Varina whispered. "You will see. But you wanted the names of the traitors and the location of the graves. I will tell you what I know." '

Dracula hesitated a moment. He was certain Varina was mad. Her mind had snapped during her stay in the dungeon. He had seen it happen often in Egrigoz. But she was all he had. He nodded for her to begin.

"When you find my Mircea, he will be undecayed, untouched by the worm, and his death wounds will have healed," she whispered, her eyes faraway again. "Your father will be the same."

"Varina," Dracula said firmly. "I want to hear no more of your hopeless dreams and superstitions. Tell me the names of the traitors and the location of the graves, or I am going to leave."

"Very well," Varina smiled knowingly, "but you will see. You will see."

12

⚜-⚜-⚜-⚜-⚜

TZIGANE KEPT WELL OUT OF SIGHT behind the thick bushes that bordered the graveyard as she watched the exhumations of Dracula's father and brother. But she did not watch the sweating men who were working to unearth the corpses. She had eyes only for him who sat aloof upon his black stallion and directed the operation.

"He is even more handsome than I had thought," the witch whispered to herself. He had a magnetism, a presence, an aura of power that fascinated and thrilled her.

Suddenly Dracula's head jerked up, and he glared directly at the spot where she crouched in hiding.

Tzigane stiffened. It was not the right time. He must not see her yet. How sharp his perceptions must be to have sensed her eyes upon him! But then, she should have expected nothing less. A predator's senses have to be sharp.

He who wore the silver dragon was now urging his stallion cautiously toward her, his hand on the hilt of his sword. The sword whisked free of its scabbard and glinted in the rays of the afternoon sun.

"No, Prince Dracula," Tzigane whispered softly, "you will not see me. Not yet." She grinned mischievously and moved her lips in a silent incantation.

Dracula came closer and closer. He stopped directly opposite the bush behind which Tzigane hid. He frowned deeply and swept the area with his gaze, examining carefully, looking for anything that might seem out of place, anything that might indicate danger. Then his eyes fell directly upon Tzigane. But he did not see her.

Tzigane struggled to keep from laughing. The spell of invisibility was one of her favorites.

Dracula's frown faded slightly as he decided there was no danger after all. He shrugged and slipped his sword back into its scabbard, then jerked the stallion around and rode slowly back to the graves.

Tzigane waited until the bodies had been placed in the new coffins and taken away to the palace crypt, then she reached into her leather pouch and removed a piece of cheese. She glanced at the setting sun. Soon it would be dusk, and then. . . .

The anticipation of the night which lay ahead was nearly too much to endure. Tzigane found she was not really hungry after all and put the cheese back in the pouch.

She could wait no longer.

She rose, brushed off her cloak and gown, repeated the incantation for invisibility to bolster the spell, then began to walk quickly toward the distant palace and her first meeting with the Dragon's son.

13

✠━╫━╫━╫━✠

DRACULA ENTERED his father's old room—the room which
he had now taken for himself—closed the door and removed his heavy cloak. Suddenly he heard the door opening behind him. He spun around with his hand on the hilt
of his sword. But it was not an assassin; it was Varina.

"You should not be walking. Your feet are far from
healed," Dracula said as he helped her into a chair.

"Do not worry about me," she said with a grimace of
pain. "My feet hurt less than they have for some time.
You have been to the graves?"

"Yes."

"And?" she asked hopefully.

"The bodies of Dracul and Mircea are now at rest in
the palace crypt."

"I want to see my husband," Varina said, her eyes bright
with expectancy.

"No. The new coffins are sealed."

"Were the vines of the wild rose wrapped around their
bodies?"

"Yes. I tore them away. But Mircea is dead, Varina.
Dead."

"And had the worms been at him?"

"Yes," Dracula lied.

"I want to see for myself."

"No."

"I do not believe you. You are lying about the worms,"
Varina said stubbornly.

Dracula shrugged indifferently.

"I intend to see Mircea," she said tersely. "He called to me again this afternoon while I slept. Let me see my husband!"

"No. I absolutely forbid it."

Varina stood without saying another word and limped painfully out of the room. Dracula did not try to stop her. He leaned against the mantel and watched the flames in the fireplace. He cursed.

"She is mad. She *has* to be mad," he whispered. "I must not let her superstitions poison me."

Dracula grabbed a bottle of wine and began drinking from it, determined to blot out his memory of the inexplicably preserved corpses of his father and brother.

Back in her room, Varina stretched out on the bed in which she and Mircea had shared their love. Tears filled her eyes.

"Mircea," she whispered with a sob. She was certain Dracula was lying. He *had* to be lying. Her husband *would* return to her, she just knew he would.

"I will not wait for you to come to me," Varina whispered, smiling in anticipation. "Tonight, when all are asleep, I will go to you, my love, my husband."

Varina looked anxiously toward the window beside her bed. The light was growing faint. The day was dying. "Soon, my love, soon," she whispered, then closed her eyes. She drifted immediately into a deep sleep. And saw her husband.

Mircea opened his pale arms and embraced her. Varina moaned in her sleep, her passion smouldering deep within her. But even in the dream, Mircea's flesh was cold and waxen, and when he kissed her with his ruddy lips, his teeth felt like icicles against her tongue.

14

✠⊹✠⊹✠⊹✠⊹✠

DRACULA BOLTED from his sleep. His eyes swept the dimly lit room, searching for danger. All seemed normal. Slowly he relaxed and tried to remember what had awakened him so suddenly.

Someone had called his name. "A dream," he whispered as he sat up in bed and rubbed his temples. His head ached. "The wine," he mumbled, then left his bed and flexed his muscles.

He decided that a breath of cold night air would make him feel better and began to pull on his boots. He was already wearing his clothing—a warrior could not afford to sleep in comfort like a common man. He buckled his sword belt, then threw a heavy, black cloak around his shoulders.

Dracula quietly opened his door, stepped into the hallway, and froze. It seemed too quiet, even for the dead of night. He glanced down the torch-lit corridor. A Turkish guard was slumped over a few feet away. Dracula drew his sword and advanced cautiously. He prodded the man with his boot. There was no response. He knelt and examined him more closely. His flesh was warm, and he was breathing deeply.

"Wake up," Dracula hissed angrily as he shook the Turk by the shoulders. "I will see you lashed for this!" But the man refused to awaken.

Dracula stood and kicked the sleeping guard. The man began to snore. Cursing, Dracula strode off toward the throne room. But in the throne room, the soldiers were also asleep.

A chill spread through Dracula's body. He shook his head angrily. "I will not be weakened by superstitions," he growled. "Someone has drugged the wine. Assassins no doubt."

Satisfied that he had the answer to the mystery but now more wary than ever of the danger around him, Dracula quickly returned to his room and locked the door.

Suddenly something creaked behind him. He whirled into a crouch, holding his sword in front of him.

There was a man dressed in a long, white shroud sitting in the chair before the fire, watching the flames.

It was his father.

15

※─※─※─※─※

DRACULA'S WARRING EMOTIONS paralyzed him for a long
moment, but then his shock and confusion were replaced by
anger.

"Impostor," Dracula hissed menacingly as he advanced
toward the man. He placed the tip of his sword beneath
the man's chin. "Since you pretend to be a corpse, I shall
help you become one."

He was now certain that he understood the plot. In the
morning some agent of Vladislav would report the dis-
appearance of the bodies of his father and brother from
the crypt. Other agents would then say they had seen
Dracul and Mircea walking in the night, searching for
blood. Word would then spread that the stories about
Dracula's father and brother were all too true, and the lies
that had destroyed his father would also destroy him for
no one would ever support a man whose family was tainted
by the superstitions of Satan and vampires.

"Do you wish to tell me who sent you before you die?"
Dracula asked calmly. "Your plot has failed. I am not
superstitious, and you do not frighten me. When I show
the people your head—the head of an impostor—they
will know that Vladislav is the true villain."

Suddenly the man thrust himself forward in the chair.
Dracula's sword passed through his neck and came out the
other side. He smiled up at Dracula, then jerked backward.
The sword came free, and the blood stopped flowing. The
wound healed and vanished.

71

"Now do you believe?" the man asked. "Won't you call me 'father'?"

Dracula said nothing. Slowly the point of his sword dipped lower and lower toward the floor. He felt a weakness spreading throughout his body. His knees began to tremble.

"Do not be ashamed of this fear," his father said. "I, too, am afraid—afraid of what I have become and of what will happen to me now."

"Where . . . where is Mircea?" Dracula asked numbly.

"Visiting his wife. She came to the crypt. Her blood gave us both the strength to rise. But I still thirst. Won't you share some of your strength with me, my son?"

Dracula's father lurched to his feet. His eyes began to glow with a hellish red light. He approached his son and embraced him with his corpse-cold arms. Dracul's icy lips touched Dracula's throat.

Dracula struggled to summon his strength and fight the foul thing his father had become. But his muscles would not respond.

Suddenly there was a hammering at the door. Dracul's head jerked up. He whirled and growled like a wild beast. Freed from the cold embrace, Dracula slumped helplessly to the floor.

The door burst open, and several Turkish guards with swords drawn ran into the room. They stopped when they saw the man in the shroud.

Dracul began to advance on the armed soldiers. One of the guards lunged forward with his sword. It passed through the vampire's body. Dracul laughed and hurled the guard aside, then pulled the sword out of his flesh and took another step. The guards cowered back toward the door, making the Turkish sign to ward off the evil eye, muttering prayers to Allah.

Suddenly a woman with long black hair pushed her way into the room. "I told you your weapons would be useless against the Undead," she said calmly. "Now get out of here. You are only in my way."

The soldiers gratefully obeyed, leaving her alone to face the living corpse with the burning red eyes.

Dracul advanced on the woman with a disdainful laugh.

The woman silently moved her lips. The effect was instantaneous. Dracul dropped the sword and fell to his

knees, clutching his heart. He collapsed on the floor and
was still.

The woman ran to Dracula and knelt beside him. She
examined his neck. "Thank Satan I was in time," she
whispered.

Dracula struggled to speak, but he was still powerless
even to move. The woman placed a hand on either side of
his head and gazed deep into his eyes. His paralysis suddenly disappeared.

"Can you stand?" she asked.

Dracula nodded, grasped his sword, and cautiously
pulled himself to his feet. An instant of dizziness quickly
passed.

The woman turned and hurried to the motionless form
of Dracula's father.

Dracula followed slowly, his sword gripped tightly in
his hand. "Is he dead?" he asked.

"Dead? The word has no meaning for him now. He is
Undead."

"How did you defeat him?" Dracula asked, trying desperately to clear his mind and make sense out of all that
had happened.

"There will be time later for explanations. Right now
we must see that your father and brother are sent on their
way."

Suddenly, the point of Dracula's sword was at the woman's throat. "I will have my answers *now*," he said tightly.

"Kill me and your father will walk unhindered by my
will. Is that what you want?" Slowly she reached up and
pushed the blade away. "I need your help. Will you carry
your father's body to the palace courtyard?"

"I may, but not until I understand exactly what is
happening."

"Very well," she sighed with resignation. "I will have
to do it the hard way." She closed her eyes. Her brow
furrowed in concentration. Sweat glistened on her face.
Her entire body trembled with the strain.

Dracula watched suspiciously in silence.

Then the woman relaxed and opened her eyes.

Dracul began to rise.

Dracula stepped backward warily, but his father took no
notice of him.

"Go to the courtyard and wait for me there," the woman

ordered Dracul, then turning to Dracula, she said, "Follow him and see that nothing hinders his passage. I must get your brother."

Dracula watched as his father slowly walked into the corridor, turning toward the courtyard.

"Will you please trust me and follow him?" the woman asked impatiently.

Dracula hesitated a moment longer, then nodded and turned to follow his father.

When they arrived in the courtyard, Dracul stopped and stood still.

"Father?" Dracula asked cautiously.

Dracul did not respond. His eyes stared straight ahead, unblinking.

"Can you hear me, father?" Dracula asked.

Again there was no response.

Soon, the woman came into the courtyard behind Dracula's brother, Mircea, whose eyes stared as blankly as his father's.

"What of my brother's wife Varina?" Dracula asked, looking with repulsion at the trickles of blood that ran from Mircea's mouth.

"She has lost much blood," the woman replied, "but she will not die. She will regain her strength. Be quiet now and do not try to stop what is about to happen. You will not be harmed, nor will your father and brother."

The woman spread her arms and began to chant in a harsh, guttural language unfamiliar to Dracula.

Then from high overhead, he heard the sound of vast wings beating the cold night air. A dark, hovering shape filled the sky over the courtyard, blotting out the stars. Three red, burning eyes glared downward. Chill gusts of wind spawned by the dark, half-hidden wings buffeted the ground. A foul stench filled the air.

"Do not be afraid," the woman told him.

"I am not afraid," Dracula answered tensely, gripping his sword even tighter in his sweating fist.

"Good. This beast is called a Strigoi. It will take your father and brother to a safe place."

"Where is that?"

"All in time," the woman replied. "Now be silent just a little longer."

She spoke again in the harsh language. The dark shape

came lower and lower. Four massive, leathery claws uncoiled from beneath the beast's body and descended into the courtyard. The woman continued to give instructions in the guttural language until Dracula's father and brother were nestled within the talons of two of the claws, then she spread her arms once more and shouted a final command. The beast ascended into the heavens as the sound of the flapping wings grew fainter and fainter and was gone.

"I am very tired," the woman said, rubbing her forehead.

Dracula slipped his sword into its scabbard and faced her. "I, too, am tired," he said coldly, "but I expect explanations, and you will give them to me freely or . . ."

He left the threat unfinished, gripped the woman's arm and steered her back inside.

16

❖❖❖❖❖

DRACULA HANDED THE WOMAN a goblet of wine, then sat beside her in front of the fireplace in his room. Her pale green eyes sparkled at him over the rim of the silver goblet as she sipped the warming, crimson liquid.

Dracula studied her suspiciously. In an oval face, beneath arrogant, arched brows, her eyes slanted catlike with heavy lids and long, curling lashes. Her nose was straight and narrow, her lips red and full, her cheekbones high and proud. She wore a hooded, dark green cloak and beneath it a simple black gown. A leather pouch hung from a thong which was tied loosely around her waist.

"It is time for answers," Dracula said. "We will start with your name."

"Tzigane," the woman replied with a smile.

"How did you get past the guards?"

"You are more concerned with the security of your palace than with your father and brother?"

"Answer the question."

"Everyone except you and your brother's wife dreamt in oblivion as I entered. Then I awoke some of the guards, convinced them you were in danger, and followed them to your room."

"You awoke the guards? I tried to awaken one but could not."

"You did not cast the spell that made him dream." Tzigane smiled mysteriously.

"A spell?"

"I am a witch," Tzigane proudly announced with a toss of her head.

"A witch? I have heard rumors suggesting that my father and brother were cursed by witches. What do you know of that?"

"Witches did not curse them. Witches blessed them and gave them the gift of eternal life on Earth."

"You call becoming a blood-drinking corpse a blessing?" Tzigane laughed.

"I would restrain my amusement if I were you," Dracula said tightly. "The Christian Dragon I wear dedicates me to killing all enemies of Christ."

"Such as witches?"

Dracula smiled coldly and nodded.

Tzigane took another sip of wine.

"What manner of creature was that flying beast, and where did it take my father and brother?" he asked.

"That beast, the Strigoi, is a creature conjured from the Unseen nether realms which lie near our physical world. They often prove useful as beasts of burden—and destruction. Only the Undead—those who are half in this world and half in the Unseen one—can safely suffer the touch of a Strigoi without injury. Your father and brother, being Undead now, were therefore not harmed. The Strigoi took them to a cave by a lake high in the mountains to the north."

"Your answers only raise more questions," Dracula growled. "I suggest you start giving me plain, simple answers before I lose patience with you."

"Simple answers do not exist. It will take much time, more time than we have tonight, before you can hope to understand the Unseen world around you." Tzigane sipped her wine and watched the flames for a moment in silence. "But do not worry for your father and brother," she finally continued. "My Sisters in the cave will care for them as honored guests."

"Sisters? Other witches?"

"Of course."

"And why should Dracul and Mircea be honored by those who cursed them?"

"Blessed them," Tzigane corrected.

Dracula's eyes narrowed dangerously. "Why did you aid me tonight? What did you hope to gain?"

"I aided you so that I might gain your trust or, at least, get your attention."

"You have my attention, witch, but not my trust."

Tzigane shrugged again. "It will do for now."

"Why should you desire my trust?"

"It would make it easier for us to work together."

"Toward what end?"

"The fulfillment of Satan's prophecies."

"I do not work for Satan, witch," Dracula replied angrily. "As I told you, the Christian Dragon dedicates me to killing enemies of Christ."

Dracula stood and looked down at the beautiful woman in the chair. "I believe my time is being wasted questioning you in this manner. Perhaps the dungeon would be a more suitable location. I think I could learn more with you stretched out on the rack."

"You will not torture me," Tzigane said quietly.

"And why not?"

"I will not allow it."

With a derisive laugh, Dracula stood and walked to the door. He called for the guards. There was no response.

"They are sleeping again," Tzigane told him with a smile. "Do you still want to know why my Sisters honor your father and brother? It is a very important question, Prince Dracula."

Dracula walked back to the fire and drew his sword. He held the tip near Tzigane's throat.

Tzigane ignored the blade and raised her goblet to her mouth, but instead of sipping, she silently moved her lips.

"I will take you to the dungeon myself," Dracula said confidently. But suddenly he found that he could no longer move.

Tzigane rose. "Your father and brother are honored because of you, because of your destiny, because of what Satan's prophecies say you shall become. You are the Chosen One of Satan, Prince Dracula."

Dracula's muscles shook with the strain, but he could not break free of the paralysis which had gripped him.

"I am tired," Tzigane sighed. "I am going to my home in the forest. Visit me soon, Prince Dracula, if you would have Tzigane tell you more. I will touch the mind of your stallion from afar so that he will know the way to my hut."

Tzigane passed her hands in front of Dracula's eyes. His

paralysis gave way to relaxation. He dropped his sword and slumped to the floor, then instantly fell into a deep sleep.

Tzigane knelt beside Dracula, bent down, and kissed him softly on his forehead, then studied his tense, frowning face with concern.

She murmured some lazy syllables, then smiled when she saw Dracula's drawn face relax. Next, she took a small, iron dagger from her leather pouch, cut off a small lock of his hair, rose to her feet, turned, and quickly left the room. She was greatly pleased with her successful night's work and her first meeting with the Dragon's son.

17

᛭᛭᛭᛭᛭᛭

DEEP IN THE FOREST, Tzigane danced naked in the moonlight, whirling, swooping and leaping as she performed the ritual which would draw Dracula to her hut. It had been two days since she returned from the palace, and he had yet to come to her. But he would come now, for no man could resist her erotic dance of beckoning—not even the Chosen One of Satan.

Finally Tzigane had finished. She ran back toward her hut, her body glistening with sweat in the silver glow of the moon, her breath frosty in the freezing November air.

She reached the clearing where her small, thatch-roofed dwelling crouched beneath towering trees and entered the hut. Tzigane lifted a folded gown bound with leather thongs from a narrow shelf over the thick layer of pine needles that served as her bed. For a moment she held the bundle to her breasts and mouthed a silent prayer of thanksgiving to Satan. Then she untied the thongs.

She unfolded the gown and held it out, her eyes growing moist with joy. It had been specially made for her to wear on the first visit of Satan's Chosen One. The gown was made of a soft, rich fabric as raven black as her hair. An intricate design of interlocking pentagrams was embroidered with silver thread on the bodice, sleeves, and hem. She slipped the long gown over her head, pulled it into place, then reverently fastened the front. Tzigane twirled happily through the hut, feeling strong and beautiful, anxious for the morrow to arrive.

"He will come," she whispered excitedly. "The Chosen

One will come tomorrow. He will remember the dream sent by my dance and come to embrace me and kiss me and . . ."

Tzigane laughed expectantly and ran back outside the hut. She breathed deeply of the cold air, then began a slow dance of joy in the moonlight, wishing for the dawn to hurry, anxious for Dracula to arrive and impatient to become the mate of the Chosen One of Satan.

18

❊❊❊❊❊

T̲ZIGANE FELT a quickening of her pulse. She smiled. "He is near," she whispered, then ran to the door of her hut and looked out.

At first the sunlit forest was silent, but then came the distant rumble of many horses galloping rapidly closer.

Tzigane frowned apprehensively. She probed with her mind. "Turks," she hissed with disgust. She probed deeper, then relaxed slightly. The soldiers' orders were only to surround and search her hut for assassins. Deciding they meant her no harm, Tzigane leaned against the door frame and waited for them to appear, her arms crossed under her breasts.

Soon a dozen mounted Turkish soldiers burst into the clearing and reined their horses to a halt in a cloud of dust. Five of them leaped to the ground and ran toward her. Two grabbed her arms and held her while the others warily entered the hut. Finding nothing, they ran back to their horses and remounted.

Dracula then appeared. Tzigane probed his thoughts but found no danger. He urged his spirited stallion closer to the dwelling, then jumped lightly to the ground. He smiled at the witch and greeted her casually, then walked toward her, still smiling.

A premonition urged Tzigane to probe Dracula's mind once again. It was now strangely and ominously blank. She hastily began moving her lips to cast the spell of sleep.

Dracula's smile faded. In a blur of speed, he drew his

dagger and brought the hilt down onto the witch's skull. Tzigane slumped to the ground and lay still. Dracula slipped his dagger back into the sheath on his belt, then turned to the mounted soldiers. "Surround the hut," he ordered. The mounted guards quickly moved away into the forest.

Dracula looked down at Tzigane, then at the two remaining soldiers. "Gag and blindfold her," he ordered, "bind her hands behind her back, tie her ankles together, and bring her inside."

The men grinned and hastened to obey. Dracula entered the hut behind them.

It was a poor dwelling even by peasant standards. There was a small fire, no windows, and only the one door. There was also a low, wooden stool near a crudely constructed table. On the table were a jug and two mugs.

The soldiers carried Tzigane inside. A dirty cloth now covered her eyes, and another, held in place by a leather thong, had been stuffed into her mouth. A second strip of leather bound her ankles together, while another cut into her crossed wrists, holding them securely behind her back. Her black and silver gown was covered with dirt.

Tzigane moaned softly beneath the gag.

"She is awakening," Dracula said. "Place her on her feet." He picked up the stool, gripped one of the three legs, and broke it off. He dropped the stool to the floor, then looked up.

"Throw a rope over that beam," he said, motioning with his black-gloved hand.

A soldier left the hut and returned with a rope, then threw one end over the beam Dracula had indicated. Dracula made a noose with the other end.

Tzigane moaned again and shook her head, fighting to regain her consciousness. Suddenly, as she felt the rope tighten around her neck, she began to struggle.

"Bring her over here beneath the beam," Dracula said.

One of the men lifted her off the floor and carried her forward. Her cries of protest were muffled by the gag.

Dracula handed the free end of the rope to the other soldier. "Keep it taut," he said as he bent down and put the two-legged stool beneath Tzigane's sandaled feet.

"Lower her," Dracula said. Tzigane's feet touched the

stool. "Good. Now tighten the rope and secure it to the adjoining beam."

Dracula stepped back and watched his men complete the task. When it was as he wanted, he stepped close to Tzigane and said, "I am now going to have my man release you. If you do not balance, you will hang. Nod if you understand."

Tzigane hesitantly nodded.

"Release her," Dracula said coldly. The soldier whose arms had encircled Tzigane's waist stepped back. The stool wobbled precariously. Tzigane fought to maintain her balance. Sweat bathed her face.

Dracula glanced at the two Turks. They were enjoying the witch's struggles. "Go join the others," Dracula ordered quietly.

The men frowned at him, then turned and left the hut, grumbling that they should be allowed to stay and watch. Still complaining, they remounted their horses and moved away to complete the ring of protection which now encircled the hut.

Dracula watched them through the doorway until he was satisfied his orders had been obeyed. Then he closed the door and turned to face the bound witch.

19

✥✦✥✦✥

DRACULA REMOVED Tzigane's blindfold. Her pale green eyes blazed down angrily at him. He removed her gag, then quickly said, "If I feel a spell being cast over me, I assure you I will knock the stool from beneath your feet before I lose my strength to resist."

Tzigane tried to probe Dracula's mind, hoping to discover a way out of her desperate situation, but as soon as she stopped concentrating upon balancing on the stool she nearly fell.

"You must be more careful," Dracula said with mock concern. "You might slip and hurt yourself. When you have done what I wish, I will let you down."

"There is no need for this," Tzigane said tensely. "I have waited long for your return so that I might help lead you to your destiny as foretold by Satan's prophecies. Have you forgotten what I said at the palace? You are the Chosen One of Satan!"

"Indeed? Well, Tzigane, I do not want to hear any more of prophecies, nor of chosen ones. Your twisted beliefs do not concern me, nor do my father and brother now that they are no longer an obstacle to my reign. I came here today seeking knowledge of a practical nature, Tzigane. Teach me the spell of sleep. I wish to use it to maintain my hold on the throne. If Vladislav returns, he and his army will be easily defeated if they are asleep."

"What you ask is not possible," Tzigane answered carefully.

"For your sake, I hope it *is* possible," Dracula said as

he slid his foot dangerously close to one leg of the wobbling stool.

"It took me years of work to perfect my powers," Tzigane protested. "I cannot simply tell you magic words to say. Witchcraft is not like that at all. And even if it were, the spell of sleep would be of no use against an army. Its range is limited. You would have to be very close for it to work. Furthermore, the more minds it must control, the weaker it becomes."

"I see," Dracula said with an indifferent shrug. "Well, it was only an idea. I suppose there is nothing more to gain by prolonging your life then. I would be foolish to let you live, don't you agree?"

"Listen to me," Tzigane hissed. "If you kill me, you will lose your chance to become more powerful than you have ever dreamed possible."

"Really?" Dracula asked sarcastically. "You would say anything to save your slim neck. I cannot believe a thing you say." He moved his foot even closer to the leg of the stool and looked up at the witch with a cruel smile. "Have you anything else to say, Tzigane?"

Tzigane fought to remain calm and think clearly. "I will help you, Prince Dracula, though not in the simple way you had thought. I will help you because it is my destiny under Satan's prophecies to do so. But you must realize that it will take years of hard work and study before your power over common men becomes supreme. I will help you to achieve undreamed of glories, but you must learn to trust me—just as I am now going to trust you. Be quick, Prince Dracula, for both our fates now rest in your hands."

Summoning all her will power, Tzigane suddenly shifted her weight. The stool fell away, and she began to hang.

20

❉—❉—❉—❉—❉

Dracula hesitated only an instant. He cursed as he circled Tzigane's waist with his left arm to lift her, slashing the rope with his dagger. He lowered her to the floor, loosened the noose, and pulled it over her head. Her neck was livid and bruised, her eyes were streaming with tears, and she was gasping for breath. He was surprised that a woman should have shown such strength of will.

"You are full of tricks, little witch," Dracula said thoughtfully. "But remember—I can still use this dagger on you if you try anything to harm me."

"Untie me," Tzigane whispered hoarsely.

Dracula shrugged and cut away the leather strap which bound her ankles. Next he freed her wrists.

Tzigane rubbed the red circles left by the straps. "Damn your suspicions," she whispered. She rubbed her bruised neck. "There was no need for that. I always intended to help you."

"I would not survive for long if I had no suspicions," Dracula answered, watching her closely. "You showed great strength for a woman."

"For a woman," Tzigane repeated, shaking her head with disgust. She went to the table, picked up the jug, and poured a deep red liquid into the two mugs. She held a mug out to Dracula. He did not take it.

With a whispered curse, Tzigane drank from the other. "It is not poisoned," she said tightly.

Dracula warily took the mug in his left hand, sniffed the liquid, took a sip, and finally nodded his approval. "Two mugs were waiting," he observed. "You were expecting me?"

"Of course," Tzigane replied, swallowing more of the wine. Its warmth began to spread through her body, and she felt her strength returning. She looked at him across the rim of her mug. "How did you know I could read your thoughts?" she asked.

"I did not know."

"You must have," Tzigane insisted, "for when I probed your mind earlier, I found no hint of danger, but then later your thoughts became strangely blank."

Dracula smiled coldly. "The trick of a hunter," he said quietly. "One's prey can often be caught unaware if the hunter keeps his mind free of thoughts of killing."

"Animals are very sensitive to the thoughts of men," Tzigane agreed. "So I was your prey today, and you kept your mind blank from habit?"

"So it would seem," Dracula replied, obviously pleased with himself.

Tzigane sipped her wine a moment longer, then set her mug on the table. "It is time to begin your lessons."

"It would be wise," Dracula said meaningfully as he studied the blade of his drawn dagger. Then he noticed that the witch was staring at him in silence. It made him uncomfortable.

"Reading my thoughts again?" he asked and consciously blanked his mind.

"No. I am sensing your emotions. Have you always been so determined to repress them?"

"I was once a child," Dracula replied. "Now I am a man."

"And emotions are only for women and children?"

"And for foolish men. You are stalling, witch. My emotions do not concern you. Begin the lessons which will give me the powers you promised or . . ."

"You will never master the forces of the Unseen world without first becoming familiar with your strongest, most basic emotions, and then learning to control and concentrate their energy. Repressing them like a Christian will keep your mind earthbound forever and will keep you from progressing toward glory."

Dracula remained silent.

"You have been with women before?" she asked.

"Of course," Dracula answered angrily.

"Yes, of course," Tzigane smiled. "Then that is where we shall begin—by helping you to become fully familiar with the sexual passions you have already experienced in a limited way."

Dracula did not reply, but the annoying memory of the dream he had had the night before flitted through his consciousness. It was a dream about Tzigane, naked, glistening with sweat, dancing in the moonlight, beckoning him, maddening him with desire. Dracula crushed out the memory and held his mind steady and blank once again.

"The controlled use of sexual passion," Tzigane continued, "is one of the more powerful forces known. It can, when manipulated in certain secret ways by witches and sorcerers, initiate a human mind into higher levels of awareness. Passion is not the only method of accomplishing this initiation, but it is certainly the most enjoyable."

Tzigane slowly began to unfasten the front of her bodice, her eyes never leaving Dracula's face. She slipped the gown from her shoulders down to her hips, then let it slide to the floor. She proudly tossed her long, dark hair, letting it frame her young, naked body, and stepped out of her sandals.

Dracula stubbornly kept his eyes locked on Tzigane's face, refusing to look at the nude beauty she was proffering.

"Why stare at my face?" Tzigane asked wickedly. "Do you want to learn or not? Look at my body and do not repress the feelings that it inspires within you. Let your passion rise. Take pleasure in it. Feel it winding tight deep inside like a coiled snake—a snake which may eventually be taught to strike down enemies or increase the awareness of your mind."

Dracula still kept his eyes on her face.

Tzigane shook her head and walked toward him.

"Stay where you are, witch," Dracula warned, raising his dagger, pointing the blade at her full, firm breasts.

Tzigane stopped and stood with her hands on her hips. "I cannot teach you if you refuse to do what I ask."

"I am not a fool, Tzigane," Dracula smiled coldly, still watching her face. "I will try to keep an open mind about the wonders of passion in which you seem to believe, but you must first satisfy me concerning one very important thing."

"Which is?"

"What do you hope to gain by teaching me your secrets? You must desire some reward other than the sparing of your life. What is it, Tzigane? What will be your reward?"

Tzigane laughed. "Of course, I should have told you before, but . . ."

"Then tell me now."

"I serve my Lord Satan. I do my part faithfully to fulfill His prophecies. You are the Chosen One who is destined to rule all the Earth. And I wish to be your mate, to sit beside you on the throne of the world. It is as simple as that."

"At last, there is some truth," Dracula chuckled and sheathed his dagger. Then he set the mug on the table and placed his hands on Tzigane's smooth shoulders. "Ambition," he smiled cunningly. "Yes, I can understand ambition. Despite all your talk of the Unseen, you are at heart merely an ambitious woman who wishes to travel a road to glory alongside a powerful man."

"I shall have to lead you a good deal of the way along that road," Tzigane quickly pointed out. "And the throne of the world is hardly the goal of a common woman."

Dracula shrugged, finally letting his gaze flow over the curves of Tzigane's body, over her proud, young breasts, her flat belly, her swelling thighs. Slowly she moistened her slightly parted lips with her pink tongue.

"You are not unappealing," Dracula said thoughtfully. "I could do worse."

"How very flattering," Tzigane said tightly.

Dracula stepped nearer and slid his arms around the naked witch. The tips of her breasts touched his chest.

"Your leather vest is cold," Tzigane complained. "You would be more comfortable without it."

Dracula suddenly crushed her to his chest in reply. He kissed her. Tzigane's tongue darted into his mouth, searing him, making him groan with impatience.

Tzigane pulled away. She smiled up at him. "Now be sure to take note of your emotions, your passion, while we are . . ."

Dracula kissed her again. "I may not find your teachings of any ultimate value, Tzigane, but I would be a fool to let an ambitious woman's beauty go to waste."

"Indeed you would," Tzigane grinned. "Your vest?"

Dracula hesitated a moment, then shrugged and began to remove his vest. Tzigane helped, and soon their naked bodies were tightly entwined upon the bed of pine needles on the floor of the hut.

21

✥ ✥ ✥ ✥ ✥

Dracula ran his fingers through Tzigane's wildly tangled hair. She took his hand and kissed the palm.

"Were my emotions satisfactory?" he asked sarcastically.

Tzigane laughed. "You should release them more often, and I intend to see that you do."

Dracula's eyes swept her nakedness. "That can be arranged," he nodded. "I could visit you each day, when matters of the throne permit. But if passion is to be our only activity, I could learn just as well in the bed of a woman in Targoviste."

Tzigane carefully concealed her hurt and anger. "We will do other things as well. I intend to begin by showing you some of the things I can do, some of the spells and dances, to make you aware of what is possible with the proper study and practice."

"I have already seen your spell of sleep, and I now know that you can read minds. Both would be of great benefit to a ruler. Tell me what else you can do."

"Raise storms," Tzigane answered, "or disperse them, weaken or kill an enemy from afar . . ."

"Could you kill Vladislav for me?"

"Do you have anything of his? Some of his hair? His nail clippings? His blood?"

"No."

"Then I cannot harm him."

Dracula shrugged. "I am ready to see a new spell."

"You already have," Tzigane smiled mysteriously. "Did you enjoy the dream I sent you last night?"

92

Dracula concealed his surprise. "So you can send thoughts as well as read them," he replied thoughtfully. "That would also be very useful. One could control an enemy's thoughts and draw him into an ambush. Could you send thoughts to Vladislav?"

"No, for the same reason as before."

"Still you sent thoughts to me so that I would dream about you, yet you had nothing of mine."

"I took a bit of your hair before I left the palace."

Dracula stared hard at the witch. "Return it to me."

Tzigane rose and picked up a small cloth pouch from the shelf above the bed, then gave it to Dracula. "I no longer need it," she said.

Dracula looked inside and saw the lock of black hair. He closed the pouch and handed it to Tzigane. "Throw it into the fire," he ordered.

Tzigane did as he asked, then returned to the bed of pine needles and knelt facing him again. "Satisfied?"

Dracula nodded. "If we have finished for today, I will return to the palace."

"Are you so anxious to leave me?"

"The throne demands much of my time."

"Stay just a little longer. I wish to tell you certain things, and since they directly concern you, you will certainly find them of interest."

"More of your prophecies of the Chosen One?"

"Yes."

"And this Chosen One is to rule all the Earth? Is that truly possible?"

"In time anything is possible."

"How much time?"

"Centuries. Perhaps thousands of years."

Dracula laughed derisively.

"Immortals never die," Tzigane carefully told him. "Centuries mean nothing to those who live forever."

Dracula hesitated. "You propose that I become a living corpse who drinks blood like my father and brother?"

"Not until you yourself so desire."

"I shall never desire to become a monster."

"Only weak, fearful minds think of vampires in that way. Servants of Satan honor and protect the living dead as sacred beings for they are proof of Satan's gift of eternal physical life on Earth."

Dracula rose and began to dress. "I am not certain that my soul is of any value—or that it even exists," he said as he pulled on his britches and reached for his boots, "but I do not plan to worship Satan and become His vampire-slave."

"One need not believe in Satan," Tzigane replied quickly, "nor even worship Him in order to control the forces you desire to possess, for the potential to control those forces already exists within the human mind. The God of Light tries to prevent humans from developing that potential so that they will remain His willing slaves, but Satan encourages the development of the powers of the individual so that mankind may grow to become their own gods."

Dracula finished dressing, then sat down on the bed and gazed into Tzigane's pale green eyes. "Your ideas and beliefs are the opposite of all I have ever been taught, Tzigane," he said. "I wish to know more about you, and why you believe as you do. How did you become a witch?"

Tzigane smiled, pleased that Dracula had asked about her. "Like my mother and my grandmother, I was born a witch. But when I was eleven, I had a vision which foretold my destiny of service to Satan. Then my parents took me to a cave high in the mountains south of the Transylvanian town of Sibiu. The women who lived in the cave came out to meet us. They were witches. My mother and father bowed to them and left me in their care. Near the cave was a beautiful lake in which slept a dragon, an emissary of Satan on Earth."

"Did you ever see the dragon?" Dracula asked sceptically.

"No."

"I thought not," he chuckled.

Tzigane ignored his sarcasm. "The cave near the dragon's lake is not unknown to Christians, though their legends twist the truth. Have you ever heard of a place called the Devil's School?"

"An old woman named Kata used to speak of it," Dracula answered. "She would try to scare my brothers and me into behaving by threatening to take us there and throw us into a lake for a dragon to eat."

Tzigane threw back her head and laughed. "You see what I mean about Christians twisting the truth?"

"How do I know you are not the one doing the twisting?" Dracula asked, raising his eyebrows.

Tzigane shook her head at his doubt. "The women from the cave," she continued, "taught me witch-secrets never dreamed of by my mother and grandmother. For seven years I practiced the spells, the dances, the words and signs of power. Then I was sent south into Wallachia to await the coming of the Chosen One of Satan, to await you, Prince Dracula."

"Why do you continue to call me the Chosen One?"

"Because the prophecies of Satan have predicted the coming of the Chosen One, and the events of your birth and life match the predictions. To begin with, the bones of your mother lie enshrined in the cave of the witches."

"My mother was not a witch," Dracula said angrily.

"Hold your anger. Let me speak. Your father did not know that Marilla, his Transylvanian bride, was a witch. But she knew that he would kill her one day, as he did."

"*I* killed my mother myself," Dracula protested. "She died giving birth to me in Sighisoara."

"No. When she knew that you, her second son, the prophecied one, were to be born, she and her sisters traveled to the cave in the mountains. You were born there on a night holy to Satan, a night when strange lights were seen in the forests and whispers were heard coming from the empty sky.

"But your father followed her. He and his soldiers profaned the cave, killed your mother and her sisters, then took you away. This was also prophesied for it was said that the Chosen One's father would kill the mother, and then, when the Chosen One's manhood neared, the father would deliver him into the hands of non-Christians. It was also predicted that the Chosen One would return in triumph, a Christian commanding infidels.

"Furthermore, the Chosen One would be called the son of the Dragon and the son of the Devil, and you cannot deny that your name means just that. Also it was said that the Chosen One would bed a witch and make her his mate."

"Which is where your ambition lies," Dracula replied dryly. "But it is easy, Tzigane, to say that everything which happens is part of a prophecy. Christians also have their prophecies and say that whatever happens is God's will."

"I did not expect you to believe so soon," Tzigane answered with a shrug, "but it was my duty to reveal these things to you so that you might begin to ponder them in your heart."

Dracula laughed disdainfully. "I am not inclined to ponder impractical things, Tzigane. I am concerned only with the life that lies before me. It does not matter to me what you believe or what you hope I will come to believe. What matters to me is my future as a living man who triumphs because of his cunning and strength. I am interested in you only because it is possible that the powers you possess could help me conquer and hold thrones.

"I will not promise to spend my time thinking about all you have said, for to me it is just a woman's tale. But I will promise you this. If you help me successfully acquire the powers needed to cast spells and control the lives and deaths of others from afar, I will keep you by my side and let you share in my glory."

Tzigane rose and kissed him. "That will satisfy me for the present, Prince Dracula, for it is my destiny to serve the Chosen One and help him onward down the road to glory. But I have faith that in time you will come to know the truth, to believe as I do and aid Satan in His battle against the God of Light.

"In time you will realize that the temporary thrones of men are nothing compared to the glory of the eternal throne of Satan's King on Earth, the King of the Undead, the Master of the Earth. You *are* the Chosen One, Prince Dracula, he whose glory will be eternal and supreme. And *I* shall share that ultimate glory."

Dracula laughed again but this time with genuine amusement. "Your ambitions may rival my own, Tzigane," he smiled, "although we have very different goals. But still, if you will be satisfied to be the ally of a man who seeks the thrones of men, then we may work well together toward my goals. Allies?" he smiled.

"Allies," Tzigane smiled. "And since we will be spending much time together, would you mind if I called you by your given name?"

Dracula started to protest, but then thought better of it and shrugged. "You may. I assume you know that name."

"It is Vlad," Tzigane stated.

Dracula nodded.

Tzigane embraced and kissed him. "Stay a little longer, Vlad," she breathed. "Let us share our passion again today."

Dracula fought a desire to agree. "I must leave," he said quickly, then walked to the door. He turned. "I will be back tomorrow," he said as his eyes raked Tzigane's shamelessly displayed beauty one more time. He smiled slightly, then left the hut.

Tzigane waited until she heard the horses of Dracula and his soldiers fade away into the distance, then went outside the hut and walked slowly down the narrow path over which Dracula had ridden, her eyes staring intently at the ground, searching for the prophesied sign.

Suddenly she gave a cry of joy, bent down, and picked up a small, silver coin. Sunlight glinted off its surface. Tzigane held the coin between her clasped hands and pressed them to her breasts.

" 'And she who finds silver in the Earth at the passing of the Chosen One shall be his mate for all eternity,' " she recited breathlessly.

And then with the coin of Satan's blessing clutched tightly in her left hand, Tzigane ran back into the hut, knelt on the bed of pine needles, and began a prayer of thanksgiving to her Lord Satan.

22

THREE WEEKS. Only three weeks. And yet at times it seemed to Dracula that it might have always been this way, riding to Tzigane's hut, making love with her on the bed of pine needles, learning things he had never believed existed.

Now riding through the forest to meet the witch yet another time, Dracula thought back over those three weeks since he had first visited her hut.

With Tzigane, he had grown to appreciate the many varied pleasures a woman could offer a man when she gave herself freely. He had decided that he preferred his sex that way rather than as he had experienced it in the dungeons of Egrigoz, taking women prisoners by force, then often killing them. But there was more to his relationship with Tzigane than mere passion. Against his better judgment, feelings of trust and friendship were growing stronger and stronger within him.

Trust. Friendship. Never had he felt that way about a woman. He had never even believed such things were possible with a member of what he had been taught to think of as the inferior sex. Were these feelings the result of some secret, devious witchcraft she was practicing upon him? It was a possibility he could not ignore, and it kept him from ever completely relaxing in Tzigane's presence. A woman with powers and abilities like hers could be just as dangerous as any armed man, and he was determined to treat his awakening emotions of trust and friendship for the witch as warily as he would treat a deadly weapon in the hands of a man.

Emotions. As she had promised, Tzigane was gradually teaching Dracula to use the power of sexual emotions to broaden his awareness of the Unseen. Their sexual climaxes had begun to be accompanied by momentary visions deep within his mind, visions which revealed glimpses of realities beyond the physical world, vistas of alien landscapes and nonhuman things beyond his comprehension.

Once he had seen the realm of eternal fire where the repulsive winged beasts Tzigane called Strigoi flew through smoky, crimson skies and heard the unending screams of those imprisoned humans that the Strigoi had stolen from the Earth and taken back to that world of eternal pain. Those cries still haunted him at times, chilling even his prison-hardened heart.

After the sex which brought the visions, Tzigane would question him about what he had seen during the climax and help him understand it and how it related to the powers he wished to possess. Next she would show him a new spell and reveal yet another of the skills she had perfected during her years of training at the cave. She would carefully describe the disciplined processes, both mental and physical, which were necessary for the successful casting of the spells.

Her explanations led Dracula to admit finally that there was no quick way for him to obtain her powers. The rituals were too complex, the mental and vocal manipulations too alien, the hand gestures and dance movements too subtle for anyone to learn in a short period of time.

But he was still determined eventually to master those powers he deemed useful. They might not help him hold the throne this first time should Vladislav return, but later they could provide the edge he might need to gain and hold absolute power over his subjects.

When the hut finally came into view, Dracula saw that as always Tzigane was waiting for him in the clearing outside the hut, wearing her gown of silver and black. But something was wrong today. Tzigane was not smiling. Dracula stiffened. That one detail, that one deviation from the way things normally were, caused him to become instantly alert for danger. He slowed his stallion and cautiously approached the witch, his hand resting on the hilt of his sword. His eyes automatically searched the forest around the hut as he strained his hearing to catch any foreign sounds from within the hut or elsewhere. Dracula motioned to the mounted soldiers behind him to take up their positions around the hut. "You look troubled, Tzigane," he said tensely.

"I had a dream last night."

"You dream every night," he answered.

"Not about Vladislav."

"Vladislav?"

"I saw him riding into Targoviste at the head of a great army."

"When?"

"I do not know, but I feel it will be soon. Perhaps today, perhaps tomorrow, perhaps a week or two from now."

"I would have preferred a dream that gave a more specific time."

Tzigane shrugged. "Dreams are seldom concerned with the exact timings of events."

"Do you know which road he will take? I could possibly arrange an ambush."

"I only saw him entering Targoviste, and his men greatly outnumbered yours."

"What else did you dream?"

"Only that Vladislav did not find you in the palace."

"Then your dream suggests what I had secretly suspected—that my first reign would not last long. Of course, this is still only a dream. A month ago I had no use at all for dreams. And perhaps you are lying about the dream?"

Tzigane looked angrily into Dracula's eyes.

Dracula shook his head. "No, I suppose you are telling the truth about the dream. Still, dreams surely do not always have to come true?"

"Mine do, Vlad."

Dracula nodded. "Very well, Tzigane. I have seen your powers. If you say my reign is nearly over . . ."

"There will be other reigns for you," Tzigane broke in.

"Of course. I will most certainly return, and when I do, perhaps I will have powers other than those of the physical world to help me hold the throne."

" 'In the year that a great comet lights the heavens,' " Tzigane recited, " 'the Dragon's son will return to Targoviste and reign in glory for many years.' "

"More of Satan's prophecy, Tzigane? Or merely hopes for your own ambitions?"

"Both, my Vlad," Tzigane smiled. "I sense that a great weight has lifted from you. Could it be that you had hoped for Vladislav to return?"

Dracula sat up straight in the saddle. "I had hoped to hold the throne. How could you suggest anything else? I have tasted the power of the throne, and I like that taste, Tzigane."

"Perhaps I have sensed a truth you will not admit to yourself?" Tzigane suggested.

Dracula's face became clouded with anger.

Tzigane quickly shrugged and tossed her head. "It is not important. Where will you go when Vladislav returns?"

"*If* he returns."

"Very well, Vlad. *If* he returns, where will you go? Back to the land of the Turks?"

"No. I do not wish to be the Sultan's prisoner ever again."

"Then where?"

"I have allies in Moldavia." Dracula studied the witch's expression. "Your eyes tell me that you have a different idea. Could it be that you want me to come to the cave of the witches with you, Tzigane?"

Tzigane's momentary surprise was apparent. "You are perceptive, my Vlad. Yes, I would like that very much. You would be safe from Vladislav's spies and assassins there, and I could continue to teach you and help you acquire the powers you desire. Also, it would fulfill another of Satan's prophecies. I cannot lie to you about that."

"Your prophecies mean a great deal to you, don't they, Tzigane?"

The witch nodded, her eyes on the ground, her body tense with expectancy. She did not want to have to use her powers to force him to go with her to the cave. She wanted him to come of his own free will. She wanted that for herself, and she wanted it very much. When the silence became too much to bear, she glanced up at him again.

"Your eyes are wet, Tzigane," Dracula said softly. He stared at her for a moment more, then asked, "What assurance would I have that this cave of yours is not a trap?"

"Only my word," Tzigane whispered so softly it could hardly be heard. The silence stretched out again.

"I must be going, Tzigane. I must send out extra patrols on the roads Vladislav will probably use and order preparations for a hasty departure should it become necessary. I will also bring two horses to you, one packed with supplies for our journey and the other for you to ride."

Tzigane's eyes grew wide. "Then you will come with me to the cave?"

"I thought you could read minds, Tzigane."

"I want to hear you say it, my Vlad," Tzigane insisted excitedly.

"Very well. Should Vladislav return, I will come with you to the cave. But if it is a trap, you will be the first to die. I promise you that."

"There will be no trap, and you may leave the cave whenever you desire. But I hope you will stay for at least . . ."

"I could not remain there for more than a month or two, Tzigane. If I disappear for too long, the Christian world might think me dead or a coward, and that would make my claim to the Wallachian throne all but hopeless."

"The powers will not be yours that quickly."

"When I leave, could you not ride by my side and continue my lessons in Moldavia? No one need know you are a witch," he smiled.

Tzigane carefully kept her face impassive. She dared not tell him about the ceremony awaiting her when they arrived at the cave for fear that he might change his mind about coming with her. "If you still want me then," she finally answered, "I will go with you when you leave."

"And why would I not still want you? If the powers are not yet mine, then of course I shall need the continued services of my teacher, will I not?"

"Of course," Tzigane said, forcing herself to smile.

"Good. Then it is decided. There may be, however, a third person in our party."

"Your brother's wife wishes to be taken to her husband?"

Dracula nodded. "She has aided me, naming many of the murderers of my father and brother so that I was able to execute them, and I promised not to let Vladislav recapture her. Therefore, if he returns, I must either kill her or take her with me, and I am certain Mircea would prefer I do the latter." His eyes narrowed, suspicious once again. "My father and brother *are* at the cave just as you've told me, are they not?"

Tzigane nodded, trying not to be hurt by his doubting. "Varina's love is strong," she whispered. "She loves Mircea even though he is Undead." The thought of Varina's love suddenly gave Tzigane hope for her own future. But did Dracula really feel anything for her? Surely he did not love her? And yet at times there was a softness in his eyes when he looked at her which led her to hope that. . . .

"I must go, Tzigane," Dracula said again, suddenly impatient. "I will bring you the horses and supplies I promised before nightfall."

Tzigane smiled again, hope suddenly in her heart. "I will try to learn something of the immediate future while you are gone, my Vlad," she promised, "and if, when you return with the horses, I have been unable to find any sign of Vladislav's immediate arrival, . . ."

She left the sentence unfinished as she toyed meaningfully with the fastenings on the bodice of her gown.

Dracula laughed, called for his men, jerked his stallion around, and galloped away.

Tzigane stood alone in the clearing for a long while after Dracula and his soldiers had gone, hoping Dracula might truly harbor feelings for her that would help him to understand why she must do what she must when they arrived at the cave. She tried to keep herself from hoping too strongly. But she *did* hope.

Sweet Satan, how she hoped!

For no matter how Dracula felt, Tzigane had fallen in love.

23

✦✦✦✦✦

NEARLY ONE WEEK after Tzigane's dream, Dracula awoke from a deep sleep and hastily began to dress in his battle gear, acting on the instincts of a warrior who has heard an alarm shouted from the battlements in the middle of the night.

He jerked on his mail shirt, drew on his heavy leather vest and pulled his boots on, buckled his sword belt around his waist, draped his cloak around his shoulders, and grabbed his gloves. Only then did he wonder at the silence in the palace. Had not a warning cry awakened him? Had he not heard the sounds of running footsteps and clanking weapons?

With a frown creasing his high, domed forehead, Dracula sat down on his rumpled bed and shook his head in confusion. A dream? Had it only been a dream? But it had seemed so real, so . . .

Suddenly he heard the pounding of heavy boots running down the corridor toward his room. Someone hammered impatiently upon his door. Dracula ran across the room, unlocked the door, and jerked it open, his hand on the hilt of his sword. It was his second in command.

The Turkish officer's expression showed his surprise at Dracula's battle dress. "Someone has already told you?" he asked as he saluted his commander.

"Deliver your report."

"A scout has reported a great army of men pressing toward Targoviste, moving at night, moving fast."

"Vladislav?"

The Turkish officer nodded. "Yes, and less than two hours from Targoviste."

"Sound the alarm and assemble the men at the encampment outside the city. I will join you there," Dracula lied.

"Then we fight?"

"Of course. We will fight unto the last man. Now go. I must finish my preparations. And don't look so forlorn. I thought you wanted to kill Christians! We may be outnumbered, but aren't the soldiers of Islam superior to those of Christendom? That is what I was told many times by the guards in Egrigoz. Now you have the chance to prove it. Yes?"

The Turkish officer snapped to attention and saluted sharply, then ran off down the corridor.

Dracula smiled coldly. Would they fight anyway even when he did not join them? Would their stubborn Turkish pride force them to fight and die beneath the swords of Vladislav's greater force?

Dracula shrugged and started to walk toward Varina's room. The Turks had served him well enough, but they were still Turks, and Dracula was still a Christian warrior. If the Turks died fighting Vladislav, Dracula would shed no tears. Nor did he feel at all guilty about deserting the soldiers before the battle. He had future battles for which he must save himself, battles he had a better chance of winning, battles which would further his goals of glory and rule.

Dracula chuckled, thinking how very angry the Sultan was going to be with his former prisoner. The thought gave Dracula a grim satisfaction as he entered Varina's room and began to concentrate on awakening her.

"Varina!" he shouted as he shook her by the shoulders.

She awoke slowly, looking at him in groggy confusion.

"Hurry, Varina," he said urgently. "Dress quickly. Vladislav is returning, trying to catch me off guard. Hurry!"

Varina did her best to hurry, but her feet had not yet healed. Finally, Dracula impatiently threw a cloak around her shoulders and carried her from the room.

He rushed to the stables where everything was a flurry of desperate activity. Dracula's black stallion and a bay mare were saddled and ready to be ridden just as they had been ever since Tzigane had told him of her dream.

Dracula galloped down the dark streets of Targoviste

and away from the city, Varina following close behind. Soon they came to a fork in the road and took the one which led to Tzigane's hut.

Tzigane was outside, saddling the spirited mare he had given her as Dracula rode into the clearing. Smiling down at Tzigane, he said, "You knew?"

"I felt it. We can leave immediately. The pack horse is ready."

"Did you send me a dream of warning?" he asked. .

"No. You had your own dream? That is wonderful, Vlad! You are making more progress than you realize."

Varina's mare trotted into the clearing. She stopped beside Dracula.

"Varina," he said, "this is Tzigane. You have her to thank for your life."

"She is the witch who had my Mircea taken away?" Varina asked coldly.

"I am," Tzigane said proudly.

"Then I shall never speak to her," Varina said defiantly. "She is a vile creature of Satan."

Anger flared in Tzigane's pale green eyes.

"Enough!" Dracula interceded. "I do not intend to travel with you two fighting all the way. Varina," he continued, calming his voice, "ride to the edge of the clearing and wait for us."

With a haughty jerk of her head, Varina turned her mare and rode off.

"She spent nearly a year in Vladislav's dungeon," Dracula whispered to Tzigane. "Her child was killed before her eyes, fresh from her womb. Her mind is not as it once was."

Tzigane shrugged.

After dousing the fire and closing up the hut, Tzigane mounted her horse. "I wonder if I shall ever see it again?" she whispered. "It will always be a fond memory, this poor hut, for it is where we first shared our passion."

"I, too, will remember it, Tzigane," Dracula replied, allowing her a moment more of sentiment. "Are you ready?"

Tzigane nodded and began to lead the way northward through the forest toward the mountains and the cave where her faith in Satan's prophecies was soon to receive the ultimate test. As she rode, she clenched a small silver

coin in her left fist. It was the coin she had found at the
passing of the Dragon's son, the silver from the Earth
which was the final proof of her destined role as Queen,
the coin which was a blessing but also a cruel burden now.

Tzigane silently cursed her foolishness. If only she had
kept her emotional distance from the Chosen One, she
would now be relishing the feel of the prophesied coin
and the satisfaction of having successfully completed her
appointed task in Wallachia. But instead she was worrying,
wondering, doubting, and . . .

Tzigane could not forget what Dracula had said about
Varina's mind. Could only an insane mortal human con-
tinue to feel love for someone who had become Undead?
Was insanity the real reason that Varina still felt love for
Mircea? And what of Dracula? He was most certainly *not*
insane. And as for any love he might feel . . .

The gypsy witch fought back a temptation to probe
his mind and seek out his feelings for her. She could have
done it easily enough, but she dared not. For if she found
that he felt nothing, her fragile hopes would be destroyed,
and although those hopes might be totally unfounded, they
would at least allow her some moments of happiness in
Dracula's arms during the few days which remained before
they reached the cave. Her hopes would also make it
easier for her to keep her faith in the prophecies once they
were there. But what if after the ceremony Dracula was
repulsed and turned away from her and . . . ?

Tzigane angrily tried to think about something else, anything else, but her mind relentlessly returned again and
again to the ceremony awaiting her at the cave and what
it might mean to her relationship with the man with whom
she had so unwisely fallen in love.

DECEMBER
1448 A.D.

24

ENRAGED that he had failed to capture Dracula by surprise, Vladislav sent out countless patrols with orders to find the usurper called the Dragon's son and bring his severed head back to Targoviste. But the patrols did not succeed. Tzigane's witchcraft proved better than the abilities of the determined Christian warriors. As he witnessed the practical uses of Tzigane's magic again and again, Dracula became more determined than ever to eventually possess those powers himself.

Finally, after nearly a week of cautious traveling, the unlikely trio composed of a dethroned Prince, a gypsy witch, and a Christian woman reached the mountains. But the most dangerous stretch of the journey still remained, for as they ascended higher and higher into the mountains, a killing winter storm descended upon them with supernatural fury. It was a storm which Tzigane was powerless to banish, a storm spawned by a magic more powerful than her own and intended to dissuade all but the most determined seekers from reaching Satan's secret mountain stronghold.

Rain lashed the narrow trail, freezing as it fell. The rocks under Dracula's boots were coated with ice. Violent gusts of wind tore at him, trying to hurl him from the face of the cliff and onto the sharp rocks far below, but he struggled on, keeping as far from the edge as possible. He tugged on the reins of his stallion, urging the beast to follow him. Its hooves scraped against the ice as it desperately fought to maintain its footing.

Ahead of him trudged Varina and then Tzigane, also walking their horses. Varina limped unsteadily, fighting the pain in her healing feet. Dracula watched her closely, fearing that each shaky step she took might send her falling to her death. The pack horse had already been lost over the edge.

Suddenly Varina slipped and fell to her knees. As she went down she bumped into her horse, and the animal lost its footing. Its hind feet slid over the edge of the cliff.

"Let go of the reins!" Dracula shouted. Why was she holding on? "Varina!" he yelled. "Let go! You must let go."

"Help me!" Varina cried. "Please help me!"

Then Dracula saw what had happened, that she could not get free. Varina screamed in terror as she slid closer to the edge. She tore wildly at the strap with her numb fingers, but it would not yield.

Dracula started forward. He slipped on the ice and fell painfully to his knees. He began to crawl, desperately trying to reach her in time. "Varina!" he cried as he saw her horse slip out of sight over the edge.

Varina's scream mingled with that of the beast. Their duet of horror faded into the distance, then was suddenly cut short as both woman and horse reached the jagged rocks far below.

Tzigane reached Dracula and knelt by his side. She put her arms around him and drew him close. "Your knees are bleeding," she said softly.

"She had wrapped the reins around her wrist," Dracula said quietly. "The wet leather froze solid. She could not get free."

"You did all you could to save her, Vlad," Tzigane said gently.

"And now she is dead," Dracula said with a weary sigh as he rose to his feet.

Tzigane also stood. "Dead?" she asked. "No, my Vlad. Have you forgotten the marks of Dracul's and Mircea's teeth on her neck?"

Dracula hesitated, then shook his head. "No, I have not forgotten."

"Then come. We must hurry. She will follow us tonight. I can deal with her easily enough, but I do not want to do it on this narrow trail. She will try to attack you, Vlad, since you are her closest relative. When she awakens, her hunger for your blood will be like that of a beast. Come, let us hurry. This storm will not reach much higher."

Dracula took one final glance at the edge of the cliff where Varina had vanished, then picked up his stallion's reins and began to follow the witch upward once again.

As Tzigane had promised, they soon climbed above the clouds. The rocks were no longer covered with ice, and the sun was shining low in the west.

Soon it would be dark.

25

✤❘✤❘✤❘✤❘✤

TZIGANE KEPT GLANCING over her shoulder at the lowering sun as she hurried up the trail, forcing her tired legs to take step after painful step, gasping and panting in the thin, cold, mountain air. Then she saw the dark opening in the side of the mountain and cried out with relief.

To Dracula following behind, it seemed that the witch had suddenly vanished into solid rock, but then he, too, saw the opening and led his horse into the darkness. Tzigane was silhouetted ahead of him against a circle of light at the end of the tunnel. By the time he emerged from the narrow passageway, she had already mounted her horse.

Dracula climbed swiftly into his saddle. He gazed over the landscape. He had never seen its like before.

The terrain sloped gradually downwards and was lost in a distant haze. It was a landscape of rocky desolation with nothing to break the monotony, neither plants nor trees. It was a land of death.

"Admire the scenery later," Tzigane laughed harshly, urging her horse into a gallop.

Dracula quickly followed the witch down a narrow path where the rubble had been swept away. Overhead the brightest stars began to shine.

Tzigane cursed at the swiftly encroaching darkness, then bent low in her saddle, stretched forward, and spoke to her beast. The animal responded and produced a new burst of speed.

After a few minutes, Tzigane reined to a halt. She

leaped to the ground and began tearing off her clothes. Dracula dismounted and watched her with amusement. She cursed him.

"This is no joke, damn you!" she spat. "You are in great danger. I must erect a circle of protection."

Dracula forced the smile from his face. He did not know why the situation seemed amusing to him. "It seems that you are overly anxious to excite me tonight, Tzigane," he said with a chuckle as he watched her finish stripping.

"Be quiet," Tzigane hissed as she kicked her clothing aside and stood naked. She looked at the sky and found the west, the brightest direction, then turned to the east and began to dance.

Dracula had seen her dance many times at the hut when showing him the movements he needed to cast some of her spells, but he had never before seen her use such grotesque gestures. Tzigane lurched around him, circling him and the horses, moving from the east to the south, then to the west and the north until she faced the east once again. She jerked around the circle twice more, then knelt and raised her arms high over her head. She began to chant in the harsh, guttural tongue unsuited to a human throat. She ended the chant with a long, raspy scream, her eyes wide and staring, her tongue lolling from her mouth, her clenched fists shaking with the strain.

As her scream faded away and the silence of the dead land around them returned, Dracula suddenly felt his lighthearted amusement disappear. He was no longer smiling when Tzigane, now sweating profusely in spite of the freezing air, walked back toward him.

She nodded with satisfaction. "Good. I see that my circle has already given you back to yourself."

"Varina was reaching out?" Dracula asked, ignoring a chill which crawled swiftly through his body.

"Yes. I could deal with her, though, as I dealt with your father and brother, but without the circle, she could have influenced you against me. That is why I was so anxious to complete the circle before twilight deepened into night."

"Then I must thank you again, Tzigane," Dracula said as he reached for her. She let him hold her close and kiss her for a moment, then pulled away and began to dress.

"Must you dress?" he asked. "I prefer you without clothing."

Tzigane laughed and smiled at him as she pulled on her black leather riding pants. "Will you hand me my boots?"

Dracula handed her the knee-high boots of thick, black leather. "Does being naked really make so much difference when you dance your spells?"

"As you have been told, my power flows at its fullest when unencumbered by clothing," she said as she pulled on the boots and slipped into her black linen shirt. "And with your life at stake, I wanted the protective circle to be as strong as possible."

Dracula draped Tzigane's black hooded cloak around her shoulders, then placed her black leather gloves in her hands.

"Thank you," she said as she pulled on the gloves. She embraced and kissed him quickly, saying, "Now we look like twins."

He laughed. "You do not wear a mail shirt or a leather vest over it. Nor do you wear a sword belt. And your hair is longer than mine. Furthermore, you have no moustache." He kissed her softly on her lips. "Tell me, Tzigane, will the other witches dance naked for me when we arrive at the cave?"

"You would wish that?" Tzigane asked, feigning jealousy.

Dracula laughed and kissed her again.

Suddenly Tzigane jerked away from him. "Be still," she hissed urgently. "Listen!"

For a moment Dracula heard nothing, then there came a faint swishing sound punctuated by the crunching of small rocks underfoot—the sound of a woman's skirts rustling as she walked, a woman coming swiftly toward them down the narrow, rocky trail.

26

VARINA APPEARED out of the gathering darkness. Her face was as pale as the white fabric of her long gown.

"She is not limping," Dracula observed.

"The Undead can heal their wounds very swiftly," Tzigane replied in a whisper.

Suddenly Varina stopped and growled low in her throat like a frustrated animal.

"She has reached the circle," Tzigane said softly. "Thank Satan she was not a witch when she was alive or she would know how to undo my protection and influence you against me."

"Those are her eyes which glow like hot embers?" Dracula asked tensely, remembering his father's burning eyes.

"Yes," Tzigane answered. "Satan's glory shines like a star in her soul. They are beautiful eyes, don't you think?"

Dracula said nothing.

"She can see as well in the dark as we see in the light," Tzigane continued. "Darkness is her element now. Satan provides."

Dracula remained silent. He placed his right hand on the hilt of his sword, but then he remembered how ineffectual his blade had been against his father and dropped his arm back to his side.

"Be silent now," Tzigane whispered, then walked forward to the inner edge of the circle.

Varina snarled and tried to claw her way through the circle to reach Tzigane, but then she grew silent. Slowly Varina turned and began to walk around the perimeter of the circle. When she had reached the path again, she walked away down the slope and was soon lost in the blackness of the night.

Tzigane returned to Dracula's side. "She will reach the cave and her husband before sunrise," she said with a sigh, then embraced and kissed Dracula. "But we shall stay here for the night."

"There is no wood for a fire. It will be a cold night."

"Not if we are wise and share the warmth of our bodies," Tzigane replied, her voice low and husky.

"I will get the furs from the horses."

"And I will get the wineskin." Tzigane was glad the darkness kept Dracula from seeing the wetness in her eyes so that her sadness would not lessen his happiness in her arms that night. She was glad he did not know that the next day would be the last she would walk in the sun.

27

❈❈❈❈❈

SHORTLY AFTER DAWN they mounted their horses and continued down the sloping pathway into the haze.

"Does your witch-knowledge tell you what could have caused such utter desolation, Tzigane?" Dracula asked as his eyes swept the rocky, lifeless land around them.

"Yes," Tzigane answered. "The legends say that once, long ago, Satan came to Earth in a ball of fire. He was like a star come to Earth, a light to lead mankind, to help mankind."

"I did not know witches read the Bible," Dracula said.

"We do not. Don't insult me."

"Your legend sounds familiar at any rate. In Christian legends Satan was an angel banished from Heaven for attempting to overthrow God."

"Satan was not banished," Tzigane replied confidently. "He escaped so that He might give hope, comfort, and pleasure to the Earth and all its children."

"I see," Dracula chuckled. Then he sensed Tzigane's icy silence and realized he should not have laughed at her beliefs. "I meant no disrespect to your faith," he said quietly. "I was merely amused by the way Christians seem to have it all backwards according to you."

"Christians are vile, guilt-ridden creatures who hate life and long for death."

"Of course," Dracula said, then decided not to comment further or point out that Tzigane's faith in Satan was every bit as fanatical and intolerant as the faith of a zealous, witch-burning Christian priest.

119

As Dracula and Tzigane moved farther down the sloping pathway, the land on each side began to curve upward slightly, and it seemed as if they were riding down the inside of an immense bowl. They kept moving downward. The slope became steeper, then flattened out.

"Look," Tzigane said, pointing directly ahead. "Do you see it?"

"That fog?" Dracula asked.

"Yes. It is called the Curtain of Satan's Tears. We are nearly there, my Vlad."

Tzigane urged her horse forward and galloped away. Soon she had disappeared into the fog.

Dracula drew his sword and followed slowly, thinking that many dangers could be concealed in the fog. He entered the curtain of thickening mist. Moisture collected on the blade of his sword, his clothing, and his skin. Then he noticed that his horse's hooves no longer crunched rocks on the path. He looked down. The path beneath him was covered by a thick carpet of spongy grass. Ahead in the distance, he heard faint laughter.

The fog began to become thinner. He emerged into sunlight in a dense forest. He saw squirrels scampering along heavily leafed branches while brightly colored birds swooped through the warm, moist air. Then he saw someone coming toward him through the knee-deep grass. It was Tzigane.

"Where are your clothes, Tzigane?" Dracula chuckled as he slipped his sword back into its scabbard.

"Isn't the sunlight glorious!" Tzigane exclaimed as she grabbed his leg and pulled. "It's always spring here, my Vlad. Satan provides. Now is the time for love and joy and laughter!"

Tzigane danced away from the path as Dracula dismounted. He swept his gaze over the forest. There was no hint of danger. Tzigane ran back and threw her arms around him. She kissed him with great passion.

"Where is the lake and the cave?" he asked as Tzigane unclasped his cloak and tossed it away.

"Not far—but far enough," she said meaningfully, then began to remove his leather vest.

Dracula examined the peaceful forest one more time, and then, satisfied as to their safety, he began helping the witch remove the rest of his clothing.

28

THE LAKE STRETCHED BEFORE THEM like a mirror, reflecting the sky and the trees. There were tears in Tzigane's eyes as she looked out over the wide expanse of water and struggled to push away her worries and doubts and concentrate on the happiness of being once again beside the sacred lake of her Lord.

"It is beautiful, don't you think?" she asked with emotion.

Dracula said nothing.

Tzigane slipped down from her horse and went to the water's edge, then walked back to Dracula and raised her cupped hands for him to drink the water from the lake. He hesitated.

"Do you still not trust me?" she asked.

Dracula shrugged, then bent down and sipped water from the witch's hands. It was sweet and cool. "I suppose you will now tell me that the Chosen One was prophesied to drink from the lake. Yes?"

"Not exactly," Tzigane said as she carefully returned to the shore and opened her hands. The remaining water fell sparkling back into the lake.

"You do not drink?" he asked suspiciously.

"In a moment perhaps," she answered tensely with her back to Dracula as she gazed out over the lake. "What the prophecy actually says is that when the Chosen One's mate gives him water from the lake, the Dragon of Satan will appear, and this will be a sign that the Chosen One has truly arrived."

"Well, I see no dragon."

"Look!" Tzigane suddenly cried. She fell to her knees and clasped her hands to her breasts. "He comes!"

Dracula looked to the center of the lake where the mirrorlike surface showed small ripples. "A fish broke the surface. That is all," he said. But then slowly, majestically, a small black head atop a long, snakelike neck began rising from the water. Shocked into silence, Dracula watched as the creature rose higher and higher in the water. Dracula could now see a humped back behind the long neck and thick fins to the sides, which propelled the creature through the water.

The beast twisted its head from side to side as if searching for something, then its small, glittering eyes became fixed upon Dracula. It began to glide toward him. His stallion shied nervously. The air became foul with an overpowering stench.

"Mount your horse, Tzigane," Dracula hissed urgently as he drew his sword.

She made no move to obey him.

"Tzigane!" he called.

She remained motionless, entranced by the approaching behemoth.

"Tzigane! The beast may be dangerous. At least move farther back!"

But Tzigane still did not move.

Dracula was about to urge his stallion forward in order to swoop her off the ground and carry her to safety when suddenly the beast lifted its head skyward and cried out.

"And Satan's Dragon shall sing praises to the Chosen One, the Son of the Dragon!" Tzigane cried.

The beast cried out twice more, then began to slip back beneath the water. Soon the surface was mirrorlike again.

Tzigane rose to her feet. She walked to Dracula and looked up at him, trembling with emotion.

"That beast could have hurt you," he said tightly.

Tzigane wiped tears from her eyes. "Surely you now believe you are Satan's Chosen One," she said softly.

"I have never seen a dragon before, if that is what that creature was. As to believing that my presence made it rise, a rock accidently rolled into the lake by an animal might also have made the beast come up for a look."

"I lived here for many years and drank from the lake

often," Tzigane said quietly, "but never once did I see the dragon. And neither have the old ones among the witches."

"Then I hope they were watching today," he said coldly.

"Oh, they were, my Vlad. They were." Tzigane pointed behind them.

Dracula turned. A multitude of women clothed in black cloaks, their faces hidden by hoods, were standing silently among the trees.

"Sisters!" Tzigane cried. "Behold he who was foretold. Behold the Chosen One of Satan! Behold Dracula! Son of the Dragon!"

And then the women silently knelt and bowed their heads in unison, worshipping him whom their Lord had chosen as their King on Earth. Worshipping Dracula.

29

·❈·❈·❈·❈·❈·

DRACULA LOOKED DOWN at the kneeling witches in silence. "Tzigane," he whispered, "I do not enjoy watching these women deceive themselves. I only desire your powers, and I do not wish to be worshipped by women whose belief in some foolish prophecy has blinded them to reality."

"You will become accustomed to being worshipped," she assured him.

Dracula did not reply.

The women finally rose to their feet, and all but one moved away toward an outcropping of rock farther down the shore. The one who remained came forward and pulled back her hood. She was a woman with graying hair, bright eyes, and a face that commanded respect. She smiled serenely at Dracula.

"Sister Lilitu," Tzigane said, bowing her head to the elder witch.

Dracula nodded to the woman.

"Welcome to both of you. You have done well, Sister," she said to Tzigane.

"It is good to be home," Tzigane said quietly, trying to smile.

"And you," Lilitu said to Dracula, "I am proud of you, so proud. I knew your mother, Marilla. I was the first to hold you after your birth."

Dracula could see that the old woman's eyes were moist with emotion. "I do not remember my father mentioning witches in Sighisoara where I was born," he replied coldly.

Lilitu looked at Tzigane with a frown.

"Satan chose a very stubborn man," Tzigane sighed.

"You were born here in the cave," Lilitu calmly told him. "The spot is now a shrine."

"A shrine of bones that you will claim are my mother's," Dracula replied.

"I told you he was stubborn," Tzigane repeated.

"Strange are Satan's ways," Lilitu said, shaking her head. "But come. A meal has been prepared."

The two witches moved toward the rocks. *I sense unhappiness within you, Sister Tzigane,* Lilitu's thoughts spoke within Tzigane's head.

It is nothing. I will not fail the prophecies, she answered silently with her own thoughts.

I also sense love for the Chosen One, Lilitu nodded, smiling knowingly.

I will not fail the prophecies, Tzigane repeated, keeping her face impassive.

You have not told him of the ceremony tonight? Lilitu asked.

Tzigane did not reply.

Lilitu nodded again. *No, of course, you have not. And you fear he will turn away when . . .*

I will not fail the prophecies, Tzigane repeated a third time. *I am loyal to my Lord Satan. I will keep faith.*

I do not doubt you, Sister Tzigane. We are very proud of you and your success. You found the silver from the Earth?

Yes.

Truly you are blessed, Lilitu noted solemnly.

Again Tzigane did not reply.

Dracula watched the two witches for a moment before dismounting. He followed several steps behind them. It was hard for him to understand how someone could bow to you one moment, then walk away and leave you to follow like a dog. He was not used to being treated so casually, especially by women. But neither was he used to being worshipped, and since there seemed to be nowhere else to go for the moment, he followed. They neared the cave. Dracula hesitated, studying the tall, narrow opening of darkness.

Tzigane noticed his suspicion and laughed. "Afraid of a cave filled with women?" she asked.

"No, but you two shall enter first," he said as he fingered the hilt of his sword.

The two women walked ahead of him through the opening, Tzigane leading her horse. Dracula cautiously followed with his stallion.

The cave was illuminated by torches. He followed Tzigane and Lilitu down a narrow passageway which gradually began to widen. They emerged into a vast cavern whose upper reaches were lost in shadow. Dracula felt as if he had entered another world.

Women were everywhere, all busy with unknown duties. In the center of the cavern was a small pool around which food had been placed. Lilitu and Tzigane walked to the pool and sat on the stone floor. They beckoned Dracula to join them.

After another quick look around, he sat down. "My stallion will require care," he said.

"As will my mare," Tzigane replied. She pointed behind them. Dracula looked and saw that two young girls were already picking up the reins to lead the horses away.

"I will go with them," Dracula said and rose to his feet, having no intention of being stranded without his horse.

Tzigane reached out and touched his leg. "Won't you trust us at all?" she asked, sounding hurt.

Dracula ignored the question and took the reins of his stallion from the young girl. She backed away shyly with a bow. He nodded to the other girl who held Tzigane's horse, and they walked toward an opening to the left of the one through which they had entered.

When Dracula returned to the pool, he noticed that Tzigane and Lilitu had still not eaten. "You have many animals, and all seem well cared for," he said to Lilitu as he sat down again. "Forgive my suspicions, but a man would not live long if he trusted everyone he met."

Tzigane sadly shook her head, then handed him bread, cheese, and a silver goblet of wine.

After they had eaten, Lilitu and Tzigane led him into a passageway on the far side of the cavern. Along the narrow tunnel, other openings branched off. They entered one. Dracula saw a recessed area surrounded by candles. On a natural rock altar was a human skeleton.

Lilitu and Tzigane bowed their heads in silence for a moment, then advanced to the sacred shrine of Dracula's mother and birth. He examined the skeleton and noticed that the bones of the neck had been shattered below the jaw of the skull.

"Your father decapitated her with his sword before he took you away," Tzigane said, noticing his interest in the severed head.

"An interesting story," he replied.

"Your mother gave her life so that Satan's prophecy would be fulfilled," Lilitu whispered respectfully, stroking the fleshless skull. "She relinquished her immortality for Satan, and we revere her memory."

"Immortality!" Dracula said with a laugh. "I suppose witches do not normally die?"

Tzigane gently pulled back Lilitu's robe, exposing the elder witch's neck. He saw two marks like the ones Varina had received from Dracul's and Mircea's teeth.

"We all die eventually," Lilitu said. "But once we have received the sacred kiss, Satan grants us eternal physical life. Your mother, by allowing herself to be decapitated, forfeited her resurrection. She was a very great woman, Prince Dracula. I wish you could have known her as I did."

"You welcome the vampire's bite?" he asked. "Why then did Tzigane protect me from my father and my brother's wife if . . ."

"It would have been against your will," Tzigane answered.

"And now you expect me to become a vampire's victim willingly?" he asked suspiciously.

"No," Tzigane replied. "Not until you yourself decide it is time."

"A wise decision," Dracula answered, relaxing slightly, "or else there might be other skeletons with shattered necks littering this cave of yours."

Tzigane and Lilitu said nothing more as they led him from the shrine down the passageway and farther into the cave. Lilitu stopped beside an opening over which a curtain of heavy black cloth had been hung. She pulled back the curtain. Inside the candlelit chamber of stone, Dracula saw a bed, a table, and a chair.

Tzigane took his hand and entered, pulling him in after her. Lilitu smiled at them from beside the curtain. "Rest," she said softly, then dropped the curtain into place, leaving them alone.

Tzigane embraced Dracula eagerly.

He pushed her away.

She was hurt, and it showed in her face.

"This is not the time for embraces," he said tightly. "I am in a strange place and do not intend to . . ."

"We are not your enemies," Tzigane assured him. "No one here is your enemy. You are safe here—safer than you have ever been."

"I cannot take your word for that, Tzigane. I must remain on my guard."

Tzigane walked to the bed and lay down. "Come and take me, Vlad," she whispered, secretly praying he would grant her this wish and make love with her one final time while yet her body remained warm with mortal life.

Dracula shook his head in silence.

Tzigane turned her back on him to conceal her tears.

Dracula paced the room for awhile, occasionally lifting the curtain to look into the passageway when he thought he heard a suspicious sound. Finally he pulled his sword from its scabbard and sat down on the chair, facing the portal.

Tzigane frowned, her back still to Dracula, listening to him move restlessly in the creaky chair. He needed to rest. It was unnecessary for him to tire himself. She closed her eyes, moved her lips silently, and soon heard his breathing become deeper. She turned. He was now fast asleep, his sword still clutched in his right hand, the blade across his thighs.

She sadly shook her head. She rose and bent over him, stroking his long, straight hair and admiring the aristocratic planes of his face in the flickering glow of the candle. She kissed him lightly on his slightly parted lips, then crawled back onto the bed. She lay facing him, watching him sleep, making sure he did not fall from the chair or hurt himself on his drawn sword.

The candles burned lower. Tzigane felt a change in the

atmosphere of the room. The sun had set. Night had come, and her final day of sunshine had ended.

She continued to watch over Dracula as he slept and was still watching when two men and a woman, all dressed in black clothing made for them by the witches of the cave, entered the chamber. Tzigane rose from the bed, then bowed to the vampires—bowed to Dracul, Mircea, and Varina.

30

❖❖❖❖❖❖

"HE LOOKS WELL," Dracul said, staring intently at the sleeping form of his son. "He has grown into a fine man. Thank you for watching over him."

"I serve Satan's will," Tzigane said quietly. "I will awaken him now." She moved her lips silently.

Dracula awoke. He glanced around the room, quickly taking in the scene. He leaped to his feet and shoved Tzigane behind him as he pointed his sword at his father's chest.

"Stop it!" Tzigane cried, pulling on his arm. "They are not going to attack, Vlad. They only came to welcome you."

"Am I such a monster to you then?" Dracula's father sadly asked.

"And I, brother?" asked Mircea.

"And I?" Varina asked, clinging to Mircea's arm.

Dracula hesitated, unsure of what to say or do, uncomfortably remembering that his sword would not hinder the Undead.

Tzigane pulled away from him and stood beside his father. "Put away your sword," she said. "If I do not fear them, why should you?"

"You are a witch," Dracula answered tensely.

"And we are not the monsters you think, brother," Mircea said quietly.

"Did you enjoy tasting the power of the throne?" Dracul asked, trying to guide the conversation onto a less troublesome path.

130

Dracula paused and stared intently into his father's face. "I felt your bones beneath me many times, but I did enjoy sitting on the throne. I intend to return and do so again."

"I am proud of you, my son."

"Varina gave me the names of those who helped to . . . to kill you," Dracula continued, "and the ones I found in Targoviste I impaled upon sharpened wooden stakes so that it took them a very long time to die. I impaled their wives and children along with them."

"Indeed, I am very proud of you," Dracul repeated.

"I too, brother," Mircea added quickly.

Suddenly the idea of calmly talking to corpses became to much for Dracula. "This is madness!" he exclaimed.

Tzigane came forward and placed her hand lightly on his sword arm. "No one here is your enemy. No one is going to attack you or me. There is no need for them to take what they need by force, not here in the cave."

"She speaks the truth," Mircea said. "The women gladly give us what we need."

"There are many Undead here," Dracul said. "It is a very practical arrangement. We are given what we need, and at the same time, the women receive the kiss of eternal life."

"We do not kill them," Mircea interrupted. "We take only a little blood each time so that they will not die. But when they die at the end of their allotted span, they rise again and walk, just as we have done."

Tzigane squeezed Dracula's hand. "Put away your sword, Vlad. Trust me just a little longer?"

Dracula hesitated, then made his decision.

Tzigane smiled softly as she watched him slip his sword back into its scabbard. But her eyes then filled with tears, and she quickly kissed him tenderly on the cheek, turned, and ran from the chamber.

"Tzigane!" he shouted, listening to the sound of her footsteps.

Dracula started forward. Dracul spread his arms to block the way. "Let her go, my son."

Dracula automatically reached for his sword, then remembered and dropped his hand back to his side. "I will fight you with my bare hands if I must," he said tightly, "but I intend to follow her."

"No. Soon you will see her again. We will take you to her when it is time. Be calm, my son. Be calm."

Dracula hurled himself at his father. It was like crashing into a stone wall. He rebounded from the impact and fell to the floor, but quickly scrambled back to his feet. He glared at his father and shouted, "Let me pass!"

"No. You will not pass until it is time to go."

"And when will that be?" Dracula replied, angry and frustrated.

"Soon."

Dracula clenched his fists at his sides. His body shook with rage.

"Be calm, brother," Mircea urged. "Tzigane goes to do what she must."

Dracula did not reply.

"Have you seen the bones of your mother?" Dracul asked, hoping to calm his son by changing the subject.

"I saw a skeleton on a slab of stone. I do not know that it is my mother," Dracula snapped.

"It is she. I killed her, my son. I lied to you about your birth because I hoped to protect you, because I hoped to spare you the knowledge of what I wrongly thought was a curse—the curse that witches placed upon Mircea and I. I was wrong. This is no curse. It is a precious gift—the gift of eternal life."

Dracula said nothing.

"Come," Dracul said. "It has been long enough now. We will lead you. They will be waiting for us by the lake. Tzigane will be there, too."

Dracula tensely followed his father, brother, and Varina from the cave. A stretch of the shoreline was illuminated with flickering torches. Black-robed figures stood in two rows, creating a path down which Dracula walked behind the three Undead.

Dracul, Mircea, and Varina stepped to the side, joining the ranks, when they reached a designated point a few feet from the water's edge.

A naked woman with long black hair was kneeling on the shoreline, her back to Dracula and facing Lilitu, who was standing with her back to the water.

"Tzigane?" Dracula called hesitantly. The woman did

not turn, though he thought he saw her shoulders quiver as if with a repressed sob. Dracula started toward her. Suddenly his arms were held from behind in the grip of fingers like steel rods.

"Be silent, my son," his father whispered close to his ear. "Tzigane does what she must. Her faith is strong."

"What is she going to do?" Dracula demanded.

"Be silent and watch," Dracul urged.

Lilitu spoke to Tzigane, her voice strong and clear. "Show us the silver from the Earth."

Tzigane raised her left hand above her head. She held a small, shiny, silver object between her thumb and first finger.

"What is she holding?" Dracula whispered to his father.

"She never told you?"

"No."

"It is the prophesied silver which she found at your passing. It marks her as your mate."

Dracula did not reply.

Lilitu took the coin and held it up for all to see. "Behold the silver from the Earth!" she cried. "Behold the mate of the Dragon's son! Rise, Tzigane."

Slowly Tzigane stood and bowed her head. Lilitu leaned forward and kissed her lightly on the forehead just above the bridge of her nose. "Blessed be, Tzigane," she said, then walked to the side and beckoned a woman with long white hair who stood waiting nearby. The woman took the silver coin. Lilitu then walked back to Tzigane.

Lilitu sank to her knees, as did the rest of the assembled crowd. The only ones left standing were the white-haired woman, Tzigane, Dracula, and his father, who still held his son's arms in a vise-like grip. The white-haired witch looked up at Dracula and smiled. Her eyes were glowing like two red-hot coals.

Understanding flooded Dracula. "No!" he yelled, struggling against his father's unyielding grip. "No! Tzigane! No! Resist her! Fight!"

Tzigane ignored his cries, bent her head to the right, and pulled back her long black hair to expose her bare neck.

The old vampire-woman looked down at Tzigane with

burning eyes, then bent forward. She pressed her lips to Tzigane's naked throat.

"No!" Dracula cried, fighting futilely to get free.

But he could not get free, and suddenly the faint, slurping sound of the vampire feeding at Tzigane's open vein told him it was now too late to matter.

31

******

THE WHITE-HAIRED WOMAN, the Undead elder witch to whom the honor of the kiss had fallen, proudly raised her head from Tzigane's neck. Her lips glistened with blood. She smiled sweetly at Dracula again, then knelt at Tzigane's feet.

Dracula's father released him. Slowly he walked forward.

"Tzigane," he whispered. "Why, Tzigane? Why?" He turned her around to face him. Trickles of blood from the wound on her throat had run down over her left breast. She looked up at him. Her face was streaked with tears.

"I had hoped you would understand when it came time for this, my Vlad. I have served my Lord Satan faithfully. I have helped to fulfill the prophecies."

"Why didn't you tell me what you were going to do, Tzigane?" he asked bitterly.

"Would you have allowed me to follow my destined path to . . . to this?" she asked. "Would you have followed me to this sacred lake?"

Dracula did not answer.

Tzigane wiped her eyes with the back of her hand. She pulled herself proudly to her full height. "I must continue to keep faith with the prophecies," she whispered under her breath. "Sweet Satan, give me strength just a little longer."

Tzigane bent down and took the silver coin from the kneeling vampire-woman's hand, then held it out to

135

Dracula. "Take it, my Vlad, and throw it far into the lake."

Dracula hesitated.

"Do it for me, Vlad? Please?"

"Why do you want the coin thrown away?" he asked suspiciously. "More of your prophecies?"

Tzigane nodded and pressed the coin into his right hand. He threw it out over the lake with a curse. It splashed into the water out of sight.

"Thank you, my Vlad," Tzigane said. She kissed him softly on his lips. "And thank you for not pulling away from me now that I have received the sacred kiss. I shall miss sharing the sunlight with you. I shall miss the sun."

Tzigane turned her back on him and began to walk rapidly toward the water. Suddenly Dracula understood that Tzigane meant to drown herself in the lake.

"No! I forbid it!" Dracula shouted and started after her, but his father grabbed his arms and held him back once again.

"Tzigane! No! I want you to stay by my side. What of our bargain?"

The beautiful young witch turned around, ankle-deep in the water, and smiled sadly. "I must fetch the coin, my Vlad," she said, then walked forward. Soon she had vanished beneath the dark surface of the water.

Dracula's father released him. He walked slowly to the water's edge and looked at the imprints Tzigane's small, naked feet had left in the mud. "Tzigane," he whispered tightly. "Damn you, witch. Damn you." His voice betrayed his emotions. Then he cursed at his lack of strength. Why should he care what the foolish woman had done? He did not care, he thought. He would not care.

But he did care. Even as he struggled to deny the truth and hide his sense of loss from himself, he knew that he cared. For once his emotions overwhelmed him.

"What will happen now?" he asked weakly.

There was no answer.

Dracula turned. He was alone by the lake. He sat down on the grass by the edge of the water and looked out over the night-blackened surface. "I will stay here no longer," he whispered to himself. "I will get my stallion and leave this night."

But he remained sitting by the lake, strangely reluctant

to rise and walk away. Suddenly he understood. Tzigane must be reaching out to him, making him want to stay until she returned from beneath the waters!

But when she returned, she would no longer be human.

Dracula shook off his desire to wait for her return. He leaped to his feet, starting to turn, to run. But then he saw something moving beneath the surface of the lake, something moving closer and closer to the shore. Two faint red lights like underwater fires which grew brighter by the second.

Dracula could no longer move his legs. He stood transfixed as Tzigane emerged from the lake and smiled at him, showing her sharp white teeth.

"Your eyes, Tzigane," Dracula groaned. "Your eyes . . . they burn!"

Tzigane walked onto the shore, her naked skin wet and glistening in the flickering light of the torches.

"Vlad," she said sweetly, her voice soft and provocative. "Vlad, my beloved."

Dracula clenched his teeth and struggled to move his legs. They did not respond.

"I found the coin, Vlad," Tzigane said proudly, holding up her left hand to show him the silver disk between her thumb and forefinger.

Dracula remained silent.

"Am I so different now than I was before?" she asked hopefully. She reached up and stroked his hair. Her trembling fingers touched his face.

"Your fingers are so cold," Dracula moaned. "Why, Tzigane? You must tell me why you have done this thing?"

"I have kept faith with the prophecies of Satan," she replied, then embraced him and held him close, "for it is written that from the lips of his destined mate shall the Dragon's son receive the crimson kiss of eternal physical life. Since I have proven myself to be that mate, and only the lips of one Undead may impart the blessing of immortality, it was necessary for me to become Undead immediately, though still young, instead of waiting for death and rebirth in the customary way at the end of a full life as Lilitu and the other mortal witches in the coven are free to do."

Dracula was silent as he continued to struggle futilely against the spell of paralysis.

"Do you think I wanted to banish myself from the sunlight so soon, my Vlad? You cannot think that," Tzigane continued quickly, still hoping Dracula might begin to understand and look at her again with that rare softness she had grown to treasure so dearly. "You know I love . . . loved the sun. Don't you also know that . . . that I feel love for you? I have done what I had to do for the prophecies, but also for you . . . so that I may bestow upon you the blessed kiss of . . ."

"And now you will infect me with your kisses," Dracula said tightly, struggling again without success to turn and flee before it was too late.

"Only when you are ready, my Vlad. Only when you are ready. This changes nothing between us," Tzigane insisted. "I will still share passion with you. I shall still teach you to acquire the powers you desire. The only difference is that now our meetings will be restricted to the hours of darkness. Say you understand, my Vlad. Please say it," she pleaded softly.

Dracula glared down at her. "We made a bargain, Tzigane. You have broken it."

Tzigane's glowing eyes became misty with new tears. "I have not broken our bargain," she said with quiet desperation. "I will still be all I ever was to you except that . . ."

"Except that now you must hide in the dark like the rats and other vermin," he said coldly. "Release me from this spell. I wish to leave this instant."

Tzigane's full red lips trembled with emotion. "Do not leave me, Vlad. Please. I will release you, but please, Vlad, please . . ."

Suddenly Dracula felt the invisible bonds that had held him immobile fade away. But he also noticed that the red fires were no longer burning in Tzigane's eyes and that she now looked much as she always had, beautiful and desirable. He tried to ignore the hurt and worry which creased her face, but could not. Then he remembered the sense of loss he had felt after she walked into the lake.

Slowly he placed his arms around her and stroked her icy skin. She raised her face to his, smiled weakly but hopefully, and softly kissed him. Her lips were deathly cold.

"Warm me, my Vlad," she whispered tenderly. "Not all my kisses are crimson."

Dracula hesitated a moment longer, then groaned and crushed Tzigane to him.

"Your vest no longer feels cold against my skin, Vlad," Tzigane said with an uncertain smile.

Clinging together, they slipped to the ground beside the lake. His warmth caressed her death-chilled flesh. Their passion grew, and together they plummeted into a vortex of desire, her ice and his fire, touching and exploding.

32

✠✠✠✠✠

DRACULA AWOKE on the shore of the lake. A bright sun glared down at him out of a cloudless sky. He sat up and flexed his muscles. Suddenly it all came back. Tzigane. Her descent into the lake. Her return.

He clasped his hand to his neck. The skin was unbroken. She had not bitten him.

He stood and looked around.

Lilitu was walking toward him.

"Tzigane," he said. "She came back from the water."

"Of course," Lilitu smiled. "Satan's blessing of eternal life is upon her. She will be happy to see you after sunset tonight."

For a moment Dracula felt intensely anxious for the sun to set so that he could be with Tzigane again, but then he remembered her burning eyes and her corpse-cold skin. Ruthlessly he repressed his desire for the witch, buried his pain, and crushed out his happy memories of Tzigane as she had once been.

"I do not wish to see her ever again," Dracula replied coldly. "I intend to get my stallion and ride away from here as swiftly as possible."

Lilitu nodded sadly. "I was afraid you might feel that way—and so was Tzigane. But yet she kept faith with the prophecy for it was said that . . ."

"Be still, old woman," Dracula interrupted. "I am going to my horse."

He brushed past the elder witch and entered the cave. Turning down the passageway where his horse had been quartered, he found the beast. He threw his saddle to the animal's back and began to cinch it tight.

Lilitu quietly entered and stood watching him in silence. "Won't you stay just a little while, Prince Dracula?"

"No," Dracula answered as he pulled the bridle over the horse's head and forced the bit into its unwilling mouth.

"Tzigane will be very lonely if you leave. Please stay awhile longer. Do not be gone when she wakens at her first sunset, I beg of you."

"Beg all you want, witch," Dracula replied bitterly. "She broke her bargain with me. I am leaving."

"You desired to possess the powers of the Unseen world," Lilitu quickly said. "You still may. Tzigane will continue to teach you."

"I want nothing more from that witch. She is no longer human. Her flesh is cold. She died when she entered the lake, and dead to me she shall remain. She betrayed me, tricked me into following her here, and led me to believe that she would leave with me when I returned to plot my way back to the throne."

"Listen to me, Prince Dracula. Please? Just for a moment?"

Dracula turned and stared at the elder witch. "Make it quick. I am impatient to be gone from this den of devils."

"Please stay for just a few days, at least. You may continue to learn from Tzigane as usual. It will also give her time to adjust to her new existence before you depart. And then when you do leave, she *can* still go with you, but only if you wish her to do so. Furthermore, since she is now Undead, her powers have been increased a hundredfold. What you can learn from her now greatly exceeds what you could before."

"I do not care," he replied. "I want no more lessons from her. I will achieve my goals with steel and cunning as befits a man, a warrior. I need no woman's magic. Satan take Tzigane and her powers to the deepest Hell!"

"She cares greatly for you, Prince Dracula," Lilitu continued, ignoring Dracula's angry, empty words. "She was tempted to betray her sacred vows because of you. Do you have any idea what that would have meant to her? To have forsaken her vows of service to Satan for fear of losing your love . . ."

"I never told her I loved her, and I do not," Dracula

interrupted. "We made a bargain and were allies. She broke the bargain. Now I am going to leave."

Dracula began to lead his horse toward the passageway. Lilitu blocked the way.

"I could stop you with a gesture," she said, "just as I could have stopped your father when he came to kill your mother. But I kept faith with the prophecies which forbade my interference and did not stop him, and neither will I stop you, though it will tear my heart to see Tzigane's grief when she awakens and finds you gone."

"Tzigane is no longer my concern. Stand aside, witch, or your own plans for eventual resurrection will come to an end," he threatened, touching the hilt of his sword.

Lilitu hesitated, stalling for time. Quickly she probed his mind. Buried deep beneath dark layers of repressed pain from what he thought was his loss of Tzigane, Lilitu was relieved to find what she had hoped might be there, a hidden spark of love. She coaxed it gently toward the surface of his consciousness.

"At least," she said carefully, "come and say goodbye to Tzigane. What harm can that do?"

"Say goodbye to a corpse?" Dracula laughed bitterly, trying to crush the rising emotion he was beginning to feel.

"Come. It can do no harm. I plead with you to at least say goodbye to her who cares deeply for you."

There was a long silence while Dracula futilely fought his emotions.

"Very well," he finally said in a harsh whisper. "Lead me to her. I will say goodbye. Perhaps she has earned that much for protecting me from the attacks of my father and Varina."

Lilitu smiled. "Thank you, Prince Dracula. Come, follow me."

Dracula dropped the reins of his stallion and followed. Lilitu led him across the cavern, then down a long passageway he had not entered before. They descended a steep path. The torches became farther apart until the dimness of the light resembled deep twilight. Then Lilitu led him into another cavern, even larger than the one near the surface. The air was heavy with silence. It was the silence of a tomb.

Upon straw mats on the floor lay the pale bodies of women in black robes. The corpses stretched away on every side, disappearing into the vast darkness of the immense cavern.

"They are all . . . Undead?" Dracula whispered.

"Yes," Lilitu said in a hushed voice as she led him farther into the sacred cavern.

In the center of the chamber was a crude platform made of flat, carefully stacked stones. Candles burned all around it, dimly illuminating the body which lay upon it, the body of a young, beautiful woman with raven-black hair and full, red lips, clothed in a silver and black robe.

"Tzigane," Dracula whispered tightly. He walked closer. She seemed to be only sleeping, but her breasts did not rise and fall. Dracula slowly reached out and stroked her long black hair. He touched her face. The skin was cold and waxen like the skin of a corpse.

"She was always so alive, so warm," Dracula stammered as he fought to keep himself under control.

"She loves you, Prince Dracula," Lilitu whispered as if fearing to wake a sleeping child. "She fears that you will no longer want her. I beg you not to make her fears come true."

Dracula said nothing. He could not take his eyes from Tzigane's beautiful face.

"Look there," Lilitu whispered, pointing to the side of the platform at three familiar figures lying motionless upon their straw mats—Dracula's father, brother and Varina. Varina was lying snuggled within Mircea's arms.

"See how Varina and Mircea smile in their sleep?" Lilitu asked. "They are happy once again. Stay with us awhile longer, Prince Dracula. Make Tzigane as happy as Varina. Do not be cruel to the one who loves you."

"Silence," Dracula hissed. "Leave me alone with Tzigane for a moment. I will find my own way out."

Lilitu nodded, then turned and left him.

Dracula gazed down at Tzigane in silence. She seemed even more hypnotically beautiful than before she had died. He touched her face once again. His fingertips tingled with cold. He groaned.

Dracula slowly bent down and gently kissed Tzigane's icy lips. But suddenly he jerked back with a sharp cry for the lips of the beautiful corpse had trembled beneath his touch!

Tzigane's eyes snapped open. They stared wildly at him.

Vlad, my beloved! Tzigane's desperate thoughts cried out inside his brain. *Don't leave me alone! Stay just a little while! Please!*

Dracula cradled his head in his hands, trying to shut out Tzigane's thoughts and pleas for him to stay with her.

I will teach you, Vlad, she declared frantically, *just as I promised, and we will share our passion every night. Please, Vlad. Please? I want to take you in my arms, but while the sun is in the sky, I cannot move! Embrace me and kiss me again! Please, Vlad? Please?*

Dracula cried out loudly in agony. He saw many other eyes snap open around him in the corpse-strewn cavern at the sound of his cry. He began to run from the tomb of living death.

Tzigane's agonized thoughts pursued him. *Vlad! No! Come back! Sweet Satan, please don't leave me! I love you, Vlad! Please!*

Dracula reached the passageway, still holding his head with both hands, futilely trying to blot out Tzigane's mental cries.

Lilitu was waiting. She moved her lips silently, and suddenly his mind was again free of Tzigane's thoughts.

"You must not think of her as a monster, Prince Dracula," Lilitu urged hopefully. "She loves you. Was the woman you loved by the lake last night a monster? No, you did not think she was a monster then, and she is not. Go back to Tzigane, please?"

"She is a corpse who lives off the blood of the living," Dracula whispered hoarsely, "and nothing will ever convince me that she and all those like her are anything other than monstrous. If not for your filthy prophecies and blind beliefs, Tzigane would still be laughing happily in the sunlight instead of lying paralyzed in darkness and agony."

"If she is in agony, it is your fault," Lilitu replied, verging on anger.

Dracula smiled coldly. "I am rather good at giving women pain. It was one of the many skills I learned growing up in a dungeon. Why should I care if one more woman feels pain because of me? Out of my way, witch."

Dracula pushed past Lilitu, sweeping her aside with his right arm. She was thrown roughly against the wall of the passageway and fell to the floor. A hot spear of pain exploded in her hip. She struggled to her feet and slowly walked forward, her hip in burning agony, trying to catch up with Dracula. But by the time she had limped painfully from the cave, he and his stallion had already disappeared into the forest.

33

Lᴉʟɪᴛᴜ ʟɪᴍᴘᴇᴅ slowly and painfully back into the sacred cavern of the Undead, then moved through the ranks of living corpses until she was again beside the platform upon which Tzigane lay. The eyes of the other vampires were closed once more in sleep, but Tzigane's were still open and staring, tears welling constantly in her pale green eyes.

Lilitu sat on the edge of the platform, trying to ignore the throbbing pain in her hip. *Be at peace, Sister Tzigane,* Lilitu urged, using her projected thoughts to reach within her future Queen's grief-stricken mind.

He is gone, Tzigane's mournful thoughts replied. *He thinks I am a monster. He hates me! He will never . . .*

He does care for you, Lilitu's thoughts interrupted. *Probe his mind yourself. Look deeply.*

I dare not!

You have trusted me many times before, Lilitu gently reminded her. *Trust me again? Probe his mind.*

Tzigane gazed hopefully into the elder witch's eyes for a moment, wanting to do as Lilitu had suggested, but still afraid of what she might find.

You have no need to fear, Lilitu assured her.

Tzigane closed her eyes. Slowly she probed outward, searching for Dracula's mind, searching, seeking . . .

She found him.

He was passing through the fog, emerging into the rocky desolation which led up out of the hidden valley, angrily urging his stallion to maintain a breakneck speed to carry him far and fast from the cave of the witches.

Cautiously Tzigane pushed into the unsuspecting mind of her destined mate, through the thick, dark layers of his strictly repressed emotions, deeper and deeper into his subconscious thoughts.

Suddenly Tzigane sensed a warmth buried deep inside the fortress of coldness with which Dracula had learned to protect himself from the hostile world of bloodshed and prisons into which he had been born, and within that warm spark of hidden emotion, Tzigane found herself.

Joy flooded her consciousness. Now she knew beyond any doubt that he thought her beautiful, even now, even Undead. She knew that even now he felt friendship for her, trust, admiration, passion, and longing. And at the very center of the warmth, Tzigane found love.

Tzigane basked in the glow of Dracula's unacknowledged love for her, warming her death-chilled soul beside the hidden flames of his desire. Desire for her! For her! Even Undead!

Tzigane never wanted to leave that center of light she had found within Dracula's self-imposed darkness, but she felt Lilitu's gentle thoughts calling to her all too soon and she reluctantly pulled away. And then she was back in the sacred cavern within her newly reborn, Undead body. She opened her eyes.

Lilitu gazed down at her, smiling and nodding happily. *You see, Sister Tzigane? The Chosen One does care for you.*

So filled was she with the joy which now flooded her spirit, Tzigane could not reply. The tears streaking her face were no longer tears of grief but of happiness.

Now you should rest, Lilitu told Tzigane.

Yes, Tzigane agreed, blinking away her tears. *I will rest. Thank you, Sister Lilitu. Thank you for . . .*

Sleep now, Lilitu urged with a smile. *Sleep.*

Tzigane closed her eyes and was soon asleep, dreaming of a secluded forest glade where she was making love with Dracula upon a soft bed of pine needles. And because impossible things often happen in dreams, there was a blazing golden sun in the sky overhead, and her flesh was as warm as his.

34

✥-✥-✥-✥-✥

TZIGANE'S LONG YEARS OF TRAINING as a witch gave her an instinctive mastery of her Undead powers. She could see in total darkness. Her mental powers could reach the mind of anyone anywhere on the face of the Earth. By an effort of will power alone, she could transform herself into a wolf, a bat, or a cloud of swirling mist. She could travel great distances quickly by commanding a Strigoi to carry her in its talons. And because the Undead were creatures of the Unseen as well as the Earth, Tzigane was now able to channel stronger currents of magical force into physical manifestation, thereby charging the spells she had perfected while human with a new and awesome potency.

But although Tzigane was pleased with her new powers, she missed the sun and she missed Dracula, both of which were now denied to her—one for all time, the other until he called for her of his own free will.

If he ever would.

If his iron-willed determination to blot out all memories of witches and the Undead did not make him hesitate too long and die without first receiving the sacred kiss of eternity from her lips.

That possibility tormented Tzigane. In spite of Satan's prophecies, death might yet separate her forever from the Dragon's son, her unfulfilled love then becoming a torture as she continued to exist in everlasting darkness alone through the unending nights of Time.

For Dracula had gone into a world overflowing with

death. Death in battle, by assassination, by accident, by disease, by old age . . .

Death.

Death everywhere without hope of rebirth into Undeath.

If only she could watch over him and use her powers to protect him from harm—from death. But the prophecies forbade her intervention. Satan's chosen were required to prove their worthiness beyond all doubts.

Only if Dracula survived on his own and requested the kiss of his own free will would Satan's final test be passed. Only then would he be unquestionably worthy to sit upon the throne of the world in Satan's name. And if Dracula failed, in time a different Chosen One and a different mate would appear, and Satan's tests of worthiness would begin all over again.

Without success, Tzigane tried not to think of that legend which was ancient when the Earth was young, the legend of the first Chosen One of Satan, she who did not survive and whose flesh became food for the worms like any common human corpse. Tzigane tried not to think that Dracula might end the same way, that her own work, study, hopes, sacrifices, and love might still come to nothing after all, destroyed by the premature death of him for whom she had suffered an early death and rebirth so that the gift of immortality would be hers to give whenever he requested it.

If he ever did.

If he did not die first.

But the prophecies did not forbid Tzigane from using her mental powers to share secretly in Dracula's thoughts and experiences as she waited for him to call to her. Indeed, it was now her responsibility to observe his thoughts at all times, even while she lay paralyzed in her day-trance, so that she would not miss his mental call.

If it ever came.

And so it was that Tzigane followed Dracula with her mind as he rode his stallion northward to the Christian nation of Moldavia where he was welcomed to live in exile by his cousin, Prince Stephen, heir to the Moldavian throne.

But although Tzigane was now spending every moment of her existence as an unsuspected spectator within Dracula's conscious mind, she soon realized that mental images alone, as real as they often seemed, were not enough. She needed to be physically near to the Dragon's son in order to be able to see him again with her own eyes and to know that should he call, she would be only moments from his side.

In late December Tzigane said her goodbyes to her Sisters at the cave. She summoned a Strigoi. She went to Moldavia.

JANUARY
1449 A.D.

35

✠╫╍╫╍╫╍╫╍╫

JANUARY. THE DEPTH OF WINTER. Moldavia lay smothered
beneath a heavy white blanket of frozen death. Waiting for
Spring. Waiting for rebirth.

And Tzigane lay in the secret crypt prepared for her
by Moldavian witches, also waiting. In darkness. Waiting.
Each sunlit day. Waiting for her nightly resurrection. Waiting for each sunset when the invisible chains of her day-
trance fell away, and the night freed her to rise from her
tomb and fly on the silent black wings of a bat to the
castle where Dracula wintered with his Moldavian cousin,
Prince Stephen, freed her to watch in secret, to hover outside the night-blackened windows of the great castle and
look within to where the Dragon's son moved and breathed
and lived and fought his memories and tried to forget the
gypsy witch who watched unsuspected in the cold and
dark, she who waited and prayed for just a glimpse of his
warm reality and the small comfort of caressing his beloved face and body from afar with the gaze from her
lonely, burning eyes.

Early January. Barely two months since their first meeting. And then only five weeks together. So little time, yet
so many memories. Memories to cherish—for Tzigane.
Memories of torment—for Dracula, because he fought so
hard to forget, because even when he managed to banish
them during his waking hours, they came back to plague
him in his dreams.

Desperately he sought weapons to battle the phantoms
of his mind, the demons of his memories.

Weapons.

He found wine; he found other women—weapons.

And within his mind, an unseen watcher felt his torment and was glad that his memories of her fought him. But she also felt the pain of loving him and being unable to comfort him and go to him. For she was forbidden even to send him a spell of restful sleep, forbidden to interfere in any way, forbidden either to follow her loving impulse to ease his torment by helping him forget or to follow her selfish impulse to strengthen his memories so that he could never forget her who loved him from within the darkness of her tomb.

His weapon of wine dulled the memories. Tzigane understood and even approved until the weapon became a crutch which weakened his body and spirit and threatened to become an end in itself.

But the women hurt her the most. They gave Tzigane constant pain and worry.

What if the love hidden within Dracula adopted a new woman and forever drove the memory of Tzigane away? What if he truly grew to care for someone else? Someone whose flesh was warm like his. Someone who could walk in the sunlight and move and speak and laugh with him both night *and* day. Someone who could be so much more to him than the witch whose once tanned and golden skin had grown pale in the darkness of a crypt.

Tzigane tried to reason with herself. Of course, he was going to bed other women. He had not sworn an oath of celibacy. He owed her no faithfulness. He owed her nothing. He wanted to forget her. To him, she was a traitor who had broken an agreement. Someone to forget. A repulsive monster.

But he could not forget for within him still burned the secret spark of love.

He drank more and more wine, and the serving maids, whores and other women of the Moldavian court continued to warm his bed.

Tzigane wanted to look away and not see. She preferred to remember her treasured time by his side and not think of the way he was now, a drunkard who bedded strange women in her place. But it was her sacred task and her curse to look, to see, to observe in secret, and to wait for him to call to her. His mind might turn back to her at any time, might it not? He might finally realize his hidden love for her, might he not? He might call.

And so, unable to look away, Tzigane watched her beloved Dragon's son slowly change from a proud Warlord-Prince into a wine-sodden drunkard who fought his memories and woke up screaming from nightmares of horribly beautiful, fiery-eyed corpses whose death-chilled lips called his name and begged for a kiss.

That first winter passed, then the spring and summer, until another winter froze the Moldavian countryside again beneath a blanket of white death. And still Dracula fought his phantoms, drinking more and more wine, scarcely sober at all now as he fought his phantoms and made love to women whose faces always seemed about to change into something else—the face of the woman who was no longer truly a woman but a pallid creature of eternal darkness, the memory of whom would not go away no matter how much wine he drank or how many women he took to his bed.

And he knew that his weapons—the wine and the women—were not strong enough. There had to be some other weapon he could use, something which would allow him to pull himself to his full, proud height again and get on with the business of life. Somewhere there must exist such a weapon. But what? And where?

And Tzigane continued to watch. The pain of seeing the other women was no longer an agony but only a dull throb which never completely went away. She cried often in her tomb. Would the years until he called her never pass? Would that time ever come at all?

Dracula's second winter in Moldavia passed slowly and then Spring again resurrected the land, but the beauty of awakening nature went unnoticed by the dethroned Wallachian Warlord-Prince as he slipped ever deeper into his own darkness. He still continued to fight the memories, refusing to surrender totally. Blindly he continued to seek a weapon that would allow him to live again, to forget the past and concentrate upon his life and his future.

Then June came. A Polish army began to mass on the Moldavian border, preparing to invade. Dracula was about to find the weapon he needed. His pain was nearly at an end.

But Tzigane's pain was, of course, only now about to truly begin.

JUNE
1450 A.D.

36

❧❧❧❧❧

"YOU ARE FALLING APART, COUSIN," Prince Stephen of
Moldavia told the half-drunken man sprawled in the chair
before the fire.

Dracula looked up and tried to focus his eyes on Stephen
but only partially succeeded. "Leave me alone," he whispered hoarsely.

"If only you would talk about it," Stephen suggested,
"perhaps then you would be able to . . ."

"I will never talk about what has been troubling me
this past year and a half. Suffice it to say that the deaths
of my father and brother affected me in an unusual manner. I should never have dug them up."

"What did you say?" Stephen asked. "Dug them up?"

"Leave me alone, Stephen."

"No, I will not."

"I do not wish to fight you."

Stephen laughed contemptuously. "Fight? You? In your
present state, a girl could defeat you easily."

Dracula angrily started to rise from the chair. But the
effort seemed greater than the need, and he slumped back
down.

"It does not matter," he whispered.

Stephen paced the room. "I have a challenge for you,"
he said coldly, "if you are still man enough to dare it."

Dracula sipped wine from his goblet without commenting.

"What you need is to do some killing," Stephen continued. "I am going to accompany my father into battle.
The Poles have sent an army to invade us. I want you to

come with me to fight by my side and help defeat this
Polish enemy. The rage of battle can cleanse a man's soul.
Well? Will you do it?"

Dracula lifted his goblet again. Stephen knocked it
away. The goblet clanked loudly on the stone floor.

"Will you come or not?" Stephen growled. "Or are you
afraid?"

This time Dracula did rise. He faced Stephen on shaky
legs, but he did not fall. "It is not fear that plagues me.
It is hate. I hate more than you can know. I hate gypsies.
I hate superstitions. I hate witches. I hate, Stephen. I hate."

"Then come with me and hate Poles as well. Let your
hate take its toll on the lives of the invaders. Please, cousin
Vlad. Come with me."

Dracula's weary, bloodshot eyes gazed at the spilled
wine on the stone floor. The splattered crimson liquid
looked like blood.

"I will come," he said quietly. "It might do me good to
see honest death once again."

37

THE POLISH SOLDIER'S WOUNDED NECK sent a fountain of blood spurting into the warm summer air. Dracula bellowed his victory cry and turned to engage with another invader.

He had been fighting atop his stallion like a madman for more than an hour and felt he could go on killing forever. The sights and sounds of battle worked on him like a fiery potion. He disemboweled a mounted Pole, then swung his sword downward in a deadly arc upon the head of a Polish foot soldier, splitting his skull like a melon.

Dracula laughed insanely as he fought on. At times the Poles he slayed seemed to change into black-robed women with burning eyes. He continued to kill. He continued to laugh.

Then it was suddenly over. No more Poles came at him. There was no one else to kill.

"The day is ours, cousin Vlad!" Stephen cried as he galloped up beside Dracula.

"Indeed," Dracula said, his trance of killing slowly beginning to fade. But something else was fading along with it, being washed away by the flood of emotions which had consumed him during the battle. Something deep within him had changed. His mind was blessedly calm and clear. He had found the right weapon.

The weapon was death and blood and the screams of the dying and the memory of those potent images—a memory stronger than the emotional memories with which he had battled for more than a year and a half. His mind and soul were once again free.

The phantoms were still there, but they no longer mattered. Their power to stir his emotions was gone. He saw Tzigane's image, and it no longer mattered. He could think of that image and feel nothing. He saw her living, smiling, weeping, and Undead. But it no longer mattered.

Dracula laughed. The sound chilled Stephen. He had never heard his cousin laugh, and it was not a pleasant sound.

"There will be a glorious victory feast tonight," Stephen laughed uncertainly in reply. "Wine! Wenches!"

Dracula's eyes glinted coldly. His face became an emotionless mask. "Are there any prisoners?" he asked.

"Yes."

"Perhaps I can help question them?" Dracula suggested. "I have certain . . . skills which might prove useful. Have you ever witnessed an impalement, Stephen?"

Stephen studied Dracula's masklike face in silence for a long moment. "And what of the celebration, cousin Vlad?" he asked. "Surely tomorrow will be soon enough to question the prisoners."

"You celebrate in your own way, Stephen," Dracula answered softly, his voice strangely flat. "I have had enough wine and wenches for some time to come." He laughed again and slapped Stephen heartily upon the back. "I'll wager my Turkish stallion can beat your Moldavian beast back to camp!" he challenged.

"Never!" Stephen replied as Dracula galloped away, his terrible laugh echoing across the death-strewn battlefield.

But while Dracula continued to laugh, relishing his victory over his phantoms, Tzigane began to weep in the isolation of her tomb. Her projected consciousness had secretly cringed within Dracula's mind throughout the battle, fearing that at any moment Dracula might be killed, and she had said a relieved prayer of thanksgiving to Satan when her beloved had survived the weapons of the Poles.

But her relief did not last long for she had also felt the change within him, and she had seen her own image appear in his mind and had felt his new, horribly cold indifference to her memory.

And so she had plunged desperately beneath the layers of his repressed emotions, searching for reasssurance, searching for that feeble flame of love which had been her comfort and hope. But she had found only darkness.

Dracula's spark of caring, which Tzigane had treasured so dearly, had flared its last.

And gone out.

38

‑‑‑‑‑‑‑‑‑

In Undeath, the body does not change. As long as there is fresh blood to drink, hair does not gray, and skin does not wrinkle. But what of the mind, its memories, its thoughts, and the emotions they spawn? They do change. Even for the Undead. Like Tzigane.

She had seen and felt the spark of love within Dracula die, and her happy memories of their time together were soon dulled by the ache of dying hope. And so she banished those memories from her consciousness as well as she could.

She submerged herself in his mind. Watching. Always. She had no need for thoughts of her own when watching, experiencing, and living within Dracula's consciousness. Only when taking strength from the blood she needed to survive, given voluntarily by the local witches who tended her, was she even aware of herself as a separate entity. And at those times when she became conscious of herself, she began to hate her task. She began to hate having to lose herself within another's mind. And she began to fear that eventually she might be unable to pull totally away, that she might become imprisoned within Dracula's mind forever and never be herself again. She would become some nonentity instead whose only hope for existence would be the thoughts and experiences of another.

One year. Two. More. Time passing slowly. The years becoming indistinguishable from each other. Now she only left her crypt rarely, for what need was there to see him with her own eyes?

Her faith in the prophecies, her loyalty to her Lord Satan, and her devotion to her sacred task kept her watching. But they were not the only reasons she continued watching so faithfully. There was also her faith in and devotion to herself, a faith and devotion to the self she feared she might eventually lose.

To have missed Dracula's calling through a weakness in her own spirit would have meant that she had not been as worthy as she had thought, and that pain, unlike the mere loss of Dracula's love, would have been unendurable. To lose hope in a lover is painful, but to lose hope in oneself is the beginning of true nonexistence. Therefore, she kept watching.

His thoughts. His experiences. Dracula's. As he plotted his return to the Wallachian throne, feigning friendships and loyalties to those who could help him return to power, making promises he only vaguely considered keeping, proving himself in battle time after time, leading armies, fighting, killing . . .

But where was Tzigane? Did she really exist anymore? Her lips, her sharp white teeth, her death-chilled throat down which the warm nightly blood from a mortal witch's veins trickled . . . were these all that was left of Tzigane? Only the act of feeding, surviving? Was that all that was left of her, for her?

Her only joy became her journeys to new locations and new crypts for Dracula moved from place to place occasionally, and she had to be near him just in case. But the Strigoi she summoned to take her to another tomb flew swiftly, and the journey was always over too soon. And even when nestled within the beast's talons, her mind was still linked to Dracula's. The journey was never her own. It was his like everything else except the feeding.

Another year passed. Then another. Or was it two? How many years had it been since he had left the cave and her watching had begun? Five years? Ten? Fifty? Tzigane did not know. She searched Dracula's mind to find out. And was shocked.

Had it really only been seven years? It seemed much longer. To Tzigane.

And her crypt? Where was she now? Transylvania? Near Sibiu? It did not matter. She was near the Dragon's son.

That was all her task required. And the watching. Always that.

It was time to feed. Tzigane nodded wearily to the young witch who had quietly entered her chamber a few moments after sunset. The witch moved closer to Tzigane's tomb and leaned down as Tzigane slowly sat up. She found the pulsating vein in the young girl's neck and pressed her sharp canine teeth against the soft, warm skin. They broke through. The good warmth, the salty sweetness, her life and strength, slowly trickled from the two wounds made by her teeth, and she began to feed. When it was over, only a little blood had been taken. Just enough and no more. The young girl bowed to Tzigane reverently as she retreated, walking slowly backward, leaving the tomb. And then Tzigane was alone. Again.

Tzigane listened. A soft and mournful howling came from outside the crypt. She recognized the sound. A blizzard was raging.

It was winter. Seven years since her watching had begun. But what did it matter? She considered rising, going into the night, and letting the freezing wind of the winter storm cleanse the smell of the tomb from her body, her hair, her clothes.

Hers. Not his. *Hers!*

But what if he had called suddenly without warning while she had been thinking those thoughts of her own? Thinking about the weather and herself! Could she have just missed the precious call?

Tzigane sighed and lay back on her soft bed of earth and closed her eyes. A moment more in which to feel her Undead flesh around her and reassure herself that she was real before she pushed her mind outward and found Dracula's once again.

She became submerged once again, lost within his mind, experiencing his thoughts and sensations once again.

And waited.

And watched.

For the call.

Just in case.

SUMMER
1456 A.D.

39

ANOTHER FEEDING WAS OVER. Tzigane drew back and smiled weakly at the young witch who had come to her after sunset. She did not even know the girl's name. It did not matter.

But the mortal witch was hesitant to leave.

"You wish to speak?" Tzigane asked gently. "Please," she reassured the girl, "please speak."

"A great light, honored Sister," the young witch said. "A great light has appeared in the sky."

Tzigane's eyes flashed with sudden interest. A great light? The comet predicted by the prophecies marking the time of Dracula's return to Wallachia? And was he not even now planning to do just that? All his thoughts and actions for months had been directed to that approaching goal. And now the comet, the great light, had appeared in the heavens. Just as the sacred prophecies had predicted.

The news truly did not surprise Tzigane, but this new proof of the prophecies—gave her renewed hope.

Tzigane smiled with sincere affection at the young witch. "Thank you, Sister," Tzigane whispered. "You have made me happy and given me new strength. Thank you."

The young witch bowed reverently and withdrew from the crypt, cherishing the warmth of Tzigane's approval.

Tzigane rose from her tomb. On impulse, she performed a few gliding steps from the Dance of Joy. The comet had appeared, and he was preparing to return to Wallachia. So far, the prophecies had been correct about everything.

"And so must they also prove correct about my future

as Queen and his future as King," Tzigane told the empty crypt, her voice sounding strong and certain.

Suddenly she wanted to see him again with her own eyes. It had been a long time since she had wanted that. A very long time.

"But I must continue to watch," she reminded herself sternly. "Especially now."

And so she quickly ran from the tomb and willed herself into bat-form, then reached out and linked minds with Dracula as she took wing and flew through the warm summer twilight toward the place where he now lived.

She flew silently and swiftly upon breezes fragrant with summer life. As she flew, her eyes beheld the prophesied comet, low in the western sky, almost like a miniature sun, its delicate tail streaming like summer smoke into the darkening sky.

And because of what it represented and the hope it had rekindled in Tzigane's heart, the beauty of that heavenly omen brought tears to her burning eyes and breathless joy to her soaring heart. And suddenly there was a realization deep within her truest self, a knowing that was as real and as solid as the Earth itself, a knowledge that she need never fear losing herself or becoming too weak to continue her appointed task.

She *was* Tzigane. Even after seven and one-half years of existing within another's consciousness, she *was* still her own separate self. Inviolate. Strong. Worthy.

And the sky grew darker, and the comet blazed brighter in the heavens, blazing for Tzigane not just with its own light, but also with her reborn hope and her knowledge that she would never prove unequal to her sacred task. And the comet blazed brighter and brighter in the dark night sky until, to Tzigane, it had become brighter and more beautiful than the sunlight she had lost.

40

Tzigane looked out through Dracula's eyes and inward into his thoughts. She felt his excitement and satisfaction in sitting on his father's throne once again. And she felt Dracula's pleasure with Vladislav's slow and screaming death. The murderer of his father and older brother had been punished at last.

And Tzigane summoned a Strigoi and journeyed to Wallachia. To a secret crypt near Targoviste. To be near him as always. Just in case.

Dracula's second Wallachian reign in Targoviste had begun. And Tzigane watched as it gradually became a reign of terror. Because of the nightmares which he could never quite remember—the nightmares that went away for awhile whenever his weapon against the phantoms was used, the weapon of death.

For Tzigane knew, even if he did not, that he still feared the phantoms, feared that they might return, and feared that his nightmares were the children of those ever waiting phantoms. Tzigane also knew why his phantoms had returned.

The spark of caring within Dracula had flared back to life. Weakly and feebly at first, but it did glow now, that spark which was his unacknowledged love for a gypsy witch long dead, but not dead. And the spark smouldered within his darkness and gave the emotion-charged phantoms strength, not enough strength to torment him as before, but enough to bring back the nightmares.

And Wallachia had rekindled that spark. The memories

of seeing the old places, sleeping in the room where he
had first met the witch when she saved him from the kiss
of his Undead father, standing in the palace courtyard
where the Strigoi had reached out to his father and brother
with its talons, finding the hut where . . .

Nightmares. So unnecessary and yet inevitable because
of his iron-willed stubbornness which would not free his
hidden love for her. Had he even suspected it was there,
he would have considered it a disgusting weakness.

But his renewed fight against the reemerging phantoms
gave Tzigane a strong hope that he would indeed call. In
time. Call to her and ask for the kiss. Just as prophesied, so
that her watching could end at last.

But for now, Dracula had an efficient weapon to use
against the phantoms, and Tzigane watched through his
eyes as the horrors of his reign increased.

So many deaths. So many screams. He killed so easily.
Laughing strangely. For so many reasons. He thought.
But really only for one.

She watched him kill and laugh and take other women to
his bed and wake from nightmares and begin to kill again
so that the nightmares would go away. She watched, and
the years slowly passed. Then it was winter again. He had
reigned for five and one-half years. Five and one-half long
and bloody years.

And then the Dragon's son embarked upon the campaign
he had vowed when he was only a child and a hostage in
the Turkish prison of Egrigoz. A time of blood and death
began along the Danube River, the southern border between Wallachia and Turkland, for Dracula and his Wallachian army had crossed the Danube in a daring invasion
of Turkland itself.

And Tzigane watched while he fought and killed and
escaped the weapons of the enemy as he pushed his army
furiously eastward along the Danube toward the Black
Sea, killing, burning, destroying, defeating all who came
against them, and impaling the survivors, and continually
asking for the aid which the rest of Christendom should
be sending to them, the men, arms, and supplies they
needed to continue the crusade against Islam to push the
Turks farther and farther toward their capital until even
that citadel could be conquered, and Islam defeated. But
the aid did not come.

And then through Dracula's eyes, Tzigane at last saw the Black Sea itself. It was spring. 1462. But the sea was not empty. The Sultan's ships had gathered, preparing a counterattack to defeat Dracula and the remains of his Wallachian army.

Then Tzigane felt Dracula's rage as he was forced to retreat. But even then he and his warriors continued to kill and harass the onrushing tide of the Turkish forces. And Dracula burnt his own land, Wallachia. He poisoned the wells, killed the livestock and destroyed the crops so that there would be nothing left for the Turks.

And Tzigane knew that the most maddening thing of all for Dracula was that his own brother, Radu, who was now called the Handsome, he who had been weak and had succumbed early to the Turks while in Egrigoz, he who was now no more than the Sultan's puppet, was leading the Turks against Wallachia and against Dracula. It was Radu the Handsome, the weakling, the whiner, the thrower of tantrums, who was pushing Dracula and his dwindling army farther and farther northward toward the mountains and the northern border of Wallachia.

But while Dracula raged and continued to fight in spite of the overwhelming odds, Tzigane watched the horrors of defeat through his weary eyes and felt the beginnings of relief for her own worried soul. For she knew his plan— the plan for escape he had hoped never to have to use. She knew that he would not allow himself be taken prisoner or killed. She knew that he would save himself for future battles, future campaigns, and future reigns. She knew that once he had left Wallachia, at least for a little while, there would be an end to the horrors and the worrying that each new battle might take Dracula's life and end forever her own plans for being Satan's Queen, her rightful due.

And then he did escape. Northward over the mountains into Transylvania. She watched and listened as he attempted to persuade the Christians there to give him a new army with which to return to Wallachia and drive out Radu, his hated, usurping brother, the Sultan's puppet.

But the Christians stalled. A letter had been found. A letter forged by some enemy Dracula had made over the years. And the letter made Dracula seem to be a traitor. And Tzigane felt his new rage. Dracula a traitor? The Christian warrior who might have defeated all of Islam with his army if only his Christian allies had sent him aid? A traitor?

But, however ridiculous, the letter was officially accepted as proof that Dracula was indeed a traitor to Christendom because the Christian leaders wanted to believe it. Dracula's campaign against the Turks had been his own idea. It had not been approved by other Christian leaders. When they did not send him aid, they had appeared cowardly. But if he were really only a traitor, then they had been right not to help him. And so the traitor was taken westward across Transylvania and thrown into prison in Hungary.

So Tzigane summoned a Strigoi and journeyed to Hungary and another secret crypt. To wait. And to watch. Just in case.

But she could still feel his anger, and his outrage at the injustice of his new imprisonment eating away at him. But she also felt his satisfaction in knowing that no one was likely to forget the six years of his reign and the atrocities and horror when one-fifth of the population of the region had died screaming at his command, the years when he had earned the grim title of Vlad the Impaler. He had impaled many thousands during those six years, becoming a demon to the Turks, who still called him the Devil's son, and a tyrant to his subjects whom he had ruled with tactics of terror and death.

But to Tzigane he was only a man who had used his weapon of death to keep the emotional phantoms of love at bay.

Tzigane continued to watch and wait. The months slowly passed, and winter came again. And she watched the spark, still glowing feebly deep within him, the spark rekindled in Wallachia, the spark which had never again completely disappeared, the spark of caring which gave her new hope that in time it might become a flame and burn brighter and brighter until it pushed back his darkness and gave him no choice but to acknowledge what it represented. Then he might call to her and end her fourteen years of waiting, her fourteen long, slow years of watching and waiting.

And her hopes grew even stronger when his nightmares returned and became more vivid. Now he could nearly remember them whether he wanted to or not.

But Dracula sensed the phantoms, his enemies, and he fought back as best he could. But now the weapon of death had been denied him.

And so he began to search for a new weapon.

But the silent watcher in his mind, alone in her hidden crypt, began to pray, in secret, that this time the phantoms would be victorious.

FEBRUARY
1463 A.D.

41

※-※-※-※-※

THE LAKE STRETCHED BEFORE HIM. Tranquil. Smooth. Streaked silver by the light of a full moon. But beneath the water, something was moving towards him. It was about to appear. He had to leave.

He had to wake up.

Dracula struggled to awaken. The thing beneath the water was coming closer and closer. Nearly to the shore.

He began to struggle and moan in his sleep. In horror. For he knew he was dreaming and wanted to awaken. But that was not the horror. That had *never* been the horror. What really terrified him was that he wanted to stay even more than he wanted to awaken. That was his terror. Of himself. Of his wanting to stay. Beside the lake. And wait. For it to appear.

And this time he did stay. And it appeared. At last. After the long years of fighting it and awakening in time, it had finally appeared.

And she was beautiful and she was coming toward him and he did not even mind that her eyes were burning with red hellfire and that her teeth were white and sharp and her lips soft and full and inviting as they smiled at him and called his name and the pale arms opened and embraced him and he felt her icy skin and he wanted her to kiss him and he knew that all he had to do was to call her name and she would kiss him and love him and comfort him and all he had to do was to call her name and. . . .

He woke up screaming.

And this time he remembered.

The phantoms had broken through. It all came flooding back. Not the images. Not the memory of Tzigane and the witches and the cavern of Undeath where she had begged him to stay and not to leave her. No, those memories had never been gone. But the emotions—the wanting to be with her again no matter what she had become—had been gone. And now those emotions had returned, the insubstantial phantoms of emotion which he had kept away for twelve and one-half years since that day of the battle with the Poles when he had found the weapon of death.

And he had almost called her name and he knew beyond all doubt that if he had called, even in the dream, if he had called her name even in the dream that she would have come to him, would have appeared to him. Suddenly he could feel her waiting and watching for the call. And he suddenly knew that she had always been there, somehow watching and waiting for him to weaken and call her name.

"But I will not weaken! I will not call you, witch!" Dracula shouted in his empty cell.

"A new weapon," he whispered as he arose from his sweat-soaked bed and began to pace his prison cell. "A new weapon. I must find it," he muttered softly.

The lonely hours before dawn crept slowly into the night, and still he paced and mumbled under his breath, seeking a weapon.

Another sleepless night. There had been many since his latest imprisonment had begun and the phantoms of emotion had begun to plague him again. The weakness of wanting to stay by the lake, of not wanting to awaken and escape her icy arms, her chill lips, and her burning eyes, had all returned.

And now he had stayed and seen her again and remembered the dream and had almost called to her and if only he was still free he could have used the weapon he had found to fight the emotions and could have washed them away in a river of blood and death and screams and. . . .

And then he knew. It was so simple, so wonderfully simple. His new weapon—memories. Memories of emotions stronger than the memories of Tzigane. Memories of the weapon which he had found to combat the phantoms. Memories of using that weapon. Many memories. Six years of memories as ruler.

If he could no longer kill and rule, he would immerse himself in his *memories* of killing and ruling, and perhaps they would crowd out the annoying thoughts of Tzigane, his father and brother, the witches, and the Undead.

"I will see if it works," he whispered excitedly, "and if it does, I will request writing materials so that I may make a record of my history on the throne."

Dracula's Hungarian prison cell was not very different from the one he had had during the latter part of his stay in Egrigoz. There was a table, a chair, a bed, a small barred window looking out to the east, and a fireplace. He now threw a new log into that fireplace and pulled the chair up before the grate. Then he reached to the table, poured himself a goblet of wine, and began to remember.

He remembered the shocked expressions on the faces of the Sultan's emissaries when he had declared what he was going to do to them for refusing to remove their turbans in his throne room at Targoviste, and he remembered their screams of agony as he had carried out his threat and nailed their turbans to their skulls.

Dracula remembered the banquet he had held for the poor and the sick of Targoviste. He had fed them well, then locked them in the hall and burned it to the ground, freeing his land of those who begged and were unhealthy.

A golden cup he had left unguarded in a deserted square in Targoviste drifted into his memories. The cup had never been stolen for no thief was so bold as to court the slow death awaiting him should he be caught.

Dracula chuckled softly as he remembered marching rebellious Wallachian nobles sixty miles on foot to the mountains and then forcing them—men, women, and children—to build his fortress on the river Arges. Not many had survived the ordeal, and those who did had finished the task naked, their tattered clothing having long since fallen from their skeletal frames.

Other fond memories comforted him, remembrances of quick revenge and merciless justice. Again he saw the thousands he had impaled outside Brasov, and again he listened to their screams, pleas, and groans as he walked through the forest of splintery death that he had erected, a forest of wooden stakes glistening red with the blood of his slowly dying victims.

And reminiscing as he stared into the fire, Dracula's mind drifted further and further away from his memories of Tzigane and the Undead. Soon he fell asleep and was comforted by dreams of blood, fire, and flashing steel, and the memories of his life as a warlord and a hero who had come to be known as the Impaler, the terror of Christians and Turks alike. He had truly found his new weapon.

And Tzigane saw his victory and felt her anxious hope begin to fade once again. It had been so close this time. He had nearly called her name. Had nearly released her from her lonely task.

It was maddening. He *knew* he wanted to call to her. He had even acknowledged it this time. But yet he would not because he thought it was a weakness.

In the morning Tzigane watched him request writing materials and begin the history of his six-year reign.

He left out nothing. There were details within details. Working tirelessly hour after hour. And slowly the stack of parchment sheets began to grow thicker.

And when the nightmare returned, he could defeat the phantoms of emotion now by merely reading what he had already written.

Slowly he completed writing the history as the months passed. Summer came, and then the fall. And now he had hours of memories, details of killings and ruling with which to drive away the phantoms.

The winter snows returned to blanket Hungary and edge the prison towers with frozen whiteness. It also buried Tzigane's secret crypt beneath drifts of winter death. But Tzigane still saw the spark glowing within him, and she knew the nightmares would always return.

And so she waited and watched, certain that it was now only a matter of time before he did what he feared so much and call her.

And she could at long last appear.

JANUARY
1464 A.D.

42

⚓⚓⚓⚓⚓

THE LAKE—always the lake—and the witch who had died
and yet still lived, coming nearer. The red fires of her
eyes glowing beneath the water, coming closer and closer.
The water beginning to ripple as she rose from its dark
depths. No longer human. Undead. Smiling at him, sweetly calling his name, coming onto the shore, and embracing him. And he wanted her to kiss him. His lips
moved, and he felt her name about to emerge from his
lips and . . .

Screaming. Awakening. Sweating. Rising from the bed.
Beginning to pace. Going to the table by the fire. Drawing
the stack of parchment sheets toward him. Starting to read
them. Again.

Dracula slowly read the first page of his history, and
his eyes began to blur and the words began to run together
and the words began to seem meaningless and he felt himself slipping off to sleep again and then he was asleep and
the lake was still there and this time Tzigane was already on
the shore and she was already embracing him and her name
was again about to be spoken by his lips and . . .

Awakening again. Another scream. He looked down.
The parchment sheets had fallen from his hands and
scattered over the floor of his cell. He reached down,
picked them up, and rearranged them in order, wearily
beginning to read again.

And then suddenly he threw the sheets onto the table
beside him in disgust. He was terribly bored by what was
written on those pages. He knew it all so well that he could

recite whole pages by memory. It had become a less and less effective weapon. More and more hours were required each time now; more and more pages had to be read to drive away the nightmare. And the nightmare was now returning more and more often. Had he not just had it twice in the same night?

"I am losing the fight," he whispered hoarsely. But he was not defeated yet. He would continue to read. He must. It was not in his nature to surrender.

But soon the words began to blur again and then he was sleeping and Tzigane was still embracing him and her name came closer and closer to his lips and . . .

"Tzigane," he mumbled in his sleep.

And awoke screaming. He had finally said her name.

A chill swept over him. He rose from the chair. The dark, barred window seemed to stare at him. He sensed danger approaching. Just like in the dream. Just like the thing which had once been human that came closer and closer towards the shore but now there was something out there in the night coming closer and closer to that window.

And he knew it was she. And he knew defeat and terror and rage.

He ran to the window and looked out into the night. Silence. Like the quiet in a tomb long closed to the light.

Dracula felt his knees beginning to shake. He felt shamed. The warlord, he who had ruled with death and terror, felt terror.

She was coming. He could feel her drawing nearer just like in the dream. But this was no longer a dream.

He continued to stare with unblinking eyes into the blackness of the night. Then there was a sound. Wings, soft wings, beating the cold winter air, coming closer. Closer.

Dracula drew back from his window. His eyes were locked upon the bars. The bars were meant to keep him in. Hope flared within him. The bars would also keep her out! Or would they?

And then he saw the eyes like two burning embers, floating closer to his window. Even though he was high above the ground, hundreds of feet above in his cell in the tower, the burning eyes—her eyes—were coming closer, hovering and watching him.

But the bars. They would keep her out. Surely the bars would keep her out.

The eyes dimmed, and for a moment it seemed that they remained looking at him from within a thickening fog. And then they disappeared.

Relief flooded him. But then he saw the fog begin to seep in between the bars of the window. He backed away until he was flat against the locked door on the far side of the room.

The fog swirled and spun in the center of his cell. Its spinning increased. Faster and faster it spun. Two long, vertical streamers of mist formed, spiraling, intertwining, a double spiral whirling faster and faster and . . .

A ghostly image began to condense and solidify out of the whirling mist.

She stood before him naked, smiling sadly. Her eyes did not glow. They wept. She did not speak, only looked at him, her arms by her sides, weeping silent tears.

His fear left him—his fear of himself and of wanting to see her again, her whom he had abandoned in the cavern of Undeath fifteen long years before.

Tzigane.

Slowly Dracula pulled himself out of his crouch. Cautiously he walked toward her. Why had he fought this for so long? Because it was a weakness? It did not seem so now.

Now he was within reach of her. He stopped and stared at her. It had been fifteen years, but she looked no different. His hair had begun to gray, and his face was lined with the strain of those fifteen years. But she had not changed. She was still as beautiful and still as maddeningly desirable. He wanted to touch her, even if her flesh were cold. He wanted to kiss her. He wanted her to kiss him.

No! Not that. He would not allow it. Surely just pronouncing her name in a dream did not automatically mean he had requested that kiss of Undeath. Or did it? Would she now infect him with her kiss? Penetrate his veins with her sharp teeth and drink his blood and . . .

"As I told you once long ago, my Vlad," Tzigane whispered softly, reading his thoughts, her voice so familiar to him that it made him ache deep inside, "as I told you by the lake, not all my kisses are crimson. I will not bless you with that kiss of eternity until you desire it."

Still he did not reply.

"Do not hide from yourself any longer," she urged gently. "You have not fought *me* all these years, my Vlad, but *yourself*. Hide no longer."

Slowly he nodded, but still kept silent.

"Yes," she smiled hopefully, "I know of your thoughts. And I want your kisses as much as you want mine. Hide from yourself no longer. This emotion is not a weakness, but a strength. A bond between us. Unbreakable for all eternity."

Dracula moved a step closer. He reached out and stroked her raven-black hair. He brushed her icy tears from her pale, waxen cheeks.

"Tzigane," he whispered, his voice strained and weak with the emotions which were boiling up inside him, violent emotions being released after all the years he had fought them. He encircled her with his arms and drew her closer. His pulse pounded in his veins.

"I am *not* asking for the crimson kiss," he said tightly. "Not yet."

"I know," she smiled again, placing her chill arms around his warmth.

And then his lips were on hers and the phantoms of emotion were dancing within his soul and it was a dance of joy and relief and strength greater than any he had ever known.

43

❊❊❊❊❊

"THE DAWN IS NEAR," Tzigane said softly, glancing at the steadily graying window of Dracula's cell. "I must be going soon, my Vlad."

Dracula looked at the lightening sky beyond his window. He nodded, then kissed her gently upon her lips once again and stroked her wildly tangled hair, tangled from their night of love.

"Back to your . . ." he began, but Tzigane reached up and placed her cool fingers against his lips, knowing he was about to say "tomb."

"Back to my . . . resting place," she finished for him.

He nodded again. "Because of the sun?"

"Yes," she whispered. "But I will return tomorrow night, if you . . ."

"Yes," Dracula said without hesitation, then rose from the narrow bed where they had made love and extended his hand to Tzigane. She took it and stood gracefully beside him.

Somewhere outside a cock crowed at the coming day.

"I must hurry," Tzigane said, stepping away from him. "You need not look if this bothers you," she added, spreading her arms, preparing to alter her form.

"I will watch," Dracula said. "Till tomorrow night then?"

Tzigane nodded and closed her eyes.

"Tzigane?" Dracula whispered.

She opened her eyes again, questioningly.

Dracula suddenly could not remember what he had been

189

about to say. He shrugged. And then he remembered something else and smiled.

"Allies?" he asked, still smiling.

Tzigane nodded quickly, her eyes growing wet and a smile breaking across her face. Then the sound of the crowing cock came again, and her eyes darted to the window. It was growing very bright.

"There is no more time," she said hurriedly, closing her eyes. Her outline became hazy, then ghostly, and then the column of whirling mist appeared where she had stood. The twin spirals formed and spun faster and faster, and then a thick mist took their place.

Dracula watched the mist seep out between the bars of his window until nothing remained in the cell, then he walked to the window and looked out. Far below the prison tower, he saw a dark shape with black wings soaring away rapidly. She was gone.

Dracula stood gazing out of his small window until the sun rose and bathed his face in its weak winter rays. Had it really happened? And was this what he had fought against for so long? This feeling of calm, relief, strength, and happiness? He watched the sun rise higher into the morning sky. And Tzigane. Where was she now? In some cold, dark . . .

He smiled. No, she was only in her "resting place." Just a resting place.

He glanced at the bed where they had slept together a short time before, their bodies intertwined as the emotions that he had tried so hard to fight had pounded his consciousness.

But he would not chastise himself for fighting. No, he had done what he thought was right. He had always done what he thought was right for himself and probably always would. But now *this* seemed right for him. An Undead witch. A lover. A friend. Still that. After all those years apart, she was still someone he could trust, a faithful ally. But she *had* betrayed him at the lake. She had broken their . . .

Dracula smiled again. No, she had done what she felt was right for herself. She had only done what she felt she had to do. She had only done what he would have done in her place. Yes, only what he would have done. For herself and her beliefs.

He walked to the fireplace and threw another log into the grate, then poked at it until it started to burn and fill the cell with warmth. He sat down, poured himself some wine, and sipped the crimson liquid as he stared into the flames.

Soon his morning meal was brought by the guards. He ate slowly, thoughtfully, his mind beginning to consider what he had at one time wanted with total determination. Tzigane's powers. She had said at the lake that she could continue to teach him. But because of his stubbornness, he had gone away and left her, his teacher. She who could have helped him to gain powers beyond those of other men. Fifteen years ago. What powers would he have now possessed if he had stayed and tried to understand?

He finished his meal and went back to the bed to stretch out. He had slept little that night, and waves of fatigue suddenly washed over him.

He closed his eyes. He would need his rest and would have to sleep during the day so that he could be alert for the lessons he intended to ask Tzigane to give him at night. What better place to study and learn than in a prison cell where there were no distractions?

He slept deeply and restfully, and there were no lakes in his dreams—only a beautiful witch with pale green eyes who danced naked in the moonlight and laughed and smiled and told him that she was going to give him the powers of a god.

44

⫘⫘⫘⫘

SHORTLY AFTER SUNSET, she returned just as she had promised. But this time there were no tears, only smiles. They embraced. And kissed.

"You want to be taught," Tzigane stated.

Dracula's surprise was obvious.

"Of course I know," she smiled mysteriously. "Did you expect anything less?"

Dracula laughed. It was a pleasant laugh. "Very well. I obviously have no secrets from you."

"None at all," Tzigane answered, looking away.

Dracula pondered her comment for a moment, then shrugged his shoulders. "Yes," he said. "I want to be taught." A grimace creased his forehead. "Did you send me that dream last night? You sent me a dream once in Targoviste." His frown deepened. "Have you been sending me dreams and nightmares all these years?" he asked tightly.

Tzigane sensed danger. She looked back into his eyes. "No, my Vlad. Those dreams were your own. They were your mind talking to itself, your hidden mind speaking to your conscious one, trying to help you realize things about yourself. I sent you one dream, only one. The one in Targoviste which first brought you to my hut."

Dracula continued to frown.

"I have never lied to you, my Vlad, not even when you thought I had," she assured him.

His frown slowly faded. "Very well," he decided. "I

believe you. And yes, I do want to be taught. But after all this time, will you. . . ."

"Of course I will teach you. It is what my appointed task requires. And also what I desire."

Dracula nodded thoughtfully. "Tzigane, you appear the same as you were fifteen years ago, but I sense that inside . . . I don't know. You were always strong-willed, but now . . ."

"Of course I have changed. There are things I have done, things I have seen and experienced, which have left me . . . changed. But yet I am the same. It is the same with you."

"But I have aged. My hair. My face."

"The years have only made you more handsome," Tzigane laughed.

"Handsome?" Dracula asked uncomfortably.

"Did I never tell you that you are handsome?" Tzigane teased. "Does it embarrass you, my Vlad, for me to call the great Impaler of Wallachia handsome?"

"You know of Wallachia?" Dracula asked, trying to change the direction of the conversation.

"I know of all that has happened to you."

"But how . . ."

"It does not matter. It was my sacred task to keep track of you and your exploits."

"And you performed your task to perfection," Dracula said.

Tzigane kissed him softly.

"As I recall," Dracula said, taking her in his arms again, "you were teaching me how to use sexual passion to see visions before Vladislav interrupted my lessons."

Tzigane laughed and nodded. "Yes. And I, too, want to start your lessons with more visions. But I will soon teach you other things as well. My powers are much greater now that I am Undead, my Vlad, and there are now ways for me to help you to learn faster. You will learn quickly, my Vlad. I promise. But first, let me help you have a . . . vision."

They embraced again, moved to the bed, and lay down. And there were many visions that night. And every night thereafter.

And as Tzigane had promised, Dracula learned quickly. His mastery of the magical forces of the Unseen was speeded by the heightened mental powers that Tzigane now possessed, powers by which she could enter his mind and cause memories to form. She implanted knowledge of incantations, gestures and body movements so that Dracula need only learn to coordinate the different aspects of a spell in order for it to be effective.

The nightly lessons continued, and time passed more quickly for Tzigane. The winters seemed closer together than she could ever remember. Soon she found that she had been visiting his cell for three and one-half years, and he had become an expert in the manipulation of the Unseen.

Three and one-half years to learn what it had taken Tzigane a childhood plus seven years of hard work to master. But now he had learned all he could as a mortal, and she hesitantly began to suggest . . . the kiss.

But still he refused. He was not ready. And Tzigane knew that his plans did not yet include the thrones of Satan, but only the thrones of men. She would still have to wait a bit longer for him to accept who he was and what he was destined to become. But time passed ever more quickly now that Dracula shared her nights. And she knew that she could now be happy waiting.

But soon Dracula began to use his new mental powers to search for a way out of prison. His lessons were over, and he was determined to be free.

Tzigane tried to ignore her annoying worry that he might want to be free of her once more, now that he had gained what he wanted from her. But all she could do was trust in the love she saw often in his eyes and hope that he also knew it was there. She could only hope that he would not want to force her out of his life a second time.

JULY
1466 A.D.

45

❊❊❊❊❊

DRACULA LAY UPON HIS BED in the cell. Bright morning sunlight was streaming through his small, barred window. A guard had just taken away the remains of his morning meal, and he was alone once again, searching with his mind. He was searching his own thoughts, but also searching the thoughts of others by projecting his new mental powers beyond the confines of his cell, seeking a way to be free of the prison walls.

And in his own thoughts, the thoughts of the king of Hungary, King Matthias, and the thoughts of a cousin of the king, a noblewoman named Countess Helen Corvinus, he finally found his answer. Yes, he was certain that by using dream-spells he could make it work.

But what of Tzigane? What would she think of him marrying this Countess, even if it were done solely to free himself from prison? Surely she would see the need for it since it would only be to get free. . . .

Dracula directed his mind beyond the prison to her resting place, toward Tzigane's mind. He found her. *Tzigane?* his thoughts called. He sensed her mind beginning to awaken from her daytime slumbers.

I am here, my Vlad, Tzigane's thoughts spoke within his mind.

I think I have found a way to be free again, Tzigane.

I am glad, Tzigane said, and Dracula could actually feel that it was true.

But, he continued, *it will mean marrying a cousin of the king.*

Tzigane's thoughts became strangely blank.

I would marry her solely to get out of prison, Tzigane, he assured her.

Still Tzigane's mind was silent.

I nearly married her once before, he continued quickly, *while I was ruler in Wallachia. But then came my Turkish campaign and this imprisonment here in Hungary, and the marriage contract I had discussed with King Matthias was forgotten.*

For a moment more, Tzigane's mind kept still, then at last, *Her name?* she asked, although she remembered the name well enough.

Helen, Dracula replied, *Countess Helen Corvinus of the royal Corvinus family.*

Tzigane was silent again.

Dracula felt anger rising within him. *I am not asking your permission, Tzigane. It is what I am going to do. I simply wanted to discuss it with you to see what suggestions you could make. I intend to use dream-spells to prepare the mind of the king to accept the letter I intend to write him, the letter in which I shall propose a renegotiation of the marriage contract. And I will also use other dream-spells on Helen herself.*

It seems to be a good plan, my Vlad, Tzigane finally said.

She is nothing like you, Tzigane, Dracula told her.

I've no doubt of that, Tzigane replied, and Dracula's mind sensed a slight bitterness tingeing her thoughts.

Will you help me send the dreams to the king and Helen tonight? he asked.

You are proficient. You do not need my help.

But I wish it, all the same.

Tzigane's mind emptied again.

Tzigane, Dracula began, a flash of insight suddenly flooding his brain, *do you fear that I will not want to see you after I am free? Do you wish me to remain a prisoner because you are certain to see me each night while I am here?*

Tzigane seemed about to reply, but then Dracula felt her pull back her thought just as she was on the verge of sending it to him.

Tzigane, Dracula said with gentle thoughts, *I want you to stay in my life and continue to fill my nights with pas-*

sion and with . . . friendship. Even if I have to marry this woman, I need not . . .

You cannot deny her her rights, Tzigane angrily cut him off.

No, of course not. But I need not . . . could not enjoy those marital duties, not with her.

Slowly he felt Tzigane's thoughts begin to relax, accept, and agree.

And we would still meet at night? Tzigane asked.

The spell of sleep, which you taught me to use, is most effective, Dracula suggested.

You mean right there? With the Countess Helen sleeping next to us in the bed? Tzigane asked with surprise.

And why not? Dracula asked. *But that need not be the way. She has a house I would share, a house near here in the town of Pest across the Danube from Buda. The house is large. There will be other rooms and other beds for us.*

Finally Tzigane's thoughts became interested once again. *Very well,* she told him quietly. *I shall be there tonight as always, my Vlad, and I shall observe your use of the dream-spells and give you any advice you may need.*

There is just one other thing, Tzigane, Dracula added. *As you know, I was born into the Orthodox faith of Wallachia.*

So? Tzigane asked, puzzled. *Your religion means nothing to you. This I know for certain. So why . . .*

Because I will undoubtedly be required to join the Roman Catholic faith of Hungary before I am allowed to marry the cousin of the king.

I still do not see . . . Tzigane started.

Well, you won't disappear into a cloud of smoke or anything when I kiss you after I'm a Catholic, will you?

Suddenly Tzigane realized that Dracula was trying to make a joke. The Impaler of Wallachia joking? She was secretly very pleased. Her return into his life had changed him in many ways.

Dracula felt Tzigane's laughter bubbling into his mind, tickling his thoughts. He was glad she was happy once again.

As long as you don't wear any silly Catholic symbols around your neck, we will not have any trouble getting together, my Vlad, she told him.

Good, excellent, he replied, suddenly impatient. *Then I will see you tonight. I must go now and compose the letter which I will send to the king tomorrow after I have sent him certain dreams.*

And I must rest, Tzigane answered. *Until tonight then, my Vlad,* her soft thoughts said to his mind.

Then their contact was broken, and with their separation, Dracula felt his now familiar emotion of unsatiated hunger.

His hunger for Tzigane.

DECEMBER
1466 A.D.

46

❊⊢❊⊢❊⊢❊⊢❊⊢

"Count Dracula," Tzigane said experimentally. "Yes," she decided, "I like the way it sounds."

"I am a Prince of Wallachia, Tzigane," Dracula protested, "and a prince outranks a count."

"Of course," Tzigane laughed, then kissed him playfully upon his cheek. "But you have married a countess and . . . very well, *Prince* Dracula," she smiled, glancing at the sleeping countess in the bed.

The light of a full moon streamed softly into the large, ornate bedroom, mingling its silver rays with the flickering crimson light from the fireplace. Except for the crackling of the flames in the grate, the night was silent. The servants in the house of Countess Helen Corvinus had also been quieted by the spell of sleep, which Dracula had cast shortly before Tzigane's arrival.

Dracula's plan for release from prison had succeeded with ease. Three months after the letter and the dream-spells were sent, he had officially become a Catholic and the husband of the countess. And though he was still technically under arrest, Helen's house in the town of Pest made a luxurious prison, and the powers that Tzigane had helped him acquire made it easy for him to do as he pleased. The spell of invisibility alone allowed him effortless access to and from his supposed prison.

He had been married to Countess Helen for nearly two months, and now he was having problems he had never anticipated—not serious problems, but annoyances which, to his further annoyance, Tzigane found extremely amusing.

"And is she still as . . . loving, my Vlad?" Tzigane asked, pulling her gaze away from Helen's sleeping form.

Dracula stared at Tzigane's smiling face for a moment without replying. "You enjoy my little problem with her, don't you, Tzigane," he stated. "And you never tire of asking me that same question. I wish you would not mention it. It is not amusing to me."

"But surely every man wishes to be desired by women," Tzigane continued to tease. "And Helen is rather beautiful. Fortunately I can read your thoughts so I know I have no reason to be jealous. But still, I can understand Helen being so . . . loving. You are handsome and an exciting lover."

"Enough, Tzigane," Dracula commanded angrily. "Having a woman practically chase you around the house, fawning over your every word, your every movement, always trying to anticipate your slightest whim, always wanting to lure you into the bedroom . . ."

"She is merely in love," Tzigane grinned.

"No. I am sure that it must have been that damned dream-spell I sent her in the beginning. I must have put too much strength into it. The first time she saw me, she acted strangely, never taking her eyes off me and . . ."

"Perhaps the spell was not needed?" Tzigane said, frowning to feign seriousness. "Perhaps she would have married you without the spell? You are very famous . . . infamous, my Vlad. The Impaler of Wallachia, the terror of Turks and Christians alike, and all those other titles that the stories about your reign have inspired. You are a legend, my Vlad. What woman wouldn't want a handsome legend for a husband, to share her bed and elevate her to the status of a celebrity among her peers?"

"You just don't know what it's like, Tzigane. She . . . if I could not cast the spell of sleep over her at night, I would go mad with her attentions. Do you know she does not ask me to make love to her, Tzigane? No! She asks me to *impale* her on my . . ."

But Tzigane's laughter interrupted his complaining. He looked angrily at the laughing witch, then turned and left the room. Tzigane hurried to catch up with him, forcing herself to stop laughing as she ran down the long corridor to the great stairway and the lower floors of the house. She caught him at the foot of the stairs.

"Where are you going, my Vlad?" she asked, pulling his arm. "Do not be angry with me. Your situation *is* amusing to a woman, but you will probably never understand."

Dracula stopped and stared at her, but much of the anger was now gone from his eyes. He shrugged. "I want to see where you spend your days," he said on impulse.

Tzigane looked away, all humor was now gone from her thoughts. "I . . . I would rather you did not."

"I know you live in a tomb," Dracula replied as gently as he could. "I understand the need for it. And I don't think that I mind. It is simply your resting place as you call it, and I would like to see it. Will you take me there? Is it allowed? I would like to be the one who leaves at dawn for a change. Or maybe even stay by your side while the sun is in the sky."

Tzigane's eyes grew moist. Never had Dracula come so close to admitting that he cared for her, and she was deeply touched. "Very well, my Vlad. If you wish it."

Dracula slowly nodded. "Good. I will get my cloak. Shall I get one for you as well? It is winter, and you look cold without any clothes. Don't you have clothes anymore, Tzigane?"

"Of course I do. In my resting place. My silver and black gown. I wear it during the day. But I have never needed any covering when I am with you," she grinned wickedly, "and the Undead cannot take clothing with them when they alter their forms for a journey."

"I see," he replied thoughtfully. "Then you do not want a cloak?"

"I will not be cold without one, but I would enjoy wearing one as we walk," she answered.

"Then I will bring you one of Helen's," he said, then left her alone at the foot of the stairs. Soon he returned and slipped a rich, pale green, velvet cloak around her shoulders. It matched the color of Tzigane's eyes, though he did not say so and perhaps he did not even know why he had chosen that color from among his wife's collection. But Tzigane understood and was deeply touched once again.

"Is it far?" Dracula asked as he pulled his own black

cloak over his shoulders and opened the massive oak door which led outside.

"No," Tzigane answered. "I moved nearer to this house once you were married." She stepped through the doorway and into the winter night. The air was cool and crisp, and the sky was clear and black. The moon and the stars blazed down in silent glory.

Dracula closed the door behind them and took Tzigane's arm. They began to walk down the snow-covered path leading to the main gate in the wall that surrounded the house. Outside the wall, the town of Pest was silent as if it, too, slept.

"I will cast a cloak of invisibility around both of us before I open the gate so that we may avoid questioning gazes," Dracula said as they walked along, snow crunching beneath his boots but silent beneath Tzigane's pale, naked feet.

"Does she really ask you to . . . impale her, my Vlad?" Tzigane asked, laughing softly once again.

Dracula shook his head in annoyance but did not reply. Then suddenly he stiffened and stopped.

"Be still," he hissed, dropping Tzigane's arm and reaching for the hilt of his sword. "Something is wrong," he whispered, automatically bending down into a fighting crouch. He scanned the interior of the walls with his eyes as well as his mind, searching for danger.

Tzigane also threw her mind into the night for now she too sensed danger—not danger to her, but to him.

Dracula's eyes and mind found the danger at the same moment. He saw a place where the snow had been disturbed at the top of the wall beside the gate, where someone had crawled over the wall, and he sensed the small, fearful mind of an assassin. And suddenly he also knew that the assassin was about to send an arrow toward his heart.

Dracula threw himself to the ground just as he heard the faint whir of the arrow in flight. Something hit his left side and sent a shaft of white-hot pain racing through his body. Then it all became a blur, Tzigane calling his name, leaning over him, weeping. He was aware that she was bending closer and closer toward his neck, her lips parting to reveal her sharp white teeth, and he knew she was going to kiss him and give him the kiss of eternity.

He tried to say no, but he did not have the strength. He sent his thoughts to her, telling her not to do it, but still her teeth came closer and closer to his neck. Then he heard her let out a strangled, frustrated cry and saw her jerk back without giving him the kiss.

He felt waves of pain and knew that he was losing consciousness, but he was still aware enough to notice Tzigane throw off her cloak, spread her arms, and change into something else. He was also aware that the assassin had not left and that Tzigane was going to do something to protect him from the assassin who was approaching with sword drawn to make certain Dracula was dead. Suddenly a huge wolf with burning red eyes was crouching where Tzigane had stood. The wolf was growling murderously. Suddenly it leaped over his body and was gone. Waves of blackness came down upon him, and he lost consciousness.

Consciousness returned a moment later. It seemed that he had just heard a man's horrible scream of terror and death. Then the wolf reappeared, and Dracula saw that its muzzle was dripping with crimson gore. The blackness returned.

"Vlad, my beloved?" Tzigane called, weeping and cradling his head in her lap.

Finally he opened his eyes. The pain was not as bad. He looked down. His side was covered with blood, but the arrow was no longer there.

"I feel better," he whispered. The effort to talk made the pain return, but not as bad as before.

"Speak with your thoughts," Tzigane urged him. "It will hurt less."

The wolf, the assassin, Dracula's thoughts said in her mind. *You? You . . .*

A wolf is another form I may employ. The assassin wanted to take your head with him to prove that he had accomplished his task. But he will shoot no more arrows, my Vlad.

You . . . protected me. My thanks.

Please do not die! Tzigane's agonized thoughts screamed in his head. *I . . . I kept faith with my Lord Satan. I did not . . . could not give you the sacred kiss without your*

*approval. Not even when I thought you were about to die.
I . . . I could not. I wanted to, but . . .*

*Do not worry, Tzigane. I can tell that I am not going
to die. The wound is not that serious. And I thank you for
not kissing me. I know that you wanted to save me from
death. I understand. But thank you for not doing it. I must
think and decide. I, too, thought I might be about to die.
I, too, saw death as an enemy I might not defeat. I do not
know who sent that assassin, but I have many enemies.
There may be other assassins in my future. I must think,
Tzigane.*

I will carry you back into the house, Tzigane's thoughts
told him. She reached out and started to lift him into her
arms.

I will be too heavy for you to . . . Dracula began, but
Tzigane had already lifted him as if he were a child. She
quickly carried him inside and up the stairs, then laid him
gently in his bed beside the sleeping Helen.

How? he asked, conquering his surprise. *So strong?*

The Undead are strong, my Vlad, she smiled down at
him, pushing his hair back from his sweating forehead.
I have the strength of many mortals.

Dracula was impressed despite his pain. *Yes,* his mind
repeated as unconsciousness began to claim him again,
*I must think of death as an enemy that I cannot defeat
without aid. Without the kiss. In time even . . . I . . . will
be defeated . . . by death . . . unless . . .* The blackness returned and his mind was calm.

Tzigane quickly went to work. She cast the spell of
invisibility around her body, then awakened the members
of the household. There was much screaming in the bedroom when Helen awoke and found Dracula bleeding and
unconscious by her side. Footsteps were heard running to
the room, and a servant was sent for a doctor. All the
while Tzigane remained unseen in a corner of the room,
watching over her beloved Dragon's son.

And she stayed until the doctor had come and dressed
the wound, pronouncing it less than fatal. She stayed until
the sun had nearly broken the eastern horizon, when finally
she had no choice but to go.

47

❈❈❈❈❈❈

THREE WEEKS OF HEALING had given Dracula his strength back, and he was once again able to leave his bed and move about. It had been horrible, confined to the bed with the Countess Helen constantly hovering over him, nursing him, bothering him with countless questions and endearments.

But now he was strong again. He had cast the spell of sleep over the household and was walking with Tzigane down the pathway to the main gate. But this time the spell of invisibility had been cast around the two of them before they left the house.

Dracula opened the gate just enough for them to squeeze through, then closed it as soundlessly as possible. But his caution was not necessary for the narrow, snow-covered city street outside the walls was empty of all life, and the homes which were crowded along the street were silent in the night.

Neither spoke as they moved through the streets of the sleeping city of Pest. Soon they were there. Tzigane's crypt.

Dracula felt a slight chill tingle his body, but he chose to ignore it.

Tzigane's resting place was a low, stone structure sitting in the midst of the graves of nobles and wealthy citizens whose bones rested in similar tombs.

And no one suspects a . . . one Undead lives within that tomb? Dracula asked with his thoughts.

The witches who tend to my needs and give me my nightly strength have cast spells of invisibility over the structure itself, my Vlad. And they are always watching—

also unseen—to turn the minds of any curious seekers away, should it become necessary to do so. I am quite safe.

Dracula nodded his approval, then followed Tzigane toward the tomb. An entrance with steps, which led down into darkness, was cut in one side of the structure.

And are the witches watching us even now? he asked, looking around suspiciously.

Yes, but as invisibly as we are to them. Do not worry, my Vlad, for I have touched their minds, and they know what we are about to do.

Dracula stopped and looked into Tzigane's eyes. *And do you also know what I am about to do, Tzigane?*

Tzigane's pale green eyes glistened with emotion. She nodded silently, then took Dracula's hand and led him down the steps into the tomb.

Of course, I am not surprised that you know, Dracula told her as they reached the bottom of the stairs. *And of course, you approve.*

Yes, my dear Vlad. Oh yes, Tzigane said, suddenly embracing him and holding him tightly against her pale body. *I have waited so long. Of course, I approve. And I understand why.*

Even so, Dracula continued, *I have words I wish to say. Such a solemn occasion . . .*

A joyous occasion! Tzigane interrupted.

Dracula shrugged uncertainly. *I have decided, and I will not change my mind,* his thoughts said, mostly to reassure himself. Now that he was here and could see the tomb, he wondered if he really wanted to do it—to condemn himself to an eternity of darkness after death, living in a place of the dead like Tzigane.

Dracula looked at the beautiful vampiress, the tears streaking her face, and the joyful smile curving her full, red lips.

I . . . he began, *I saw death when the arrow entered my body, Tzigane, and I must not allow that enemy to defeat me when the time comes for me to die. I have always saved myself, given myself an escape route, when I came face to face with an enemy I could not hope to defeat. I had an escape route from Vladislav when he returned to drive me from my first reign. And I had an escape route when my brother Radu led the Turks and drove me from*

*my second reign. And now I have seen death and felt my
true mortality for the first time, and I recognize death as
merely another enemy whom I cannot hope to defeat without your help. And that is why . . .*

"Vlad," Tzigane whispered softly, her voice sweet and
loving, "speeches are not necessary. I know what lies in
your heart, and I understand. You look upon death as an
enemy and reason your decision like a warrior. But I think
of your decision as something glorious and wondrous, the
fulfillment of hopes and dreams after centuries of prayer
to our Lord Satan. But more than anything else, I rejoice
because for me it will mean an eternity by your side. Together always and forever, Vlad, my beloved."

Dracula looked past Tzigane to the open tomb surrounded by glowing candles, the tomb where she spent her
days. "I do not wish to leave the sun just yet, Tzigane."

"I know."

"You will not . . . ?"

"I will only break the skin and taste a trickle of your
blood. That is all that is required to bless you. Nothing
more."

Dracula nodded solemnly.

"There is something else you should know, my Vlad.
Once the kiss has been given, your ties to the Unseen will
be stronger, and you shall be able to wield the powers you
have mastered with greater force than before."

Dracula tried to smile. "An admirable benefit to be
sure," he said, a faint trace of nervousness tingeing his
voice.

"And there is a way to become even more powerful
while still in the flesh of a mortal, my Vlad," Tzigane continued carefully. "If you were to . . ." But then she hesitated.

But Dracula could also read minds, and he knew what
she was about to ask. And although for a moment he
was repulsed, the idea soon began to appeal to him for he
understood what it would mean to Tzigane and that it
would make the bond between them even stronger than
it already was. He also knew that perhaps what she desired would lessen the emotional hunger he felt whenever
she was not near for it would bind them together with
stronger chains than ever before.

"I wish it to be so, Tzigane," Dracula told her gently,

lightly kissing her on the forehead. He felt joy engulfing her mind. "Shall you go first or shall I?" he asked softly.

Tzigane led him to her open tomb. She looked deeply into his eyes for a moment, then leaned close to the pounding vein in his neck.

He felt the icy touch of her lips as they caressed the bare flesh of his throat. A faint shudder crept through his body as her freezing tongue stroked the skin covering his jugular vein. And then her teeth, like sharp, pointed icicles pressed harder and harder against the skin. Suddenly a flash of dark pain seemed to penetrate his entire being and shake his soul to its core.

Tzigane moaned softly. It was done.

Dracula noticed that his fists were clenched so tight that his arms were aching with the strain. He tried to relax. He heard a soft, sucking sound. The sensation of his own warm blood upon the skin of his throat was now mingling with the cold touch of Tzigane's teeth and lips. Then she drew back, gazing up at him, her eyes filled with tears and emotions he could not begin to fully comprehend. A small trickle of his blood ran down from the left side of her mouth.

Dracula reached up and wiped away the crimson trickle from Tzigane's face. He smiled as best he could.

"I love you so much, my Vlad," Tzigane suddenly sobbed as she embraced him and held him close.

Dracula clumsily stroked her hair and patted her back. He let her hold him close as he tried to grasp the significance, of what had happened, what he had just allowed to happen. Feeling closer to Tzigane than he ever had before, he suddenly wanted to be closer still, and he knew how that could be done.

"And now the other thing that you wanted, Tzigane," he whispered.

She looked up at him again, smiled, and wiped her tears. "A woman's tears," she laughed. "I think myself so strong, and yet . . ."

"You *are* strong," Dracula interrupted. "You are not weak in any way, Tzigane. I do not understand it, but I know it is true. You, a woman . . . I feel that you are as strong as any warrior I have ever known or fought. I do not understand, but I know it is true."

Tzigane kissed him quickly on his lips. "And you really want the other?" she asked quietly.

"I do."

Tzigane nodded. She slowly brought her left hand up and rested her sharp thumbnail just above the swelling of her left breast. Suddenly she pushed the nail inward, penetrating the skin, then jerked it downward until a small wound had been made, and her blood had started to flow.

"Hurry, my Vlad," she urged. "The wounds of the Undead heal very quickly."

Dracula hesitated only a moment as he watched the blood welling out of the wound. His conscious mind fought his desire to be closer to Tzigane than ever before. Then he found that he was bending closer and closer to the wound above her breast. His lips touched her death-chilled skin, and her blood was mixing with his saliva. Her blood was as cold as the water from a frozen winter stream, but also salty and sweet. It also tasted of Tzigane herself, and Dracula felt a wave of emotion explode within him, which made the tomb around him spin as if caught in the vortex of a tempest. He swallowed and felt Tzigane's Undead blood slide smoothly down his throat, a warmth beginning to spread outward through his body. New strength poured through his veins, and he felt his senses sharpening to a razor's edge. Then she gently pushed him away, and he realized that the blood had stopped flowing into his mouth. The wound above her breast had already healed.

And then he embraced her and held her close and they made love upon the bed of earth. In her tomb.

JANUARY
1476 A.D.

48

-ıı̇-ıı̇-ıı̇-ıı̇-ıı̇-

IT WAS JANUARY, the depth of winter, but now Tzigane
and Dracula shared their nights. Time continued to pass,
but ever more quickly.

Nine years since that night in Tzigane's tomb. Nine years
of passion and friendship. Was there ever a time when
it had been otherwise? A time when Tzigane had been
alone? Had those fifteen years of watching and waiting
really happened?

Nine years since the night of the kiss. Now it was winter
once again, and those other years of pain, doubt, watching,
and waiting were like a bad dream only dimly remembered
because nine years of happiness had crowded them from
any place of importance. Nine years of happy memories for
Tzigane.

But happiness also for Dracula—except during the day.
For in his nine years of marriage to the Countess Helen,
she still plagued him even though he had given her two
sons. The Countess Helen's attentions still annoyed Dracula and still made Tzigane laugh.

Transylvania. The town of Sibiu. Near the southern
border between Wallachia and Transylvania. Sibiu. And
south of Sibiu in the mountains was the cave of the
witches, which Christian legends called the Devil's School,
where Tzigane had become Undead over twenty-seven years
before. Twenty-seven years without sunlight. But although
her once tanned and golden skin had now become pale
in the darkness of the tomb, her beauty remained un-
changed. Her hair was still raven-black. Her forehead was

still smooth and unlined. Her breasts were still high and full.

But in twenty-seven years Dracula *had* changed. His hair had faded from black to steel-gray. His forehead was now lined from all he had done and experienced. But his body now flowed with more strength than when he was young because nine years before he had tasted a vampire's blood— Tzigane's blood. Salty-sweet and icy-cold. Undead blood. Immortal blood.

Nine years. And Dracula now lived with his wife and two children in the Transylvanian town of Sibiu. He had been given a captain's rank by the Hungarian king and was commander of the border guard. But he was still determined to reclaim his Wallachian throne for the third time in his life. Before . . .

"We could do it now, my Vlad," Tzigane whispered hopefully as she walked beside him from the room where the Countess Helen dreamed in oblivion with the spell of sleep strong upon her.

Dracula hesitated outside the room where his two sons slept and reached out with his mind to be sure they were all right and sleeping soundly. Then he continued down the hallway and turned right toward the door which led outside. His heavy black cloak was already around his shoulders, and there was a new, pale green one around Tzigane's, a cloak he had had specially made for her to wear when they went walking in the night.

"Vlad?" Tzigane whispered. "Did you hear what I said? We could do it now and avoid the risk of . . ."

"Not now, Tzigane," he said. "Let us talk later." Dracula closed his eyes and moved his lips in a silent incantation. He opened his eyes and nodded. A spell of invisibility now cloaked them both.

He opened the door, and they went out into the beautiful winter night. Snow glistened silver beneath the light of a full moon. The stars glowed coldly. Dracula and Tzigane began to walk unseen down the streets of Sibiu.

"Tzigane," Dracula said when they had reached the outskirts of town, "I know there is a risk, but I must do this for myself. You know that I am tired of the affairs of mortal men. You have seen my rages of frustration over the last nine years as I have tried to use my new powers to manipulate and control my destiny. Using my powers has been such a delicate matter, trying to manipulate minds and control the thoughts of those in power, but without arousing suspicions. So many minds to control. So many twistings of luck and chance to anticipate and allow for in my spells, having to be so careful and subtle and . . .

"It is not my way. It has never been my way, Tzigane. I have never been one to hold back, to restrain myself, to be subtle. I could attack, but I dare not. I dare not use the unrestrained power of the Unseen. I dare not summon Strigoi armies to destroy the armies of my enemies. I dare not summon demons to bear arms for me. For as strong as my powers are, I acknowledge that they are not strong enough to defeat every army the world would throw against me. And I also know this is the reason why witches and sorcerers do not already rule the Earth.

"But with more power? Undead power? And with centuries at my disposal in which to plot and plan and gain more and more power and strength? Centuries in which to organize the witches and sorcerers of all the nations of the world, they who will give homage to me, the one their prophecies have led them to believe is their rightful king? Perhaps then I *can* do as I wish and attack, destroy, and conquer all who come against me.

"I have said that I will soon be ready to become Undead, Tzigane, to become stronger and have even greater powers at my command, and I will soon do just that. But I must exit this world of mortals in my own way. And that way is to make the world think me dead in battle after regaining my Wallachian throne for a third and final time. And that is exactly what I am going to do."

Tzigane smiled. "Yes, my Vlad. I know. And I also know that you talk of this more to convince yourself than to convince me. But I do not like your risking battles where you might . . ."

"I will not forego my immortality by allowing someone's blade to sever my head from my body, Tzigane," Dracula laughed. "I promise."

Tzigane was silent.

"I may not accept all your beliefs and prophecies, Tzigane," he went on, "though I would be a fool if I were not grateful for the opportunities they have given me. But I do trust you, Tzigane, and I trust myself. Even without the prophecies to give us acceptance as King and Queen,

I trust that together we might still achieve powers and thrones which will make the thrones of mortals seem worthless by comparison. But the prophecies do exist, and we will use them just as they have always used you until now. Your sacrifices for your beliefs and for me will be richly rewarded in time, Tzigane. I will see that this is so."

"At least, you will not have to kill your own brother when you invade Wallachia," Tzigane sighed wearily. "Yes, I know how you feel about Radu. You hate him, but still you would not like to kill a brother. No one would ever guess that the dreaded Impaler of Wallachia would feel that way."

Dracula shrugged. "I would have done it all the same if it had been necessary. But you are correct. I am glad that others drove him back to Turkland before I returned."

"And your sons?" Tzigane asked gently.

"Mihnea and Mircea will stay here in Sibiu with Helen. They seem to be worthy sons, but they will have to learn to survive and conquer thrones on their own. Their mother is of a powerful, royal family. They will be fine. But I suppose I shall miss them—at times."

"And your eldest son? He who was born to your first wife during your reign in Wallachia?"

Dracula frowned thoughtfully as he gazed at Tzigane. "Is there anything you do not know about me, Tzigane? I've never spoken about Ilona, my first wife. Nor about Vlad, my first son."

Tzigane merely shrugged.

"Then you also know that Ilona was weak, and that she committed suicide rather than attempting to escape with me when Radu drove me from Wallachia?"

Tzigane nodded.

"And you also know that Vlad escaped with me?"

Tzigane nodded again. "And I know that when you were imprisoned in Hungary they took Vlad away to be raised by others."

This time it was Dracula who nodded. "I've neither seen nor heard from him in a very long time. Any feelings I had for him died long ago. He learned to live without me, and I learned not to think about him. So it is unlikely that I would start missing him now."

Tzigane seemed about to speak, but did not. Dracula, however, knew her thoughts were about children of their own. "There may be a way, Tzigane. Just because an Undead woman has never given birth does not mean .. "

"I knew everything I was giving up when I walked into the lake, my Vlad," she whispered flatly.

"But there may be a way. We will learn new things and in time go beyond the limits set by those before us. In time, all things may be possible for us. Even sunlight and children, Tzigane "

She looked up at him and smiled sadly. "Perhaps."

"If there is a way, we shall find it," Dracula solemnly vowed.

Tzigane embraced him and held him tight.

"Soon, Tzigane. I promise. Once the summer is here when I meet with my allies and the details for my return to Wallachia are drawn up . . ."

"Your cousin, the one you stayed with in Moldavia, who now rules there? He will send aid?"

"Stephen will send aid. Or rather 'Stephen the Great,' as they now call him," Dracula chuckled. "Stephen has done well with his life."

"But in time his life will end; yours will not," she smiled.

Dracula laughed softly. "Yes, Tzigane. Mine will not end. Thanks to your kiss. Soon—within the year—I will have reconquered my Wallachian throne, and then we can go to that castle you have spoken about and given me visions of so often, the one waiting for Satan's King and Queen."

"We will be very happy there, my Vlad."

"And very powerful, Tzigane," he reminded her with a smile. "Come. Even if you do not feel the winter cold, I still do."

"There is always the spell of heat," she teased. "I once felt warm in the waters of an icy lake by using that spell."

"I have not forgotten the spell of heat, Tzigane. But tonight I prefer to use the spell of *passion*."

Laughing softly together, the two unseen walkers in the night reached Tzigane's secret tomb on the outskirts of the town. And soon that chill house of death was filled with the sounds of passion and life.

NOVEMBER
1476 A.D.

49

━┼━━┼━━┼━━┼━━┼━

THE YEAR FLED, and winter returned. November was now
one week old. Dracula's invasion force was camped in an
open field, an army on the move without time to enjoy
the comforts of nearby Targoviste, the city which was no
longer the seat of Wallachian power.

A skirmish with the army of the current ruler of Wallachia, another Turkish puppet called Laiota, had been
won earlier that day. At dawn Dracula planned to lead his
men southward in pursuit of Laiota's retreating army to
the new capital of Wallachia—Bucharest, a city founded
and fortified by Dracula himself during his second reign.

Dracula waited until the night had come, then he silently
mounted his stallion and recited the incantation for invisibility, hiding himself and his horse from all mortal eyes.
He rode unseen from the camp.

He rode slowly, thoughtfully, across the snow-covered
ground, his stallion's breath frosty in the silver moonlight.
Soon he came to the familiar fork in the road which led
through the forest to the hut where he had spent so many
happy hours with Tzigane.

He came into the clearing and reined to a halt. It had
been twenty-eight years since he, Tzigane, and Varina had
ridden away from that hut on the night of Vladislav's return, and during those years, the hut had fallen into total
ruin. There was little left to show that a dwelling had ever
stood in the clearing at all. But at least one part of the
scene was familiar.

Tzigane stood in the center of the clearing, smiling up

at him, dressed in her black and silver gown. And other than the fact that she cast no shadow in the moonlight, for the Undead are their own shadows, she looked just as she had twenty-eight long years before.

"Tzigane," Dracula smiled. He nodded at the ruins of the hut. "I don't think we will be able to use your hut this time, do you?"

Tzigane laughed. "No, my Vlad."

"But I have furs tied to my saddle," he said, "and there is always the spell of heat."

"And passion," she laughed again as she watched him slip from his horse and land lightly on the ground.

Dracula embraced her and held her close. "It almost seems like we had never left this clearing, Tzigane."

"But we did, my Vlad," Tzigane whispered. "And now we are back, and I am happier now than I was then."

"Yes," Dracula said and kissed her lips.

"The furs?" Tzigane asked impatiently.

Dracula laughed. "Very well, Tzigane. But remember, this was your idea. Such sentiment from one so strong."

"You did not object," Tzigane pointed out with a grin. Tzigane watched as he spread the furs on the ground. And soon Dracula's warmth was pressed tightly against Tzigane's chill flesh.

At the climax of their passion, Dracula saw that Tzigane's eyes were burning red with fiery light, and he wondered—not for the first time—how he ever could have thought those glowing eyes repulsive. For he now believed them to be more beautiful than any mortal woman's eyes could ever hope to be.

At dawn Dracula and Tzigane parted, she to her secret crypt near Targoviste, and he to lead his army southward toward more battles, victorious battles. And within the month, Dracula had achieved his goal. He was once again the ruler of Wallachia, now for the third time.

The final time.

For now, the Warlord-Prince called the Dragon's son was ready and impatient to become a King.

DECEMBER
1476 A.D.

50

⫞⫞⫞⫞⫞

ON A MARSH NEAR BUCHAREST in a small clearing in the forest of Vlasie, the new ruler of Wallachia was reaping lives with his flashing sword. His black clothing was splattered with blood. The silver dragon on his chest seemed to be weeping crimson tears.

Dracula saw his chance. The soldier was about the right height and weight—Dracula's height and weight. Quickly Dracula recited the incantation for invisibility and moved unseen toward the unsuspecting warrior. Dracula whipped out his invisible sword. The warrior's head flew from his shoulders. The headless body slumped in the saddle, then fell heavily to the ground.

The battle continued to rage around Dracula. His men were being cut to pieces just as he had known they would be when he had led them into the obvious ambush set by his enemies. For his own secret purposes.

Dracula jumped to the ground beside the headless corpse and began to strip. When he was naked, he extended the spell of invisibility to include the head and body of the dead warrior he had picked to take his place. Then he set to work.

Soon he had exchanged clothes with the beheaded soldier. His silver dragon shirt now adorned the headless corpse. He made the redressed body reappear, but not the head. Dracula picked up the man's severed head and moved away unseen through the forest, keeping out of the way of the rushing horses and battling men. Dracula kept moving, and soon the din of battle was a faint memory on the cold winter breeze. Dracula glanced at the gray sky. It would soon be dark.

When he could no longer hear the sounds of battle, Dracula climbed to the top of a low hill and sat down, then tossed away the head of the soldier whose corpse was now impersonating him. It began to snow. Dracula wrapped the cloak of the dead man around his shoulders.

When it was dark, Dracula stood and concentrated his thoughts, calling to Tzigane. Soon he chanted a guttural phrase over and over until he heard the sound of vast wings beating the air above his head, and also heard a woman's laughter.

Tzigane leaped to the ground from the extended talons of the Strigoi which hovered overhead. Small whirlwinds spawned by the creature's flapping wings scattered the snow along the sides of the hill. The stench of the nether realms fouled the air.

Dracula and Tzigane embraced and kissed. Then, without speaking a word, Dracula removed a dagger from the sheath at his belt and poised it over his heart.

Dracula glanced into Tzigane's eyes. They were moist with tears. He looked down at the dagger. It was poised to end his mortal life.

He hesitated. The dagger was positioned for a killing stroke. He glanced back at Tzigane. He could see the tension in her face.

"Worried that I will change my mind, Tzigane?" he asked tightly.

"Vlad . . . I . . . if you are not certain this is what you want . . ."

Dracula looked again at the ready blade. "To take one's life—a forbidden thing. To do this forbidden thing? But I have always done things forbidden to most men."

Tzigane marveled at Dracula's hands. The hands which held the dagger were as steady as iron.

"No escape route this time, Tzigane," Dracula said softly. "And if I am wrong . . ."

The dagger struck, shearing through flesh and muscle into the heart of the Dragon's son. Pain flooded Dracula's chest. His breath hissed between his teeth. He jerked the dagger free and even replaced it in the sheath on his belt. And then he fell.

Tzigane caught his body and eased him to the ground.

Dracula's blood poured from the wound, staining the pure white snow around him.

His body grew cold. Tzigane waited. She sensed a change. She bent down and softly kissed his icy lips. They trembled beneath her touch.

Dracula's eyes snapped open. A hellish red glow burned in his eyes. He gazed at Tzigane for a long moment in silence, and then he began to laugh.

51

-)(--)(-*-)(-*-)(-*-)(-*

THE STRIGOI TOOK DRACULA AND TZIGANE swiftly northward away from Wallachia and the mountain cave and
into the Carpathian Mountains of northern Transylvania
to a massive castle atop a mountain.

Dracula watched the courtyard of the castle grow nearer
as the Strigoi descended toward the ground. The beast
hovered a few feet above the stones of the courtyard and
released him. He landed solidly on his feet, then turned
to see Tzigane do the same.

Dracula raised his arms above his head and began making complex gestures with his hands. Then he uttered a
harsh, guttural word of command.

The Strigoi's powerful, leathery wings lifted it higher
into the thin mountain air. For a moment it glared hate-
fully down at Dracula and Tzigane with its three fiery
eyes, then it began to fade until only a ghostly outline remained, and finally that too was gone. A clean mountain
breeze swept away the last of the Strigoi's stench. Dracula
and Tzigane kissed. He then began to examine first himself, and then his surroundings. He was pleased to note
that he felt no overpowering craving for human blood.
He felt hungry, but no more than he would have after a
day of battle. The only difference was that he no longer
hungered for the food of mortal men.

Dracula slowly reached up and touched his teeth with
the fingers of his right hand. They had become sharper,
and the two upper canine teeth had grown slightly longer.
He raised his shirt and felt the skin where he had given

himself his death wound. The flesh was smooth and unbroken. His senses were also sharper than ever before. By
concentrating, he could detect the sounds and scents of
animals in the forest surrounding the castle.

"There are many wolves," he said to Tzigane.

She nodded silently, pleased to see him exploring his
new awareness with such calm authority.

Dracula looked up at the sky. There were no clouds.
The stars burned with a greater brilliance than he could
ever remember. The brighter ones made him silently uncomfortable, but he was not surprised. Through his knowledge of the Unseen, he knew that stars were merely distant suns like the one that shined in the daylight skies
of the Earth, like the one whose rays the Undead were
forced to shun.

Dracula closed his eyes and reached out with new
senses, which now seemed instinctive and completely normal. He sensed vibrations in the ether, and powerful forces
gathered about the mountain top.

"The protective spells are strong," he said with approval.

Many of Tzigane's teachings had dealt with this castle.
It was a stronghold of Satan, built by witches, sorcerers,
and Undead souls many centuries before to await the coming of the Chosen One, to await the coming of Dracula.

The castle was surrounded by wolves and protected by
potent spells. The wolves protected it against living enemies. The spells kept the powers of the God of Light at
bay.

Dracula turned as he studied the courtyard. It was just
as he had seen it in his sex-inspired visions. Several dark
passageways led away from the courtyard beneath rounded
arches. On three sides loomed walls with tall, narrow windows from which no light gleamed. The fourth side, the
north one, contained the gateway and drawbridge to the
castle, now drawn up into place sealing off the castle from
the outside world.

The narrow windows in the walls were too high to provide entrance to the castle proper. There was only one
way to enter from the courtyard—through a great door
that was studded with large iron nails and set in a projecting doorway of massive stones.

Tzigane embraced Dracula again. "Are you pleased?"
she asked excitedly.

"I am. Let's go inside," he said, then kissed her brow.

Dracula strode to the nail-studded door and ran his fingers over the massively carved stonework in which the door was set. The carvings depicted grotesque, non-human creatures.

"You recognize them?" Tzigane asked.

Dracula nodded. They were also familiar from his visions, creatures from the nether realms.

"Yes," he said thoughtfully. "It is very familiar. I feel as if I am coming home, instead of just arriving for the first time."

Suddenly Dracula held up his hand near the surface of the stones. It cast no shadow in the light of the moon. He chuckled with amusement. "A most interesting effect," he observed. "It will be a challenge to explain how it is possible."

"Is it necessary to explain it?" Tzigane asked.

"Of course," Dracula answered immediately. "I will strive to explain everything."

"But why?" Tzigane asked. "Is the awakening of the Undead any more miraculous than the first cry of a new-born babe? Isn't it enough to know that a thing exists and to know how to use or control it according to your will?"

"By explaining things," Dracula replied, "I may find new uses for them. In the case of dangers specific to the Undead such as crosses and garlic, finding the reasons for their harmful effects may eventually allow me to counter-act and nullify them. Yes, Tzigane, I intend to explain everything eventually."

"Warlord, know thy weapons and those of thine enemy," Tzigane teased.

"Of course," Dracula nodded. "Merely because I have changed sides, so to speak, does not mean that I . . ."

"I love you, my Vlad," Tzigane said, quickly kissing Dracula's lips. "Come, let us go inside."

Dracula studied the door. "There is no knocker, no chain, nothing to grasp in order to open it. That is good. Unless one knows the secret . . ."

"No one but you can open it," Tzigane reminded him.

"Yes," he chuckled. "That is the secret. Very well." Dracula reached out and placed his hands flat against the rough wood of the huge door. He closed his eyes and concentrated his thoughts. The door began to open smoothly and silently.

Dracula stood back. When the door had opened all the way, he took Tzigane's hand and led her over the threshold.

Suddenly from all around the castle, wolves began to howl.

"They know you are here," Tzigane smiled. "They know their Master has come to his new home. They are the first to sing the praises of Satan's King on Earth."

Dracula nodded and smiled with approval, then closed the door.

52

❊❊❊❊❊

DRACULA SLID THE MASSIVE BOLTS into place. He turned the key in the lock, removed it, then slipped it into a leather pouch on his belt.

He eyed the narrow hallway in which they stood. There was no light, yet he could see. A ghostly blue glow outlined the stones. He looked at Tzigane. She, too, was tinged with the cold, blue light. "I am pleased with my ability to see in the dark. It will be very useful," he said.

Tzigane nodded, saying nothing.

Dracula led her down the passageway, his steps ringing heavily on the stone floor. They came to a great, winding staircase. Passageways led away on each side of it. Dracula ran his fingers along the balustrade of the stairway. "There are no spider webs," he observed, "and no dust. Another useful spell, don't you think?"

"Very useful," Tzigane agreed with a laugh.

Dracula went down the passageway to the left, turned right down a short flight of stairs, then walked along another passageway lined with doors on each side. He stopped in front of one.

"Here, I believe," he said thoughtfully, then opened the door and entered the room. It was a small room. A window looked out to the south, revealing a vista of forests and distant, snow-capped mountains.

In the left-hand wall of the room was another door. Dracula opened it. They went through the doorway, then down a stone passage with a low ceiling. They came to a spiral stairway which descended steeply.

Dracula and Tzigane went down the stairs. At the bottom was a dark, tunnellike passageway, and at its end another heavy door.

They passed through the door at the end of the tunnel and entered a large, windowless room. It gave every appearance of being a chapel but had no cross above the altar. Along the left-hand wall were two dark archways with steps leading down into vaults. Dracula led Tzigane to the nearest one.

At the bottom of the stairs, they entered a vaulted crypt. Except for the fact that there were still no spider webs or dust, the crypt was exactly as Dracula remembered it from his visions.

Other archways led away on all sides. Dracula strode confidently through one, turned, went through another, turned again, and then went through yet another, leading Tzigane through the intricate maze of passageways. Finally they emerged into a crypt of vast proportions. In the center was a dais, and upon it an open tomb, carved from a single, massive block of stone.

Dracula walked to the tomb. On the side of the tomb, a name was carved, his own name—DRACULA.

Tzigane slid her arm around his waist and kissed his cheek. "And how do you feel about prophecies that can even predict the correct name on the tomb of the King?" she teased.

"I do not mind using the belief in the prophecies to further my . . . our power, Tzigane," he replied solemnly, "but I will not let the prophecies use me. You wish me to believe that my name has been upon this tomb for centuries because that is what *you* believe. But for all I know it might have been carved *after* my birth, after I was decreed the Chosen One."

"The inscription is very old, my Vlad."

"Perhaps," he answered with a shrug.

Dracula stepped onto the dais which supported his tomb. Tzigane followed him. They looked into the tomb.

A recessed area, the length of a tall man and twice a man's width, was cut into the top of the stone to a depth of about two feet. The bottom was covered with soil.

"Certainly large enough for two," Dracula said as he slid his arm around Tzigane's waist. She nestled close and kissed his cheek.

"There are still several hours before dawn, are there not?" he asked Tzigane.

"You are hungry?"

"I am," Dracula admitted. "Come. There is still time for a hunt before we sleep."

"It would be so much easier, my Vlad, if you would let mortal witches serve you as they have me."

"We have talked of this before, Tzigane," he replied sternly. "I will find my own . . . food. Hunting keeps the senses sharp."

Dracula and Tzigane hurried back into the upper wings of the castle. They ascended the winding staircase at the end of the entrance passageway, then made their way to a tower which rose along the south wall of the castle.

"This is the highest tower," Tzigane stated as they reached the top of the narrow stairway.

"Yes. From here it will only take a moment to survey the castle. Then we will hunt."

There was a small balcony on the tower. Dracula walked around the tower, studying his new home. He was pleased and impressed. It was everything Tzigane had promised it would be.

Castle Dracula sat on the summit of a mountain. On three sides—the south, east, and west—the walls of the fortress edged on sheer, vertical walls of rock which plummeted down for a thousand feet or more.

"Only one side need be defended from invaders," Dracula said with approval, motioning to the north. "I will examine the north wall in greater detail when we leave on the hunt."

Dracula turned his attention to the land around the castle. To the south, closely packed trees created a dense forest broken here and there by deep chasms and occasionally by deep gorges which bordered the silver threads of rivers. In the distance, snowy mountains rose like sentinels of stone. The terrain to the east looked much the same as that to the south. In the west, the forests dropped away into a great valley whose far side rose to peaks of jagged rock. The land to the north looked similar to that of the south and east except that it gave access to the castle by way of a narrow, winding road which crawled steeply toward the fortress from out of the forest a few hundred feet down the slope.

"Very well," Dracula said. "Now we may hunt. I wish to experiment with the form of the bat. The idea of flying free from the binding Earth appeals to me."

"It is my favorite form," Tzigane laughed and began to remove her clothing.

Dracula hesitated to follow her example. "I intend to explain this transformation, Tzigane," he said, "and someday I will find a way to make the transformation and still arrive at my destination wearing my clothes. It is improper for a King to go naked."

"I love you naked," Tzigane teased as she slipped out of her black and silver gown to stand nude before him.

Dracula shrugged and began to undress. At last he, too, was naked.

"You should have picked a victim with better taste in clothing," Tzigane said, kicking the pile of clothes Dracula had discarded, the clothes he had taken from the dead soldier. "I will not have you wearing these again." Suddenly, before Dracula could stop her, she picked up the pile of clothing and threw it over the edge of the tower.

He glared angrily at Tzigane. "You will retrieve my clothes for me at once. I will wait for you here."

Tzigane laughed and kissed him. "When the castle was originally constructed, clothing for the prophesied King was also made. You will find they fit you perfectly. And each stitch was sewn while uttering sacred incantations, so that time will neither weaken nor destroy them. The clothing of the King should be as special and immortal as he, don't you agree, my Vlad?" Tzigane then kissed him again, playfully nipped at his ear, and ran her hands downward over his body.

Dracula pushed her away. "It is time to hunt," he growled, still upset. "You can go first."

Tzigane laughed and walked to the center of the tower. She dropped her arms to her sides and moved her lips in a silent incantation. Her outline became diffused and smoky. For a moment, a thick cloud of mist enveloped her human form, then it condensed into a vertical column and began to whirl.

The spinning increased in speed, and as it did, the mist condensed into two tendrils of milky-white smoke. The streamers became two intertwining spirals and spun even faster. Suddenly the tall column of whirling spirals began to shrink in length until a globe of spinning whiteness was formed. It darkened and began to stretch outward. It grew even darker as the spinning gradually slowed.

Tzigane's form became solid again. A furry, thinly winged, delicately veined bat soared and dove through the interior of the tower for a moment, then in a blur of speed, suddenly darted out of the tower and was lost in the night.

53

Dracula laughed and ran to the center of the tower, anxious to join Tzigane in the sky. He spread his arms and repeated the incantation while twisting his thoughts down a maze of potentialities until he found the correct one, then locked his consciousness onto it and began to change.

There was a moment of cramping pain before he soared away from the tower. A yawning gulf opened beneath him. He soared and dove, exhilarated and thrilled with the joy of flight.

Tzigane circled him as he experimented with his new ability. The instincts of a bat guided him, making him feel as if it were the most natural thing in the world to be able to fly.

Suddenly he became aware of Tzigane's consciousness touching his, talking to him through her thoughts.

I am hungry, she told him. *There will be plenty of time later for you to test your flying skills.*

It is quite wonderful, Dracula answered with his mind, his excitement barely under control. *Come. We will survey the walls of the castle from the outside and inspect the north face, then find our prey.*

Below the tower, the south wall, because it was totally impervious to a ground attack, was generously lined with stone-mullioned windows of shapes and sizes that varied from room to room. There were squares, diamonds, tall rectangles, and a few circular windows of stained glass. Along the east and west walls, there were fewer windows, and none near the corners where the north wall began.

The north wall, which held the drawbridge, was without any windows.

With the inspection completed, Dracula and Tzigane soared away from Castle Dracula and downward along the road which led to the north. The road twisted and turned through the forests around the castle. As they skimmed the treetops, wolves began to howl below them, singing praises to their Master.

The road eventually emerged onto the Borgo Pass. In one direction, the pass led into Moldavia, while the other direction led to Transylvania.

I traveled this road many times with my cousin Stephen, Dracula told Tzigane, *never once suspecting the presence of the castle from which we have come.*

The spells are strong, Tzigane agreed. *There are Christian legends about a house of the Devil in this region, but only servants of Satan know of its reality.*

And now even they may not come near if I do not wish them to do so, Dracula replied. *It is a good, secure fortress. I have never seen a better one.*

They flew above the Borgo Pass toward Transylvania. Soon Dracula veered from the well-traveled road and soared away into the foothills of the Carpathian Mountains.

My hunger burns strongest in this direction, he told Tzigane with his thoughts.

Mine too, she agreed. *Can you tell what form the prey takes?*

Dracula reached out with his mind. He cast about, discarding the weak consciousness of animals as well as those of old and very young humans. Then he found the girl.

A young girl, he told Tzigane. *She is strong and full of life.*

A thatch-roofed peasant hut came into view at the edge of a clearing in the forest.

Dracula and Tzigane hovered over the trees opposite the hut. The process of transformation began to reverse. The twin spirals formed and spun again, then suddenly two naked humans condensed out of the dual clouds of whirling mist. Dracula and Tzigane walked to the edge of the clearing and looked across at the hut. No lights shined within.

"I detect two consciousnesses inside," Tzigane whispered.

"Yes," Dracula agreed, "but there is also a small insolent awareness which seems to know we are here."

"A cat?" Tzigane asked.

"Possibly," Dracula nodded. "I will cast the spell of sleep over the hut, then we can find out."

Dracula closed his eyes in concentration. "It is done," he announced a moment later. He led the way across the frozen ground to the door of the hut and tried the latch.

"It is barred from within."

"We need an invitation to enter," Tzigane reminded him.

"I know of that superstition. I intend to test it."

"I have tested it myself," Tzigane assured him. "We will need an invitation to cross the threshold. It is easily obtained by entering the dreams of the sleeper and . . ."

"I know how it is done," Dracula interrupted. "Be still."

Tzigane shrugged. "Do not take too long with your tests," she urged. "Dawn will come soon, and it is a long way back to the castle."

"I also know the distance and the time," Dracula growled. "Now be quiet, Tzigane."

Dracula reached out with his mind and located the consciousness of the young girl. Slowly she rose from her bed and walked toward the door, her eyes still tightly closed in sleep. She lifted the bar and opened the door.

Dracula and Tzigane looked in at her. She was in her early teens and not particularly attractive. But she was healthy and strong. By listening closely, Dracula could hear the pumping of her heart and the rush of her rich blood through her young veins. Unlike lifeless objects which glowed blue in Dracula's night vision, the young girl's body was tinged with the warm red radiance of life.

Now at his mental command, the girl stepped away from the door. Dracula raised his right foot and carefully extended it toward the threshold. A sharp pain shot through his foot as it neared the entrance. He gritted his teeth and forced the foot closer. The pain became an agony.

"A great annoyance," Dracula hissed between his clenched teeth as he drew the foot back. "Very well, Tzigane. You may have the honor of obtaining the invitation."

Tzigane grinned and touched the girl's mind with her own. She probed deep into the girl's memories and found an image of a smiling man with gray hair—the girl's dead father.

Tzigane manipulated the image of the father within the girl's consciousness. The girl began to dream that her father was outside the hut, cold and in need of a fire. The girl invited him inside. The father told her he had two friends with him and asked her to shelter them as well. The benevolently smiling faces of Dracula and Tzigane came into view behind the father. The daughter told her father that his friends could also enter.

"Finished," Tzigane said softly.

Dracula again extended his foot to the threshold. This time there was no pain. He walked into the hut and took the sleeping girl by the arm, then quickly led her back to her bed.

Tzigane entered behind him. The hut was even poorer than her own had been, but no doubt it was just as dear to those who lived in it. She saw the cat, now asleep under the influence of the spell Dracula had cast. The girl's aged mother slept near the small animal.

Tzigane walked to the bed where Dracula was kneeling beside the reclining girl. He was bending forward toward the girl's neck, following his instincts with calm self-assurance.

Dracula's lips touched the girl's neck. She moaned softly in her sleep. She moaned again as his two sharp canine teeth punctured her skin and pierced her jugular vein.

Dracula sipped slowly from the vein, fighting a strong impulse to tear the girl's flesh and let her hot blood pour down his cold throat. Warmth and strength soon began to fill him. His vision became tinged with red.

When he was no longer hungry, he stood and flexed his muscles. He felt stronger than he could ever remember. He turned and smiled at Tzigane. "Her blood is sweet," he whispered.

Tzigane nodded, then impatiently knelt by the bed and leaned forward to the wound he had opened. Soon she, too, was satisfied.

Dracula looked at Tzigane. Her face and chin were stained with blood. In several places the rich liquid had dribbled down over the smooth skin of her breasts. He pulled her into his arms and began to kiss her.

Tzigane responded immediately. They plumbed each

others' mouth with their tongues and licked the remains of the young girl's blood from each others' lips and teeth.

Then Dracula used his tongue to clean the blood from Tzigane's face, neck, and breasts. She moaned and swayed in his arms as he made her body burn with desire. She could wait no longer.

Tzigane pulled Dracula down onto the dirt floor of the hut. She arched upward beneath him, pulling him into her, encasing him in her flesh. He crushed her in his embrace and began to move like a madman within her.

Suddenly the night was split by their cries as they exploded together in the throes of a scarlet passion greater than any they had ever known.

54

✻✼✻✼✻

"YOUR FLESH DOES NOT FEEL COLD," Dracula whispered as he stroked Tzigane's naked skin.

"Would an icicle call the snow cold?" she replied with a smile.

Dracula shrugged and rose to a sitting position. He glanced at the girl whom they had bled. She was still smiling sweetly, lost in her dreams. He stood and offered Tzigane his hand. She took it and stood up beside him. They looked down at the girl. The wound on her throat had stopped bleeding, but her neck and gown were stained with blood.

"She will know she has been attacked," Dracula said thoughtfully. "It may not be as easy for us tomorrow night."

"They will put up protections," Tzigane said.

"Garlic and crosses, I should imagine," Dracula agreed. "I am surprised they do not at least have a cross in the hut. I would have liked to have tested that superstition, too."

"The mother is wearing a poor wooden one around her neck," Tzigane said, pointing to the sleeping form of the older woman.

"Excellent," Dracula said, walking to the woman. "And they should have some garlic for their cooking. See if you can find it, Tzigane. You would know where women keep such things."

Tzigane began to search for garlic while Dracula examined the wooden cross on the leather thong around the woman's neck. At first there was no reaction, but as he reached out to touch it, the cross began to glow with a pale white light. As his hand moved nearer, the glow became a fire which threatened to sear his fingers.

Frowning, he withdrew his hand. For a moment, the cross continued to pulsate with a blinding white glare, then it faded to a soft glow and finally became a piece of dark wood once again.

"It would be useful to learn the reason for this effect," he said, "Does this power come from the woman's faith? Or is there an independent power responsible for this, some emanation from the God of Light?" Was he going to be forced to take religious superstitions about Gods and Devils more seriously?

Tzigane returned to stand beside him. "I would guess that it is caused by the God of Light, my Vlad. Satan's enemy is also ours. I found the garlic."

"Show me where," Dracula said, turning away from the old woman on the bed.

"It is there," Tzigane said, pointing to a shelf along the far wall of the one-room hut. "I will go no nearer. The stench is overpowering. It sickens me."

Dracula nodded, then walked forward warily. When he was about four feet away from the shelf, the odor of the garlic began to burn inside his nostrils. He whispered a curse and took another step. His eyes began to water. He could no longer breathe. He felt nauseous and dizzy.

"Go no nearer," Tzigane pleaded.

"Just one step more," Dracula replied tensely. He took another step. His legs began to tremble and he staggered back to stand beside Tzigane. Finally his head began to clear. He cursed again and looked back at the shelf. He considered forcing the older woman to destroy her cross and the garlic, but then decided it would do no real good, for she would no doubt simply get more garlic and make another cross.

"It is getting late," Tzigane said. "Dawn is coming. I can feel it."

"I, too," Dracula agreed. "Very well. But tomorrow night we shall return, and if they have armed themselves against us, it will provide us with an interesting and instructive challenge."

From the outside, the hut looked no different on the following night. But when Dracula cast his mind within

the structure, he found himself hindered by waves of
turbulence beating against his consciousness. He persevered
and cast the spell of sleep.

"They have smeared the doors and windows with garlic,"
he said in disgust as he pulled his mind back to the edge
of the clearing. "And there is a man, the girl's betrothed.
All are now sleeping, though not as soundly as I would
have wished since their protections have weakened the
spell."

"There is easier prey in the forests," Tzigane suggested.
"Many peasants have strong children."

"I will not be defeated, Tzigane," Dracula growled.
"Come."

Dracula strode across the clearing toward the hut. When
he was a few feet away, he stopped, his fists clenched at
his sides in anger.

"Damn their garlic!" he hissed. He took a step back.

"Let's forget her, Vlad," Tzigane said hopefully.

"Never," Dracula snapped. "If the enemy lies safe
within a fortress and one does not have time to lay siege,
the only way to victory is to lure the enemy outside."

He led Tzigane back to the edge of the clearing. "I will
make the girl walk outside the hut, to come for our kisses,"
he said with a cunning smile. "I have tasted her life. I
know her. Their protections cannot shield her mind from
me now."

Dracula reached out and fought his way through the
turbulent interference. He touched the girl's sleeping mind
and found the image of her betrothed. He used it to call
her, making her want to leave the hut and join the young
man she was to marry for a moonlight walk in the forest.

Soon the door of the hut opened, and the young girl
emerged. Around her neck was a cross and a string of
garlic flowers.

Dracula commanded her to remove the protections. She
did, then walked to the edge of the clearing and stood before them, seeing only the smiling image of her betrothed
in her mind.

"You may go first, tonight," Dracula told Tzigane. "I
will continue to hold her dreams in my grip. The spell of
sleep is weak, and I do not want a cry from the girl to
awaken those in the hut."

Tzigane laughed and bent toward the girl's neck. Her

teeth found the wounds of the previous night and reopened them. She began to feed.

Soon Dracula was also bent over the girl's soft throat. When he too had fed, Tzigane embraced him and kissed his blood-stained lips. Dracula pushed her gently away. "There will be time for our passion after I have finished with the girl. I do not want those in the hut to know how we reached her. I want them to doubt the value of their protections."

He commanded the girl to return to the hut. Outside the door, he forced her to reach down, pick up the garlic necklace and the cross, and replace them around her blood-smeared neck before going back into the hut, sliding the bar into place, and stretching out on her bed.

"There now, Tzigane," he chuckled as he pulled the witch into his arms, "you see—victory has been obtained. But our feeding has greatly weakened the girl. Tomorrow night may be the last time we can use her. It will be necessary for us to decide what will become of her then. Shall we allow her to rise from her grave? Or shall we . . ."

"We shall discuss it later," Tzigane growled impatiently as she took Dracula's hand and led him deeper into the forest, anxious to quench the passion burning deep within her Undead flesh.

On the third night, the hut still looked the same from the outside. But inside . . .

"They have tied the girl to her bed," Dracula growled in disgust. "Her betrothed is clever. I touched his mind for a brief moment and learned that he found signs that she had left the hut last night."

"Then she cannot come to us, and we must go elsewhere for our strength," Tzigane concluded.

"Not at all," Dracula grinned. "This peasant boy tries his wits against mine, I who was commanding armies before he was born. We can use his help, I think."

The young man's mind was stubborn. It resisted Dracula's mental commands for nearly an hour. But at last, it yielded. The boy rose and walked to the bed of his betrothed. In his mind he dreamed that the sun had risen, and she was safe. The boy untied the bonds which held the girl to the bed.

Soon the girl's pale body lay on the ground at the edge

of the clearing. Dracula and Tzigane had fed, and the girl was now a corpse.

"I left the boy with the ropes in his hands," Dracula chuckled as he smoothed his long, straight moustache thoughtfully. "His pain will be great. He believed himself to love the girl. I have changed his future. It is exhilarating to have such power over the lives of others."

"How cruel," Tzigane teased as she kissed his glistening lips. "Come into the forest with me, my Vlad."

"In a moment," Dracula said quietly, "in a moment. First, let us decide what to do with the girl."

"We have no need for her at the castle," Tzigane said quickly. "If you wish to have servants, I shall call to the witches in the cave. They would be honored to serve their King and Queen."

"No, we do not need her at the castle," Dracula agreed. "But neither do we need servants. At least, not yet. Perhaps later I will invite the witches to come. My father and brother could come, too. But for the moment, I prefer the castle to remain empty except for us."

"I am not lonely with you by my side," Tzigane said. "The two of us are enough. At least for the moment, as you say."

"But the girl?" Dracula asked. "If we leave her, it is doubtful that she will rise. These peasants will drive a wooden stake through her heart and cut off her head at the very least. It is a great disadvantage living among those who fear the powers of Satan. It would be good to live among the nonsuperstitious, if such a nation exists. Their nonbelief would then be our greatest protection and our greatest advantage over them."

"Wishful thinking," Tzigane laughed. "Where would you find such a nation? I know of no country populated by people as stubborn and sceptical as you."

Dracula shrugged, "Nor do I." He gazed down at the girl. "We could awaken her now," he suggested, "and send her away. She would instinctively find some hole or grave in which to crawl during the day, and then return after sunset to drain the life from her mother and her betrothed."

"She is like us now, my Vlad. Why should we punish her? She would be hunted and tormented by guilt. It would be terrible for her."

"She is *not* like us," Dracula replied harshly. "We are

her masters, and it is the right of the master to do as he wishes with his subjects. Do not be weak, Tzigane," he warned.

"I am *not* weak," Tzigane snapped. "It is not a weakness to care for one of your own."

Dracula remained silent for a moment. "I have decided," he said. "We will awaken her and send her on her way. I am King of the Undead, and I wish to have more subjects with which to build my power, my armies. I desire more slaves to do my bidding."

"She will not survive," Tzigane said angrily.

"Then I would not want her for a subject," Dracula answered without hesitation. "Only those clever enough to avoid destruction are worthy enough to bow to me."

Without another word, Dracula knelt by the girl. He reached out, grasped her head in his hands, and probed with his mind. Her consciousness was a faint shimmer of light hiding at the bottom of a deep, dark well. He called to her consciousness, coaxed it to rise, commanded it to come out of hiding and throw off the shackles of death.

Suddenly the girl's eyes jerked open. Seeing the two naked vampires with their burning red eyes staring down at her, she opened her mouth to scream. Dracula swiftly raised his hand in an imperious gesture. The girl closed her mouth and remained silent. Dracula stood and pointed away from the hut and into the forest.

The girl staggered to her feet. With a soft moan of agony, she ran away from the life she had known and the dreams she had nurtured, away into the lonely forest, away from her mother and the man she had loved and hoped to marry.

But even as she fled in horror at what she had become, she began to feel a hunger smoldering deep within her, a desire to return to the hut, to bend low over her mother and her betrothed, to kiss their warm, pulsating throats, to open their veins with her sharp pointed teeth, and drink their sweet blood.

55

✳✳✳✳✳

THICK CURTAINS OF LIFELESS AIR hung motionless around the tomb where Dracula and Tzigane lay entwined in each others' Undead arms. Within the crypt, the darkness was total, the silence complete.

Outside Castle Dracula, the sun slowly crept closer to its nightly grave beneath the western horizon. Fingers of purple shadow stretched farther and farther across the valleys, clutching at the dying light of the day.

The sun touched the rim of the horizon. The fiery orb slipped lower. Its light grew dimmer. Then it was gone.

A subtle change stole over the oppressive atmosphere within the crypt. The ether began to quiver with tense anticipation, with eager expectation. The trance of Death grew weaker. Whispers of life escaped into the imprisoning silence of the crypt for the third time since Castle Dracula had received its King and Queen. Breath hissed in and out, in and out, softly, faintly at first, then louder, stronger, more certain. Outside Castle Dracula, wolves began to howl.

Dracula and Tzigane opened their eyes.

He climbed from the tomb, turned, and offered his hand to Tzigane. She slid down and stood beside him. They embraced and kissed. She noticed he was shaking.

"Vlad?" she asked apprehensively. "Are you all right, Vlad?"

Dracula looked down at her. His face was drawn and tense. "I . . ." he began, but then faltered.

Tzigane began to feel fear. She had never seen him like this. Not her fearless Vlad. Never.

Dracula pulled himself out of his slouch and began to

pace the crypt, trying to think, trying to overcome his emotional shock. And as he paced, he sent his thoughts to Tzigane for thoughts communicated much more quickly and accurately than speech.

It was only a dream, Tzigane. Do not be worried. Only a silly dream. But it affected me. Strongly. Even after all your teachings, I had no idea that a mere dream could be so powerful.

And you remember this dream? Tzigane asked with her thoughts. Her worry increased for she *always* took dreams seriously. And for one to affect her Vlad in such a fashion . . .

I remember it. Oh yes, Tzigane. I shall never forget it. I saw a man, a dead man, wrapped in a long white shroud, lying on a slab in a dark place, a cave. The entrance had been blocked by a large boulder.

As I watched, the man came back to life. He struggled to a sitting position, then stood. He began to walk stiffly around the cave, working the stiffness of death from his limbs. There were wounds on his hands and feet, and another wound in his side.

And then he raised his arms and began to shine as brightly as the sun. I was nearly blinded by the light. The boulder which blocked the entrance rolled away. He ceased to glow. Then he left the cave.

But once outside he turned and looked back into the darkness. A newly risen sun was shining behind him, and I had to hide from its rays as they streamed into the cave.

And he saw me in the darkness and pointed at me and . . . laughed. He laughed! At me! Because he had the sun and I did not. Because he represented the Light and I did not. And because he thought the Light superior to the Dark.

Dracula stopped pacing and grabbed Tzigane's arms in a viselike grip. She grimaced with pain but kept silent.

You know that it was Christ I saw, do you not? Dracula asked with his turbulent thoughts.

Tzigane nodded slowly. *We are safe from Christ here, my Vlad. The protective spells keep the powers of Light away. You need not fear . . .*

"I do not fear Christ!" Dracula shouted, his voice echoing around the crypt. He shook his head and released his grip on Tzigane's arms.

"I do not fear Christ, Tzigane," he said, quieting his voice. "And I am ashamed that I should be so upset because of such a silly thing as a dream."

"Dreams are very powerful, my Vlad."

"At any rate, this one was," he said, trying to smile. His legs still felt shaky. He shook his head again. "No, Tzigane, I do not fear Christ. I . . . did you know that I never really believed in Christ, Tzigane? I placed Christ and his religion in the same category as other superstitions which weaken the rational mind."

"Such as witches and the Undead?" she asked.

Dracula nodded. "Yes. I was certainly wrong about those superstitions. But somehow, even with all the knowledge of the Unseen you gave me, I did not really believe in the *big* superstitions, the ones to which all the others are subservient. I still did not *really* believe in God and Satan."

Tzigane held him close, trying to comfort him. "Until now?" she asked gently.

"A mere dream will not make me accept them immediately, Tzigane. But . . . that glowing cross in the hut the other night . . . I wondered then if I might have to take religious superstitions more seriously because crosses and the like are obviously, undeniably, dangerous to my continued existence now that I am Undead. And a warrior who does not know and understand the weapons of his enemies will not survive long.

"So perhaps this dream is merely another instance when my hidden thoughts are talking to my conscious ones. Telling me to beware of dangers ahead. Telling me to take God and Satan more seriously because to do otherwise could mean my defeat and my destruction."

Dracula pulled away from Tzigane's arms and began to pace the crypt again. He began to feel stronger once more, as if talking about the dream slowly washed away its effects.

"No, Tzigane," he continued as he paced, "it was not Christ who made me fearful, but my own sudden conviction that there *was* a God and there *was* a Satan! It was my sudden belief in the reality of religion that affected me so strongly. But perhaps it was not fear so much as . . . awe . . . or surprise? Yes, surprise that I could have ever ignored the reality of God and Satan.

"But the effects of the dream are passing, Tzigane, and I no longer feel so certain about God and Satan. Yes, I am feeling more like my old self every moment."

"Vlad," Tzigane began hesitantly, "would you have become . . . Undead, one of Satan's Undead, if you had had this dream before you . . ."

"You mean would I have picked the side of God instead?" Dracula laughed softly as he took Tzigane's hands in his. "No, Tzigane, I do not think so. And it is best I think that way, is it not? As I said before I plunged the dagger into my heart, there is no escape route this time." He smiled. "I am all right now, Tzigane. But I shall not foolishly forget this dream. I shall take Satan *and* God more seriously from now on. Anyway I must appear to do so if I am to have the respect and homage of my new subjects, for the King whom everyone believes to have been chosen by Satan should at least give lip service to the Devil, should he not?"

Tzigane laughed with relief now that he was once again himself and no longer shaking. "Yes, my Vlad," she smiled. "Satan's King on Earth should at least partially believe in the Devil."

"At least partially," he agreed, still smiling, thankful that his memory of the dream was no longer charged with such overpowering emotion.

Tzigane kissed him on his lips. He embraced her for a moment, then pulled away.

"I intend to bring my subjects together here at Castle Dracula for a great council of war. It is only proper that they should come and pay homage to their new King. I also wish to begin organizing the witches and sorcerers from every corner of the Earth into an effective fighting force. If *they* all believe God and Christ to be their enemies—and if I . . . partially believe it—then I as their King must plan and coordinate the battle for them. The followers of Satan from all over the world must work together to defeat the power of the God of Light. Perhaps then the cross of Christ will not burn when I come near.

"It is rather amusing, Tzigane," Dracula chuckled thoughtfully, "don't you think? I thought to conquer only the Earth. But in order to do that, it seems that I may first have to conquer Heaven."

AUGUST
1477 A.D.

56

✳❉✳❉✳❉✳

THE WINTER SNOWS slowly melted and gave way to spring
and summer. And with the summer, they began to arrive.
The followers of Satan—some mortal, some Undead—
coming to pay homage to their long awaited King and
Queen. And now the windows of Castle Dracula blazed with
light whenever the night freed Dracula and Tzigane from
their tomb.

Dracula sat upon his throne in the great hall of Castle
Dracula. At Dracula's left, Tzigane sat upon her own
throne, listening to the suggestions and discussions taking
place in the vast chamber and offering her own ideas when
she felt they were needed.

Beside Dracula, to his right, stood his father and brother,
whose opinions he consulted from time to time. To Tzigane's left stood Lilitu and three other mortal witches
from the cave.

Many of the guests in the hall had traveled for months
to reach the fortress high in the Carpathian Mountains of
northern Transylvania. There were witches, sorcerers,
alchemists, thinkers, doubters, servants of Satan, worship-
pers of life, joy, and pleasure.

From all over the Earth they had come, from the nations of Europe, from the mysterious Orient, from the unknown South, and from the frozen North, all representing
their native lands at Dracula's Satanic court, bringing with
them their knowledge and power, their devotion to Satan,
and their loyalty to Dracula, Satan's King on earth.

Dracula had waited impatiently for them to arrive, for

his summons to be received, for the winter snows to melt, for the war council to begin, a war council whose object was to plan the defeat of Satan's enemy, the God of Light. Now for nearly a month, the discussions had continued as the guests combined their knowledge and ideas under Dracula's stern control. He was about to announce his decision. But while he ordered his thoughts in preparation for his decree, he allowed his guests to talk.

He stroked his long, straight moustache and pretended to listen to the words of a man with yellow skin and narrow, intelligent eyes. The man finished talking and took his seat at the long table. Several other voices sprang up, clamoring to be recognized. Dracula pointed to a red-haired woman wearing a long, green robe.

The woman, who represented an island nation far to the west, rose with pride and began to talk in the language of her homeland, and although only she knew the language she spoke, no one in the throne room had any difficulty understanding her, for all the guests had long since developed the skill of reading the thoughts of others and conversing in the universal language of Satan, the language of the human mind.

When the woman had completed her speech, Dracula rose to his feet. The room grew quiet. All eyes were fastened upon him.

"You are all worthy servants of Satan," he told the assembled guests and saw a ripple of pride flow over the faces stretched out before him in the great hall. "For all your knowledge and suggestions, your King and Queen thank you. But it is now time to cease our talking and to act.

"It would please me greatly if we could simply attack Satan's enemy and destroy the power of the Light. To attack and destroy without mercy was always my way when I was a mortal. The events of my reign in Wallachia are well-known to all of you.

"But your knowledge of the conditions in your countries has now forced me to hold my desire to have the battle over with quickly. As powerful and as numerous as the followers of Satan are, we are still greatly outnumbered by the followers of the religions of Light. And only a foolish warrior orders an attack against an enemy who outnumbers him.

"We must, as so many of you have suggested, first weaken the religions of the Light. Where possible, we must bring the people of the Earth into Satan's fold. The kiss of Undeath shall aid us greatly in that task. But where that is not possible, we must weaken the beliefs of the people who follow the Light until their religions become no more than empty, indifferent superstitions.

"It has not been easy for me, a hardened warrior who always scorned superstitions, to believe that the power of mere faith could be a threat to those who wield weapons, either weapons of steel or of magical powers. But I have seen the cross of Christ burn in my presence, and I cannot deny the evidence of my own eyes. The cross burns when the Undead, the children of Satan, come near. *And something must make it burn.*

"And you all have answered my question—'Why does the cross of Christ burn?'—in similar ways. You have all answered, 'It is faith which makes it burn.' Faith. The faith of those who believe in its power. The faith of those who follow the religion of Christ.

"And you have also suggested that perhaps this faith does not directly affect the cross, but like the powers we receive from Satan, the power of the faith of our enemies is somehow channeled through the God of Light, who in turn causes the burning. And I believe you are correct. I have had new dreams since these discussions began, and they tell me to believe you, to trust your knowledge. And they tell me that by weakening the faith of our enemies, we will also weaken the God of Light Himself.

"I am your King. Satan chose me to reign. But He chose a man who was first a warrior and only second a believer in and manipulator of the Unseen. Why? Why did Satan not choose one of you? Why did he choose me?

"It is because I *am* first a warrior, experienced in conquering the armies of enemies, armies which are well organized and entrenched. He chose me. A warrior who nearly brought all of Islam to its knees without the help of my allies. I, Dracula.

"Satan chose me for my warrior's experience to organize, to coordinate, and to lead. For although you are all powerful witches, warlocks and wielders of Unseen powers, you are isolated within your own countries, cut off from the others of the world who follow Satan, cut off because you must be suspicious of others in order to survive in a world the religions of Light control, cut off from others who think and feel as you do because of those who faithfully follow the Light.

"But here we are all together! And by using our powers of mental communication, we need never be apart again.

"And I will be the center of this new unity. It is I to whom you will report, and it is I who will issue new orders to keep our efforts coordinated and working smoothly. Yes, I will plan our strategy.

"But the individual tactics? You know better than I which tactics will most effectively weaken the religions of Light in your own lands. So I shall leave those tactics up to you.

"And my strategy—your strategy—is simply this. Do all that is possible to weaken the religions of Light by weakening the faith of the followers of the Light. Remain passive no longer! Attack in secret and gradually break the back of Satan's enemy. And in time the cross of Christ will no longer burn in my presence. In time the Holy Water will not boil when the Undead come near. In time the Undead shall walk boldly into the sanctuaries of the Light, into the churches and temples of the Light, and we shall rip the crosses and icons from the walls and stamp them underfoot!

"*Then* we shall attack, together in Satan's name. And we shall be victorious!"

Cheers filled the hall. Dracula smiled and nodded to the throng, pleased with their reaction. They would make good warriors. All they had needed was a leader, someone to bring them together and make them work toward a single end.

Dracula raised his hands for silence. "Four times each year on Satan's high holy days, you shall gather together the followers of Satan in your regions and wait for my mental call. And I shall touch your minds and ask for your reports. I shall consider all your reports as a whole, then when I am ready I will contact you again in your thoughts or in your dreams to tell you of the progress of our unified battle and give you new orders, if needed, so that our fight against Satan's enemy may continue in unity toward our mutual goal.

"And," Dracula added with a humorless smile, "be assured that I will know if you lie to me or attempt to deceive me in any way. No one can hide the truth from Satan's chosen King. My thoughts reach far, and my vengeance is swift for any who betray me. So continue to be loyal to me and to your Lord Satan, and in time working together, we shall truly triumph.

"Now only one more thing remains, and it is this. I shall convene a second council of war five years from this month, and all of you will, of course, wish to attend," Dracula said, his tone of voice leaving no doubt that this was not a mere request but a royal command.

"Your King has spoken. Now come forth to the throne, all of you who are not already Undead, and receive Satan's gift of future eternal life, His sacred kiss from my lips and the lips of your Queen. The war council is now ended.

The still mortal guests moved forward reverently, expectantly, and one by one bowed to Dracula and Tzigane, baring their throats, anxious to receive the sacred crimson kisses of the King and Queen of the kingdom of Satan, secure in the knowledge that only a drop of their blood would be taken so that they would not die from the kiss, and comforted by the knowledge that when, in the fullness of time, Death came to claim them, the grave would hold no fear but only the glory of immediate ressurection into the immortal ranks of Satan's Undead.

DECEMBER
1477 A.D.

57

✦✦✦✦✦

OUTSIDE CASTLE DRACULA, a winter storm howled and moaned, its heavy curtains of whirling whiteness isolating the mountaintop from the rest of the world, steadily burying the towers and battlements of the fortress under thickening drifts of icy, wind-whipped snow as the dull grayness of the day sluggishly brightened toward noon.

Far beneath the blizzard-besieged castle, within the darkness and silence of the crypt, Dracula and Tzigane lay side by side in their trance of death, once again alone in the castle, unaware that their sanctuary of Undeath was about to be invaded.

At the exact moment that the sun reached its noon zenith, the silence of the crypt was disturbed by a faint, rumbling sound like distant thunder. The thunder grew louder. The castle itself began to tremble and shake as the violence of the airquake increased. Then two lights suddenly invaded the crypt's dark sanctity.

The lights—one crimson, one white—hovered above the tomb of Dracula and Tzigane. They grew brighter. Within the red light appeared a cloud of boiling blackness. Within the white light, a white cloud also began to boil.

The black, crimson-haloed cloud slowly descended toward the tomb and protectively covered Dracula's body. The white cloud remained hovering above Tzigane.

Suddenly a bolt of blinding white lightning shot downward from the center of the whiteness. It struck Tzigane between her breasts. Her body shuddered from the blow and began to smoke. Her black and silver gown burst into flames. Her skin blistered and blackened. Her flesh melted away from her bones.

The white cloud faded and vanished.

The dark cloud faded and vanished.

The crypt returned to darkness.

But within the tomb, only Tzigane's smoldering skeleton rested upon the bed of soil. The body of Dracula had vanished from the face of the Earth.

AUGUST
1482 A.D.

58

FIVE YEARS PASSED. Again it was summer and again it was night, and again the throne room of Castle Dracula was crowded with the servants of Satan. The air was filled with the confused sound of mingled languages talking loudly to one another, no one knowing what to do.

All had visited the crypt and seen Tzigane's skeleton in the tomb, a black cross burned into her breastbone. But for nearly five years, five long and tormenting years, there had been no sign of their King.

They had persevered in their assignments and sent their mental reports to Dracula's father and brother who, along with Lilitu, had come to Castle Dracula and done all they could to reassure the servants of Satan across the world that they should continue with Dracula's tactics and have faith in Satan and his King on Earth.

But now doubts filled many of the faithful. If the power of the God of Light could enter the stronghold of Satan and penetrate the most powerful of protective spells, could they ever again feel true faith in the power of their Lord Satan?

Many did not think they could. Many wanted to leave, to slip away, before a similar fate left their bones resting atop the ashes of their bodies. As they talked and argued about what they should do, many eyes glanced toward Dracula's empty throne, the symbol of the defeat of Satan.

Suddenly the sound of thunder rose over the voices in the chamber. With fearful eyes, the servants of Satan saw a pale red light begin to form above the empty throne.

271

The thunder and the glow grew more intense, and then a black cloud began to boil beneath the halo of crimson light. The castle shook with the thunderous roar. The cloud descended and covered the throne. The light and thunder faded. Then it was gone.

Where an empty throne had been a moment before, now sat a man with iron-gray hair, burning red eyes, and a long straight moustache, dressed all in black.

Dracula slowly rose and faced the assembled crowd. The awed servants of Satan fell to their trembling knees and covered their faces with their shaking hands.

"Off your knees!" Dracula shouted. "Rise and stand like proud men and women! Follow," he commanded.

He stepped down from the throne and strode through the great hall, never looking to the left or right. The crowd cautiously followed Dracula through the castle and into the crypt.

Dracula stood over the tomb and looked down at Tzigane's skeleton. Something bright glistened within the ashes beneath the naked bones of her ribs. Dracula reached down and picked it up. It was the silver coin Tzigane had always clutched in her left hand while she slept, the coin that she had treasured for it was her sign that she was the chosen mate of Dracula.

Dracula placed the coin out of the way on the edge of the tomb. He stretched out his left hand, then reached across with his right, pressing his thumbnail into the vein of his left wrist and jerking downward. Blood from the wound began to drip onto Tzigane's skull.

Dracula began to hiss like a serpent, intoning soft, sibilant words. Then he began to chant in a harsh, guttural language. He circled the slab three times, all the while being careful to let the drops of his blood fall onto Tzigane's bones and ashes.

Dracula withdrew his bleeding wrist. His concentration left the slab for a moment as he stared at the gash in his flesh. The hand and wrist became misty momentarily, then returned to normal. The wound was gone. Nodding with satisfaction, Dracula looked again at the blood-splattered skeleton in the tomb.

He bent forward and kissed the skull, then stood back and quickly stripped naked. He spread his arms and willed his smoky spirals of metamorphosis to form. Then he floated his whirling column of mist into a horizontal position and carefully lowered his essence into the skeletal remains.

When he felt himself within the bones and ashes, he began to concentrate with every ounce of his energy, visualizing Tzigane as she had once been, seeing every detail of the beautiful body he remembered.

Slowly and gently, Dracula willed his mist to rise. But within the bones and ashes of the remains, he left a small, serpentine whisp of thick smoke, a minute portion of his own existence.

Dracula returned to human form and stared intently at the streamer of smoky existence which he had left within Tzigane's skeleton. The thin column wound in and out of the bones and ashes, like a worm searching for food.

Dracula willed the whisp of smoke to separate into two identical streamers. He willed them to intertwine. He willed them to whirl about each other. He willed them to expand, to feed off the blood he had dripped onto the bones and ashes, to gain substance from the crimson ooze.

Soon the spirals had grown to the length of the skeleton. Dracula nodded with approval and willed them to condense and reform the body of Tzigane.

Veins, muscles, tendons, organs, all began to appear. Last came a fleshy covering of smooth, pale skin.

Tzigane finally lay before him, once again as he remembered her. Dracula bent down and kissed her full, ripe lips. Then he forced his mind down a torturous maze of non-existence and oblivion, searching, probing, calling her name.

Suddenly a feeling of desire swept over him. He felt his manhood begin to stiffen. He had found her soul.

Reverently Dracula led the spirit back through the maze, back to the crypt of death, back to the body he had created for her to inhabit again.

The body before him in the tomb began to tremble with the vibrations of reawakening life. Swiftly Dracula climbed into the tomb and forced entry into the cold flesh of Tzigane's body. He moved violently, calling her name over and over and over again, commanding her to awaken.

Suddenly he felt her arms gripping his back, her nails clawing at his flesh, her thighs pressing inward against his sides. Then he heard her familiar moans and sobs as she neared the climax of passion. He moved faster with more and more violence, ignoring the stinging wounds she cut into his skin, ignoring his own pain as he struggled to bring her fully into alignment within her body.

Suddenly Tzigane's eyes snapped open. She screamed as her body convulsed with the explosion of her orgasm.

Dracula eased himself away from her, then climbed back down onto the floor. Tzigane's body continued to shake with small convulsions as the last of her passion faded away. Her eyes stared unblinking at the ceiling of the crypt.

Dracula bent forward and kissed her once again, and continued to kiss her until she began to respond. Then he drew back and whispered her name.

"Tzigane," he called softly. "Come back to me, Tzigane. Come back."

Tzigane slowly turned her head to the side and looked with wonder into Dracula's eyes. He picked up the silver coin and pressed it into her left palm. Her trembling fingers closed around it.

"You are my mate, Tzigane," Dracula said tightly.

Tzigane began to weep.

59

Dracula again sat upon the throne at Castle Dracula with Tzigane again by his side. The crowd waited, watching him in silence, waiting for him to speak. But he sat without moving, his brows drawn together in a grimace of deep concentration.

Why don't you speak, my Vlad? Tzigane asked him with her thoughts. *Tell me what has happened. Was I really no more than ashes and bones until an hour ago? Has it really been five years since we last hunted?*

Dracula did not reply.

Now and then one of the assembled servants of Satan would venture to whisper to a neighbor, but instantly he would feel the eyes of Dracula bearing down upon him and fall silent once again.

All through the night, the crowd waited in anticipation. Finally, just as the dawn drew near, Dracula rose to his feet.

"You have seen your King return from out of the cloud of Satan," he said quietly. "You have seen me raise your Queen from the dead. Has any of you ever done such things yourself?"

There was silence in the throne room.

Dracula nodded. "Do any of you now doubt the power of Satan? Is your faith still as weak as it was before I returned?"

Again there was silence.

"Satan can do all that His enemy can do. His power is the equal of the enemy. He allowed the entry of the Light into His stronghold so that He might demonstrate His power to you. Your resurrected Queen is proof of that power."

Dracula extended his hand to Tzigane.

She looked up at him and smiled uncertainly, then took his hand and rose to her feet.

"There is yet one ultimate proof which remains to be revealed. Those of you who still walk in the day will remain in the throne room. The Undead who are here, all who have died and been reborn since receiving the sacred kiss or who were Undead before our first council of war, will now go below to their resting places in the crypt, but their minds shall watch even as they sleep."

Dracula's father, brother, Varina, and other Undead among the assembled crowd had been apprehensively feeling the coming of the dawn. Now they quickly and gratefully obeyed Dracula's command and went below to their resting places.

Tzigane tugged on his hand to get his attention.

Dracula ignored her.

We, too, must go below, she reminded him with her thoughts, fearing that his experience in the cloud, about which she yet knew so little, had damaged his mind.

Have faith, Tzigane, Dracula told her with his mind. *Trust me. Satan provides.*

Tzigane struggled to conceal her nervousness from the assembled crowd. She started to plead with him to be reasonable, but then did not.

"All the Undead who must shun the sun have now left our midst," Dracula said to the crowd, "all, that is, except your King and Queen. Come. Follow us. Satan will now give you the ultimate proof of His power!"

We cannot! Tzigane's thoughts exclaimed in alarm, suddenly perceiving his intent. *The sun will destroy us!*

Have you so little faith, Tzigane? You who have kept faith for so long? You who walked naked into the dragon lake to retrieve a coin, trusting in your rebirth in Satan's name? There is a reason for all I do, Tzigane. Have faith. I will allow no harm to come to you. I thought you once loved the sun.

Dracula walked from the castle with Tzigane at his side, tightly grasping his right hand. He stopped in the center of the courtyard.

Tzigane looked up at the sky. It was painfully bright. She felt a sharp pain in her chest. Her limbs began to stiffen.

Dracula sensed her fear. *You will not be harmed, Tzigane. Hold on tight to my hand. I have been with our Lord Satan. He will not forsake us.*

When the crowd had assembled around Dracula and Tzigane in the courtyard, Dracula spread his arms. Tzigane clung to his right hand as if gripping onto a precipice. Suddenly warmth flowed from Dracula's hand into her body, giving her strength, removing her stiffness and pain.

Then she suddenly felt her body begin to transform into the whirling spirals which preceeded a metamorphosis. She gasped in shock. *We must be naked!* she cried out in Dracula's mind.

Really? Dracula asked. *Are you certain, Tzigane? I thought I once told you I would find a way to circumvent the need to be naked.*

The crowd watched as the whirling spirals of Dracula and Tzigane condensed into bats. The two winged creatures soared upward, then hovered above the eastern battlement of the castle.

On the battlement, Dracula and Tzigane became human once again.

"It is all a matter of having enough power and energy to change the clothes along with your body, Tzigane," Dracula told her as they looked at the rapidly brightening eastern horizon.

Tzigane was beyond words.

"Hold onto my hand tightly and have faith," Dracula whispered.

Suddenly the orb of the sun broke the eastern horizon. Scarlet light the color of blood bathed Dracula and Tzigane. They felt a wave of nausea and a brief cramping pain in their stomachs, but their skin did not burn.

The crowd below in the courtyard gasped in awe as they heard laughter drifting down from the eastern battlement of Castle Dracula where Dracula and Tzigane stood proud and unafraid in the crimson rays of the newly risen sun.

60

✣ ✣ ✣ ✣ ✣ ✣

"THIS IS WONDERFUL, MY VLAD!" Tzigane exclaimed as she reveled in the warm rays of the sun.

"Do not grow too fond of the sun, Tzigane. Satan taught me how to suffer sunlight, but only for short periods of time, for He wished to demonstrate His power to his servants, His power and my authority as King. None of Satan's followers will doubt His power or mine after seeing this miracle."

"Satan really taught you?" Tzigane whispered in awe. "Then the thoughts of the throng are true. You have been with Satan, and I was a blackened skeleton and . . ."

"We must go into the castle now, Tzigane. The daylight is already beginning to take my strength, and there is one more thing I must do in Satan's name before we can rest today on our bed of earth. Later I will speak to you with my mind and explain all I can while our bodies are at rest in our tomb. Come. We must go back down."

The crowd again watched their King and Queen become bats, swoop into the courtyard, and change back to human form. Without another word Dracula brushed by the awed and bowing servants of Satan with Tzigane walking proudly by his side.

Dracula and Tzigane entered the castle and went directly to the great hall. "You must sit down now," Dracula said to his Queen, motioning to her throne, "so that your strength may be conserved. I am weakening and therefore must draw away the strength I have been giving to you so that I can fulfill Satan's final command. You must stay awake through the force of your will power alone when I withdraw that strength."

Tzigane nodded and slowly sat down upon her throne, clenching her fists in her lap, waiting for it to happen. Then Dracula pulled away his strength, the strength Satan had given him, and Tzigane's body began to ache and burn. She stubbornly kept her pain from showing on her face.

Dracula looked down at her with concern, then turned to face the throng which had followed them into the throne room.

Dracula raised his arms for silence. "I have been with Satan," he said in a loud voice. "You have all seen me appear from out of Satan's cloud of crimson fire. You have all seen me raise Tzigane from the dead. And you have all seen your Undead King and Queen standing unharmed in the rays of the sun. Do any of you now doubt that your Lord Satan has the power to protect you and strengthen you so that victory over the God of Light may eventually be yours?"

The room was silent.

Dracula nodded. "Excellent. Your faith is now stronger than it was before. Faith. In Satan. Faith in Satan which in time will help us to overcome the lesser faith of those who follow the Light."

Dracula turned and looked at Tzigane. Her body was trembling, but her face still showed no signs of the pains which were racking her body. *Just a little while longer, Tzigane,* he told her secretly with his thoughts. He raised his hand and gestured toward the seated Queen.

"Tzigane was burned in her tomb by the God of Light just as you had thought," he told the crowd. A fearful murmur began to spread through the throng. "Silence!" Dracula shouted angrily. And there was silence.

"Tzigane was burned by the God of Light," he continued, "but Satan's enemy was only permitted to enter this stronghold because Satan Himself allowed it.

"Satan allowed the invasion of the Light not because of weakness, but because of superior cunning," Dracula explained, "for He has taught me that the realm of the gods is much like the realm of men on Earth. Deals must be made and compromises reached between enemies. And that was why Satan allowed the God of Light entrance, for only by compromising with His enemy, by sacrificing His

Queen, could Satan take His King, take me, into the cloud of crimson fire and give me superior knowledge, strength, and powers.

"But Satan is more clever than the God of Light for He also gave me the knowledge to bring Tzigane back. I have been with Satan, learned many forbidden things, and gained many new strengths, and yet Tzigane again sits before you unharmed.

"Yes, servants of Satan, our Lord is more cunning and clever than His enemy, and this is why our forces in time will be victorious, for though the powers commanded by Satan and His enemy are equally balanced, Satan's superior cleverness and cunning will eventually bring about the downfall of the God of Light.

"And just as Satan is clever so must you also be clever as you continue to fight to weaken the God of Light.

"Ours is a sacred fight. And there are sacred tasks you must all individually perform, sacred tasks which in a moment will be given to you *by your Lord Satan Himself!*"

This time Dracula's command for silence had to be given three times before the crowd quieted and he could speak again. "The tasks you are about to receive will enter your minds when I open the gateway from our world to the realm of Satan," he continued, and again those in the crowd began to talk among themselves.

Dracula quieted them again. "The tasks you will soon receive *must* be accomplished if we are to be victorious in our battle. Some of you will be required to find rare Satanic manuscripts or write new ones yourselves, grimoires in which Satan's power can be focused. Others among you will be responsible for destroying sacred objects and buildings that are potent focuses for the power of the God of Light. Others will be asked to assassinate or pervert leaders of the religions of the Light, or to start wars between nations.

"But in many cases, it will take centuries to complete your tasks because in many cases the manuscripts, the sacred objects and buildings, the religious leaders, even the nations which will be named to you *do not yet exist!*"

Dracula quieted the crowd a fourth time. "Yes, you and those you command may have to wait until centuries have passed before your tasks can be accomplished. But time is not your enemy. You have all received the sacred kiss, and when in time you die, you will be reborn Undead into eternal physical life.

"Above all, remember that it will be your cleverness, your cunning, and your ability to accomplish your sacred tasks in secret that will insure our victory. The religions of Light must never suspect our worldwide, organized actions. They must never suspect that they are being weakened from within and that the disasters which befall them are anything other than the acts of men or their own God.

"Finally, you will continue to report on the high holy days of our Lord so that I may coordinate our efforts, but you need never return to this castle again.

"Now kneel, servants of Satan, and receive the sacred tasks of your Lord!"

Slowly, fearfully, the people of the throng went apprehensively down onto their knees, nervously wondering what was about to happen.

Dracula raised his arms above his head and began to chant in a guttural tongue. His body began to glow with a hellish red light, and soon his image became ghostly and transparent as if he were no longer totally in the physical realm.

And then the rumbling of Satan's thunder again intruded onto the plane of the Earth. But this time no cloud formed. Instead, the great hall began to fill with thick, black smoke which smelled of burning sulfur and boiled into existence from out of the empty air itself. The black smoke also appeared in the underground crypt, where the Undead among the guests had been following the speech of their King with their minds.

The smoke began to whirl around each guest, mortal and Undead. Only Dracula and Tzigane remained untouched. The smoke made eyes burn, and nostrils ache, and throats scream with pain as each guest was covered by a whirling black cocoon. And the screaming of Satan's followers increased as Satan's burning spirit seared their souls, marked them, and made them His own as the walls of the castle shook from the shock waves of thunder crashing about the mountaintop.

And then the screaming and the thunder faded away, and the whirling black clouds of Satan's sulfurous smoke also began to vanish. But as they disappeared, the cocoons of blackness also took away the bodies they had covered.

It was over.

And Dracula and Tzigane were alone in Castle Dracula once again.

61

DRACULA QUICKLY LIFTED TZIGANE into his arms and carried her from the throne room, his own day-weakened limbs aching from the strain. Tzigane was only barely conscious. Her face was bathed in sweat, and tremors had begun to shake her body.

Dracula felt somewhat stronger once he was beneath the castle where no light could reach. But it was not until he had finally laid Tzigane on the bed of soil and then joined her in their tomb that he was finally free of the agony of moving about during the day.

Dracula reached out with his mind and touched the mind of his mate. *Rest, Tzigane,* his thoughts gently told her. *We are in our tomb. You may rest.* He waited until he saw her body relax, then let himself also fall into the state between waking and death, the state in which the Undead were normally forced to spend their days. His body stiffened as the trance of Undeath stole over him. Strength began to pour back into his tired body. But he could not allow his mind to rest.

Tzigane, he called softly with his thoughts.

I am here, my Vlad, her mind responded weakly. *I do not think seeing the sun was worth such agony.*

No. But it was necessary to strengthen the faith of Satan's followers. Did you see the smoke of Satan take away the bodies of His followers, Tzigane?

Yes, I saw. Where did it take them, Vlad?

To their own lands—returned them in an instant to their homes.

283

Arriving so far away in an instant should greatly impress them, Tzigane observed.

Yes, and they will never forget witnessing the miracles Satan helped them to perform.

Satan. . . , Tzigane thought with reverent excitement. *You were with our Lord!*

Satan was the name that He called Himself.

To be taught by our Lord Himself, Tzigane thought with awe. *It is glorious, my Vlad. Now you must truly believe as I do, that our Lord . . .*

Your Lord Satan is a liar and a traitor, Dracula's bitter thoughts intruded.

But . . . how can you say that when . . .

I only told the crowd what He wanted me to tell them, Tzigane. And that was less than the total truth. Yes, I must *now believe there is a Satan, or at least a thing which calls itself Satan. But during all the time I was in His realm of darkness, I saw only a boiling cloud of blackness shot through with thin bolts of crimson lightning. Tzigane, Satan is not even faintly human.*

Of course not, my Vlad, Tzigane protested. *Satan is a God.*

Whatever Satan is, Tzigane, He is a traitor to those who have sacrificed and worked for His cause. To you, Tzigane. To me?

You have spent your whole life in service to Him. You have sacrificed greatly for His prophecies. You have worked and sweated and wept because of your loyalty to Satan and His prophecies. But now? Now!

For a moment, Dracula's anger overcame him, and he could not continue. But then he brought his hate-filled emotions under control.

Tzigane, he continued to explain, *Satan allowed your destruction by the God of Light. He allowed His Queen to be destroyed! After all you had sacrificed for Him, He bargained away your existence as if all your work and devotion meant nothing at all. You had faithfully served His purpose in guiding me to my destiny, but when he no longer needed you, He just tossed you away like a . . . a . . .*

Please, Vlad, Tzigane urged. *Do not think badly of my Lord Satan. He allowed my destruction, but that was just another sacrifice for me to make. I remember nothing of it.*

No pain. Nothing at all. I did not suffer. And now, through Satan's mercy, I am back by your side for all eternity.

No, Tzigane, Dracula's angry thoughts told her. *No. Only until the next midnight. That is what I did not tell the assembled guests. Had I told them the whole truth, they would have seen Satan for the foul thing that He is, and then His plans would have been thwarted. His plans as well as . . . mine.*

Midnight? Until midnight? Tzigane asked, fear suddenly creeping over her consciousness. *What do you mean?*

I could not tell the throng. I could not. There is no escape for me from this existence, Tzigane. I must use this Undead Kingship. It is all I have, Tzigane. You must understand. You must! If I had told the crowd the whole truth—as I wanted so badly to do—not only Satan's plans of victory but also mine would have been ruined. Don't you see, Tzigane? That is why I could not tell them about the next midnight. And by not telling them, I still have a chance to succeed. But the price? The price!

Tell me, Vlad. Please tell me about the next midnight! Tzigane pleaded, pushing her thoughts through Dracula's seething emotions and into his mind.

Dracula slowly calmed himself again. *Satan's enemy destroyed your body, but He merely sent your soul to a realm of gray waiting, Tzigane. That was part of the bargain because only from the gray realm could your soul be brought back to the plane of the Earth when I performed the miracle of your ressurection.*

But there was more to the bargain Satan made with His enemy, which I did not tell the crowd. In exchange for the privilege of training His King to do the miracles by which the faith of His followers could be strengthened, Satan had to promise the God of Light that He would send the soul and flesh of His Queen into eternal torment. And in fulfillment of His promise, Satan will send a Strigoi at midnight to take you to its . . .

No! No! Tzigane cried with her terror-ridden thoughts. *To the Strigoi's realm? Oh sweet Satan! Those screams of the ones who are there . . . I can still hear them from my day at the cave! Please, Vlad? Say you are making a joke?*

You know better, Tzigane. Now do you see why I call your Satan a worthless traitor? Only a traitor would do such a thing to one as faithful as you! But He is a traitor whom I must both serve and hate because I have no escape. Nor do you. Unless . . .

Unless? Tzigane asked hopefully, reduced to grasping at the slimmest of hopes.

At sunset, we shall draw protective circles and pentagrams in the chapel above this crypt, Tzigane. Perhaps I can bargain with Satan. I know how to make Him appear. He taught me how. I can speak with Him and perhaps . . .

And if He does not wish to bargain? Tzigane asked, her hope fading away as her terror returned.

Then I could . . . fight Him.

But you could not win! All our powers and spells could not turn away a Strigoi commanded by Satan Himself!

Dracula did not answer for a moment. *He is testing me, Tzigane. He would not have told me about the Strigoi if He had simply wanted to fulfill his bargain with the God of Light. No. He is testing me. Will I be loyal and simply give you to Him? Or will I fight for you to remain by my side, even though it might mean my own destruction? Yes, He is testing me, Tzigane. And He thinks He knows what I will do. What I have always done. That I will not fight a battle where there is no escape and no hope of victory.*

But . . . would Satan destroy His chosen King? Tzigane asked apprehensively.

I don't know, Tzigane. He might. I have organized His followers, performed His miracles, and opened the gateway between His realm and the Earth. In Satan's traitorous eyes, I might be just as expendable as you now that He has reached through the gateway and directly touched the minds and souls of His followers.

But He may bargain with me, even yet, Dracula thought with determination. *I may not have to decide whether or not to fight a losing battle. I did not tell the whole truth to His followers. I did not betray Him with the truth. That might mean something even to Him. And if I can bargain with Him for your continued existence by my side, we may still spend the centuries together.*

Tzigane was silent in her thoughts for a long moment. *Vlad,* she finally thought to her mate, *if . . . if Satan will not . . . bargain, you must promise me that . . . that you will not fight Him for me. You must not risk yourself just to . . .*

Tzigane, Dracula broke in gently, *I . . . I care for you. Even . . . even love you. I do not like to think of spending an eternity without you by my side.*

Dracula's thought of love swept through Tzigane's consciousness, and for a moment, her terror lessened. *Vlad . . . how long I have wanted you to admit your love for me! It means so much. But . . . but you must promise me you will not fight Satan. Please, Vlad. My torment will be great in . . . in the realm of the Strigoi, but it would be much greater if I knew that I had also been the cause of your destruction!*

It would *be foolish to fight,* Dracula admitted.

Promise me, Vlad. Now. Please? Tzigane pleaded with her thoughts. You must not fight! You must not!

But Dracula would not promise for he did not truly know what he might do if Satan refused to bargain. And as the day wore on toward night, he continued to battle with himself, his emotions fighting his rational mind, his love for Tzigane struggling against his knowledge that he should—as he always had before—save himself for future battles and not attempt to fight foolishly when the outcome would be his certain defeat.

62

᪂᪂᪂᪂᪂᪂

ONCE AGAIN the gypsy witch called Tzigane, she who had become Satan's Queen, was waiting for midnight. But this time she was not looking forward to its arrival for midnight now held only terror.

Dracula and Tzigane stood in the exact center of a pentagram which they had drawn upon the floor of the unsanctified chapel above their crypt. A pentagram, a five-pointed star drawn with their own blood. For protection. And around the pentagram they had also drawn a circle whose circumference was embellished with magical names of power.

"A pentagram will not stop a Strigoi sent by Satan," Tzigane mumbled numbly for the third time in the last few moments. Her growing terror was nearly unendurable. Her face glistened with nervous sweat, her knees weak from the emotional strain of the waiting.

Dracula squeezed her hand tighter but said nothing. He understood her fear for he had seen visions of the Strigois' realm and heard the never ending screams of those imprisoned there. He had seen the tortures those prisoners had to suffer, tortures which slowly, so very slowly, destroyed their bodies, bodies which then reformed so they could be destroyed once again and again without end for all eternity.

The thought of Tzigane imprisoned in that realm of pain made Dracula ache with hatred. Hatred for Satan who would do such an injustice to a servant as loyal as Tzigane. Her religion had been her life, but now her God was about

to send her to a realm where she would scream forever
without hope of release. Religion. Faith. Gods who made
bargains with each other—Dracula hated them all. And he
now knew for certain that the God of Light was no better
than Satan for it was the God of Light who had *requested*
Tzigane's coming torment.

But despite his hatred, Dracula still did not know if he
would defy Satan and fight a hopeless battle, or . . .

"Vlad?" Tzigane asked with a trembling whisper. "Can
you feel it building?"

"Yes," Dracula replied tensely. "Midnight nears. It is
time to call to Satan."

"Vlad?" Tzigane said again, then suddenly threw her
arms around him and kissed him. He returned her kiss,
long and deep and filled with passion. The contact of their
flesh said so much more than words or even thoughts, the
contact of their flesh, even Undead and chilled by death,
singing silent songs of love.

Dracula finally pulled away. "There is no more time,
Tzigane," he said urgently. "Midnight is nearly upon us. I
must conjure Satan."

Dracula spread his arms wide and began to chant the
same guttural phrases which he had used to bring the black
sulfurous cloud into the throne room. Again his body began to glow with a reddish light, and again his body and
black clothing became transparent.

Thunder rumbled within the chapel. A black cloud boiling within a halo of crimson fire materialized above the
pentagram. The thunder increased in volume until it
threatened to shake the castle apart.

Dracula dropped his hands, and his body ceased to glow.
Satan! he called out with his thoughts, his face turned upward to the black cloud. *I wish to bargain for Tzigane's
continued existence by my side!*

Dracula and Tzigane waited, fists clenched, sweat glistening on their pale cold skin, their Undead eyes burning
with red light. Suddenly words exploded within their brains.
Satan's words.

There will be no bargaining, Satan's thunderous thoughts
announced. *Bargains between Gods take precedence over
bargains with lesser beings. Bring the woman to the courtyard. A Strigoi awaits her.*

She is your Queen! Dracula screamed with his thoughts.

"You must not destroy your own Queen!" he shouted with his voice.

I would destroy you, too, Satan replied with frozen indifference, *but you may still prove useful to me later. Bring the woman to the courtyard.*

"No," Dracula stated quietly, suddenly chilled by the knowledge that his decision had finally been made. And his emotions had won.

Dracula pulled Tzigane into his arms and held her close. "We are mates," he told the boiling cloud. "We will not be separated. And I will fight you if you try to take her from me!"

Dracula heard Tzigane begin to weep against his chest. He looked down and saw that she was pitifully clasping the small silver coin which had meant so much to her, the coin which had meant future glories in payment for her loyal service to Satan, the coin which was now only a small piece of silver that marked her as the target of a Strigoi.

"Vlad," Tzigane whispered between her tears, "you must take me to the courtyard and stand away. Please do not let yourself be taken, too."

"No, Tzigane. I know it is foolish to defy Satan. I know it with my mind. But my emotions tell me otherwise! It defies logic, but I know, I *feel* it is right to fight this hopeless battle. Is this what you have felt all your life? Am I beginning to understand what drove you to sacrifice so much for your religion? If so, if what I am now feeling is a religious conviction, it is a religion not of Gods but of ourselves. We are mates for eternity, Tzigane, no matter where that eternity is spent. We shall be our own Gods, Tzigane. We shall be our own religion. We shall be together, we shall . . ."

Suddenly the floor jerked violently beneath them. A huge section of the chapel roof fell inward, and the stench of the nether realms fouled the air. Then through the opening in the roof, the talons of a Strigoi appeared and moved downward toward them.

Only the woman, Satan's thoughts commanded the Strigoi.

"No!" Dracula screamed out. But suddenly an unseen force tore him out of Tzigane's arms and threw him against the far wall of the chapel.

He struggled painfully back to his feet. He heard a scream. A woman's scream. Tzigane's.

Dracula ran toward her. She was already within the grip of the talons. A searing bolt of crimson lightning shot outward from the boiling cloud and struck her body. Her black gown burst into flames. She screamed in agony as the fire engulfed her. But her flesh did not blacken! It had begun. Her gown turned to ashes and fell away. The Strigoi began to pull her upward.

"Tzigane!" Dracula shouted, suddenly realizing that Satan did not even intend to give him the honor of a battle. "Tzigane!" he cried out in desperation.

But she was now beyond answering. All she could do was scream and scream and scream.

The talons continued to ascend, pulling the now naked body of Dracula's mate to her doom of eternal pain.

Dracula raised his arms and prepared to throw all the Unseen powers at his command against the Strigoi and at the cloud of Satan itself, determined not to allow Tzigane's abduction to proceed without a fight, but suddenly the unseen force grabbed him again, and threw him to the floor. And pinned him there. Helpless. Staring up. Seeing the talons beginning to fade as the Strigoi returned to its realm with its screaming prize. And Tzigane's image was fading, too. Fainter and fainter and . . .

And then she was gone.

But her screams still continued a while longer.

Then they, too, were gone.

And Dracula was alone. With the black and crimson cloud of Satan still boiling above him.

The force which had held him to the floor faded. Dracula stood and glared furiously at the boiling cloud. Tremors of naked hatred shook his body.

"I don't know how," he hissed, "but I will find a way to destroy you. Hear me, Satan! You are now as much my enemy as the God of Light! And I vow to destroy you and get Tzigane back! I vow this upon the sacred soul of my lost mate!"

Be still, Satan's exploding thoughts commanded. *You defied me and lost. As you knew you would. Curious. To risk so much? For a mere woman? Very curious.*

"I will destroy you," Dracula repeated. "Somehow I will

destroy you and the God of Light as well! I swear it by
Tzigane's soul!"

Very curious indeed, Satan replied. And then the boiling
black cloud faded away and was gone.

And Dracula was alone. Truly alone.

Midnight stars gleamed in the black night sky through
the hole in the chapel roof. Dracula looked up at that
opening where his mate had vanished from the Earth.
Tzigane. His friend. His faithful ally. And his love.

"Tzigane," he whispered, and on the cold night breeze
which had begun to moan outside the castle, he thought
he heard the echo of a scream.

By The Author of
COLD MOON OVER BABYLON
and **THE AMULET**

GILDED NEEDLES

MICHAEL McDOWELL

In the 1880's Lena is queen of The Black Triangle,
Manhattan's decadent empire of opium dens,
gambling casinos, drunken sailors and gaudy
hookers. With her daughters and grandchildren,
she leads a ring of female criminals—women skilled
in the arts of cruelty.

Only a few blocks away, amidst the elegant
mansions and lily-white reputations of Gramercy
Park and Washington Square lives Judge James
Stallworth. He is determined to crush Lena's evil
crew, and with icy indifference he orders three
deaths in her family. Then one Sunday, all the
Stallworths receive individual invitations—
invitations to their own funerals.

When you cross some people you may wind up
dead. When you cross Lena you will end up wishing
you were...and wishing you were...and wishing...

"Readers of weak constitution should beware!"
Publishers Weekly

**"RIVETING, TERRIFYING,
AND JUST ABSOLUTELY GREAT."**
Stephen King, author of THE SHINING

AVON Paperback   73698/$2.50